'Provocative and creativ[...]
of narrating a grand so[...]
blazing new trails into v[...]
— Amir Ahmadi Arian, author of *Then the Fish Swallowed Him*

'*You Must Believe in Spring* is knotty, hopeful and heartful as it explores Egypt's oppressive regime over the generations, and what liberation might be.'
— Yara Rodrigues Fowler, author of *there are more things*

'A visionary work from a remarkable new voice. Tonsy's use of speculative fiction to archive the past gives us a mesmerising new lens onto the 2011 revolution in Egypt.'
— Akil Kumarasamy, author of *Meet Us by the Roaring Sea*

'A beautiful and assured debut, masterfully pulling apart the complexities of a singular moment in time. Mohamed Tonsy is a hugely exciting new writer, and I can't wait to read more.'
— Heather Parry, author of *Orpheus Builds a Girl*

'With rare lucidity and lyrical precision, this critical contribution to contemporary Arab literature quietly keeps the flame—and the bruises—of a concussed Egyptian revolution alive. To the vanishing beat of protests, Tonsy's prose bears witness to the stubborn reverberations of trauma while inventing a temporality to survive a suffocating present. His voice of resistance prospers in the expansive future of fiction, the home of a generation that remains pained yet proud.'
— Farah Abdessamad, writer, critic and essayist

'At a time when emancipatory possibilities seem to be closed off, *You Must Believe in Spring* opens a much-needed avenue to reclaim memory and narrative control amidst defeat and

fatalism. Fiction and nonfiction intertwine in an increasingly absurdist way not dissimilar to present realities in Egypt. In this excellent work of speculative political fiction, Tonsy succeeds in making us rethink the events of the revolution and other stories that exist in history's margins.'
— Nihal El Aasar, Egyptian writer and researcher

'*You Must Believe in Spring* evokes a sprawling, dense and simultaneously intimate portrait of a traumatised Cairo. The characters seem to speak in hushed tones, but their whispers echo throughout the city.'
— A. Naji Bakhti, author of *Between Beirut and the Moon*

'Reading Mohamed Tonsy's *You Must Believe in Spring* is a reminder that to imagine the future based on what we know of the past, it is to those who were there whom we turn, and this too is where the most exciting fiction is at this pivotal moment of global political turmoil.'
— Elizabeth Chakrabarty, author of *Lessons in Love and Other Crimes*

YOU MUST BELIEVE IN SPRING

First published in the United Kingdom in 2022
by Hajar Press C.I.C.
www.hajarpress.com
@hajarpress

© Mohamed Tonsy, 2022

The right of Mohamed Tonsy to be identified as the author of this
work has been asserted by him in accordance with the
Copyright, Designs and Patents Act, 1988.

All rights reserved. No part of this publication may be reproduced,
distributed or transmitted, in any form or by any means,
without the written permission of the publisher.

ISBN 978-1-914221-18-7 Paperback
ISBN 978-1-914221-19-4 EPUB eBook

A Cataloguing-in-Publication data record for this book is
available from the British Library.

Cover and interior art: Hanna Stephens
Cover design: Samara Jundi
Typesetting: Laura Jones / lauraflojo.com

Printed and bound in the United Kingdom by
Clays Ltd, Elcograf S.p.A.

YOU MUST BELIEVE IN SPRING

MOHAMED TONSY

This book includes descriptions of military, police and sexual violence, imprisonment and death by suicide.

AUTHOR'S NOTE

'This is what you get for protesting.'

The 25 January revolution was a landmark uprising. Egypt has seen many massive popular revolts, but most of this history is locked away in inaccessible archives or was long ago destroyed. In 2011, for the first time, activists had the means to create their own archives, documenting events as they happened, independently of institutions and their investment in certain narratives. Still, even in the age of the internet, no archive can be exhaustive, and to claim to have the complete picture of anything is its own form of tyranny, since it denies others the ability to add their experiences to the mix. This is the first reason why I chose the form of a fictional narrative set in the future to tell a story about that historic time.

President Mubarak fell on 11 February 2011. The Supreme Council of the Armed Forces stepped in to govern Egypt, with the Muslim Brotherhood expected to do well in elections. In March 2011, a referendum was held to decide whether to pass amendments to Egypt's outdated 1971 constitution and leave the task of drafting a new constitution till after parliamentary elections, or whether to draw up a new constitution before holding elections so as to limit the power vested in the new government. Only 23 per cent voted for a new constitution to be drafted before elections. It was the first time I had ever voted. Though most of the people I met in line at the polling station were in the opposing camp, there was a common feeling of celebration: at long last, we held the reins; no one else was in control of our fate. Of course, none of that was true.

As the protests continued, women demonstrating in Tahrir Square were arrested, beaten and sexually assaulted by the Egyptian military, who groped them, stripped them and subjected them to so-called 'virginity tests', abuse that was defended publicly by a senior general. The ruling army's brutal repression of protesters included campaigns of mass slaughter, as in the Maspero Massacre in October 2011 and the Battle of Mohamed Mahmoud in November. The Muslim Brotherhood, too, whose candidate Mohamed Morsi won the presidential elections in June 2012, used the long arm of the Central Security Forces to attack protesters for the duration of their brief rule. Of course, when you strike a deal with the devil, he is going to come back to collect. Sure enough, in July 2013, army chief Field Marshal ʿAbdelfattah el-Sisi led a coup against Morsi, who, refusing to cede power, repeated the word 'legitimacy' in his final televised address as president as if it were a right owed to him. On 14 August 2013, shortly after Sisi's takeover, the military unleashed its deadliest terrors in the Rabʿa Massacre, in which a thousand demonstrators were killed in a single day.

This kind of history, a chain of events enacted by leaders and masses of people lumped together in homogeneous groups, is often how people tell the story of the Arab Spring in Egypt, but it wasn't my experience of it. By the time Morsi was overthrown, I had already moved to France, where I was racing for a French triathlon team, Olympic Nice Natation, and working as an architect. It had been a while since I had been able to run for the Egyptian Triathlon Federation, which was largely managed by ex-military officers who disapproved of my participation in the revolution. Protesting between 25 January and 11 February 2011 was forgivable, easily dismissed as youthful passion. But people who carried on protesting after Mubarak's fall were agitators who wanted to bring the country to its knees.

I lost 18 per cent of my lung capacity during the gas attacks of the Battle of Mohamed Mahmoud. When security forces launched a vicious assault on demonstrators gathered nearby in Tahrir Square, my undergraduate alma mater, the American University in Cairo, allowed police snipers into its buildings to shoot at protesters and refused to give refuge to injured civilians; the university was *neutral*. More than forty people died in the clashes, in which one police sniper rose to infamy for deftly targeting bullets at protesters' eyes.

Lung damage doesn't rear its head until a few months after the initial trauma, so I only realised the extent of my injury in mid-2012, half a year later. It was manageable during swims and runs but dangerous on the bike. I started blacking out during training sessions. As the effects on my health became graver and more apparent, I told coaches and administrators in the Egyptian Triathlon Federation about what was happening. 'This is what you get for protesting,' they told me.

Disappointment weighed heavily on me, clouding all my thoughts. I was disappointed in Egypt, the government and its institutions; in my country-people, friends and family; in those telling me that one had to exercise patience with tyrants, as though they were tantrum-prone children whom we ought to indulge. Most of all, I was disappointed in myself. I had survived when many others hadn't; I escaped when still more were languishing in prison.

When I came to know more about trauma, I realised that my memories of that time will always be cloudy, with just a few persistent episodes recurrently rising to the surface in vivid detail. This is the second reason I decided to set this novel in the future: it was the only lens through which I could look back at what happened without feeling like I was running in circles. I found that this setting and structure offered me a way of writing that honoured my experiences. Instead of my trauma being a hurdle that I needed to overcome, the blind spots of the past became part of the narrative design. The choice also came from my need to imagine, for my own sake, a time beyond the one I was living in, even—or especially—one in which the traumas of the past live on. The future in this story is one prefigured by the suppression of this very process: a denial of Egyptians' right to archive the collective traumas of the revolution.

A persistent challenge I faced was how to position facts within a fictional narrative, particularly as more of this imagined future was being revealed with every news story. This also raised the question of activism and the text, given that it is currently illegal to challenge the authority of the Egyptian government. In the end, rather than providing clear answers as to 'what really happened', I decided to trust my readers and let them do their own research to tease apart fact and fiction. I wanted the narrative to remain open to interpretation, and in any case, I felt the distinction to be arbitrary. Whatever the violent categorisations of the archon's archive, fiction is capable of conveying knowledge about reality that might fall outside of official, documented fact.

Throughout the writing process, I had a terrifying sense that crucial little details were slipping away from me and that I was therefore always on the verge of losing the knowledge I gained from that time. But, as mentioned at the start of this note, the truth is that it's impossible to create an exhaustive narrative. Setting this book in the future was my way of launching an arrow forward into the dark, accepting that whatever account I have inherited and whatever the future will inherit about the past is partial. The story then becomes about the resilience needed to combat the state's hegemony, so that even when important information is gone, we won't ever lose what we have gained.

The revolution has had its setbacks, and many failures, but it is not lost, and it is not over. The final reason I set this novel in the future is to attempt to renew my own faith, to visualise how even from the midst of the forces of counter-revolution, the revolution can be revived, and the people's cries of *'Aish! Horreya! 'Adala 'egtema'eya!* will ring out, again.

PLAYLIST

Eskenderella – 'Youhka Ana [1]'

Youssra El Hawary – 'Ghareeb An El Medina (Brenk Sinatra Remix)'

Maryam Saleh & Zeid Hamdan – 'Watan El Akk'

Omar Khairat – 'Leilat El Kabd Ala Fatma (Original Score 5)'

Eskenderella – 'Eini Fi Einek'

Sheikh Imam – 'Shayed Koussourak'

Maryam Saleh – 'Wahdi'

Marcel Khalife & Oumaima Khalil – 'Sparrow (Asfour)'

Ghalia Benali, Romina Lischka & Vincent Noiret – 'Mosabbeb al Asbab'

Mashrou' Leila – 'Tayf (Ghost)'

Ramy Essam feat. Malikah – 'Segn Bel Alwan'

Orange Blossom – 'Mexico'

Alsarah and the Nubatones – 'Ya Watan'

Egyptian Project – 'Soufi'

Abdelbaset Hamouda – 'ElDonya Garalha Eah'

Najat Al Saghira – 'Ana Bashaa El Bahr'

Farid al-Atrash – 'Ya Habaybi Ya Ghaybin'

EL-BAB EL-'AWWAL

Turning the last corner before Teita's house, I find myself at a fresh barricade. On the other side, the drab beige of squat residential buildings, Ramy's kiosk, which he took charge of managing when I still lived here, and these trees, whose shadows I would furiously trace in chalk on the pavement as a child, all feel like a mirror in which I can finally see myself again.

I take my ID card out of my prayer book, which has been doubling as a wallet, to ready it for inspection, examining the back to check when it expires. *23/05/2034*—a few more years. All the important bits of information are here. *Sex: Male. Religion: Muslim. Marital status: Single. Occupation: Student.* Holding the card in one hand, I quickly turn to pages fourteen and fifteen of the prayer book and press the Polaroid embedded among the sheets further into the spine, so that the binding strains audibly like a taut string.

It's secure, I think, folding the pages over again before returning the book to my coat pocket.

This checkpoint can't be more than a few days old. The concrete blocks haven't sunk far into the road. A bit more heat in the air will soften up the asphalt and help it find its place. Give it a week.

The guard has turned to face me now. He's holding his walkie-talkie at chest level and scans me from head to toe with his eyes, trying to ascertain whether I'm trouble, terror, timid or treacle-sweet.

I hold up my ID card and try to breeze past. Often, this gesture is enough to get me through. If guards stopped every single person crossing at every single checkpoint, the city would be at a permanent standstill.

The mesh sports bag I'm carrying usually helps me pass through checkpoints quickly, allowing guards a clear view of the excess of tubes inside. They scarcely look at me.

Broken glass, potholes and the heat cause tyres to burst frequently in the city, so I've started walking and using public transport to get around. It takes longer, and I get stopped at checkpoints more often on my feet than on my bike. My progress on foot is slower, and the whiff of petrol coming from my gym bag more obvious.

'Why do you smell like petrol?' the guard asks. Walking around me, he lifts the bag and feels its weight sink in his grip. His words are posed like a question, but I can tell he's made up his mind. No answer I give will be sufficient. I am trouble.

I'd like to keep quiet just to see what he would do, but I know his intentions, and my reply comes out like a reflex. 'The swimming pool where I train has run out of chlorine, so they've been using benzene to disinfect the water.'

Striped shirt, tan trousers—the guard is playing at being a civilian—a gun at his hip and a walkie-talkie buzzing with static and warbled voices. I'm playing at innocence too, but it doesn't seem like repeating well-worn prayers will cut it. The black rubber snaking its way around my bag, see-through or not, raises suspicion, and he asks me to empty it out.

I wonder what gave me away. A stiff-legged walk, as if I'm not used to my legs yet. An uptight way of breathing through the nose. I'm wearing my finest calico: the Sufi disciple's uniform, burlap sacks with sleeves. And, of course, there's that smell of petrol.

'Why does this smell like petrol?' the guard asks again, as I lay my bag on the ground and bend down to open it. Either he didn't listen the first time, or he wants to see if I'll contradict myself. 'What are you carrying?'

Chlorine tanks were supposed to be delivered to us, but the technicians bringing them were arrested at a checkpoint when they couldn't prove their employment, making their canisters incendiary in the eyes of the guard who stopped them. A fresh crew showed up at the pool the next day. In the absence of chlorine, they recommended benzene to purify the water. I suspect they didn't know how to work the pumps, but it's not for me to suspect. Since then, my speedo and towel have been soaking up the benzene-infused pool water, giving me the faint aroma of trouble.

I can't explain this to the checkpoint guard, implicating people like him in needless harassment of the innocent. He's here to keep me safe, and if I don't convince him that he's doing a good job, then I don't go home.

'The pool where I swim has run out of chlorine, so they use benzene to help disinfect the water.' I loosen the noose cinching the bag closed. 'I'm just carrying my training gear.'

I'm quite sure I won't get arrested today and will make it home safely. If necessary, I can ask the guard to contact Lieutenant Colonel Khodeir, the director of the swim team. He'll tell this nameless official that I've represented the Armed Forces in national championships and international competitions, that I train in the same swimming pool as officers and heroes.

It's what he once said to an interviewer visiting the swimming federation's offices. It was hoped that my quiet, spiritual demeanour would appeal to the media and show the federation in a good light, offsetting the fact that it's run by a bunch of ex-army officers looking for an easy administrative job where they can take advantage of other people's achievements to raise their own profiles. I was expected to charm the reporter, but I'm not much of a natural charmer.

'Money isn't the only measure of value, ya hanem,' the director said when the interviewer asked about athletes' financial compensation. The director isn't a charmer either. He wreaks destruction when he perceives the slightest offence against him, which includes any offence against me—*his swimmer*. As a tyrant, he's largely ineffectual; his thoughts are written all over his face. 'This boy,' he pointed at me, 'swims so he can hear the national anthem from the top of the podium, not to prim himself up. He's not that sort of man.' The journalist raised an eyebrow and laughed as she scribbled her notes.

A week after the interview, when Colonel Khodeir passed by the pool to watch his athletes train, I asked him when the piece would be published. He followed me into the locker room, massaging my shoulders firmly, and sat down on the wooden bench opposite me as I changed.

'Never,' he said, dusting off his hands, as though disappearing the article and the interviewer herself. The other athletes moved around us silently. 'You should've seen what she wrote,' he went on, his voice echoing off the ceramic tiles. 'The ugliest things. But don't worry. I'll always protect my boys.' I tried to remember if I had said anything in the interview to jeopardise myself. I thought I had been pleasant, even too benign; with the director there, it had been impossible to be anything but unassuming.

I heard him heaving his body off the bench. A slap on my back left my skin stinging, and he sniffed his palm before going to wash it clean of the petrol stink. The outline of his hand glowed red where it had landed, like cave art shimmering on stone, pushing into the future. My body is a landscape, vulnerable to people like the director who try to stake their claim to me.

So, when a guard stops me because he smells petrol, I know I have someone to call who can make the problem disappear. I've had my difficulties with the federation, but Colonel Khodeir will always be keen to help out an athlete in distress. Special favours guarantee future compliance.

'Is he wearing sandals?' he'd ask the guard, intending levity.

'Yes,' the guard would reply, unamused. It doesn't happen often, but I have been made to remove my shoes before. In sandals, I just wiggle my toes at anyone curious so they can see I have nothing to hide.

'That's him,' Khodeir would confirm. 'Let him go.'

I've only had to resort to that once, and I'd rather not make a habit of it. I race for the director and don't want to owe him any more than I already do. Favours are counted and need to be repaid. The chlorine tanks were confiscated and sold back to the pool managers. The technicians didn't come back with them. 'This is the way things go,' the director said.

Barring Khodeir, I'd have to call my parents and ask them to call a colonel of their own, anyone with a brass eagle, a star, or at least a dragonfly on their shoulder who can help me out.

But I can't do that. They worry.

'Benzene can't be good for your skin,' the guard says, unconvinced by my story.

'It's not,' I say, scratching my back, trying to scare him into releasing the bag.

'Already rotting at your young age?' he asks.

A superior radios him, and the guard nudges my bag with his walkie-talkie to shift its visible insides around. Finally content that whatever I'm carrying isn't dangerous, he waves me on as if he's directing traffic.

'Get home,' he says, squinting at my ID to try and make out my name. He might need glasses, he might be illiterate, he might even be one of the blind innocent people of the city.

That's not true, I correct myself. The blind innocent—that's how our president wants us to see ourselves, as if innocence were an ailment that necessitates our powerless acquiescence to tyrannical rule. If we start thinking of tyranny as something malleable, something that can be broken, then we're not so innocent anymore. In the real world, outside of pointless axioms, it's the innocent who are unpredictable.

'What's your name?' the guard asks, giving up on the ID.

'Shahed.'

'Get home, ya Shahed, before curfew starts.'

'Is something going on?' I ask. 'This is a new checkpoint.'

'La nabeeh,' he shrugs, waving me forward. 'What could happen?'

'Rabbak bass ye'lam el-gheib,' I reply, pointing up at the concerned parties.

*

I have a letter that lets me stay out past curfew inside my prayer book, behind my ID. It is folded and enclosed with the Polaroid of a makeshift morgue in a mosque that my grandmother told me displays the grief and horror from a massacre of civilians— not of soldiers, as I first thought. Men and women in white coats stand beside tables that seem to be holding themselves together only for the photo and not for the corpses they're carrying. Buckets are scattered across the ground. Most of the dead are shrouded in white sheets and can't be seen. Blocks of ice are wrapped in black bin bags and placed on their torsos. Those who aren't covered in cloth have their jaws tied shut to keep water from entering their mouths when their bodies are washed. Big toes are bound to keep both feet side by side. Hands are fastened at the wrist and folded over the chest. With their eyes closed, I can almost imagine them praying.

Crouching in the far side of the room, out of focus, are two veiled figures dressed in black. One of them holds a pen to the surface of a large placard, filling a numbered list of the dead with names and addresses that her neighbour is dictating. The placard is to be placed on the door of the mosque for families and friends coming to claim their kin.

Teita took the photograph in a moment of calm when everything was more or less still. It was before the soldiers burst into the mosque—*wearing their boots!*—and ordered everyone out, then proceeded to set everything on fire: the prayer room inside the building, the makeshift wooden stage nearby on the corner of Nasr Street and Tayaran Street, Teita's field hospital, the protesters' tents, even some of the dead.

In the bottom right corner of the picture, sneaking below the scaffolding holding up one of the beds, there is a bird. It's a hudhud, adorned with a crown of feathers, dressed for death. The tips of the bird's feathers look like they've been dipped in black, but they're just that colour. If an abandoned feather is found, it can be used to make a mark of wisdom on a dead body. Incense is burned; the feather is dipped in the embers and grazes the skin of the dead. This is to ensure that they remain faithful to themselves, and to their path, even beyond death. A rabbit's foot.

On the back of the Polaroid, my grandmother wrote that the hudhud is the king of the birds, which isn't true. 'Attar's epic poem *Mantiq al-Tayr* tells us the hudhud led a flock of birds on a search for their king, Simorgh, who is the only imaginary creature in the fable.

*

It's November, and I can still smell the rice ash burning.

We're straddling two months: Baba, Enter and Close the Gate, and Hatoor, the Golden Spread, when wheat is supposed to turn to gold. I can't say I've ever seen the golden fields in real life, but I can smell the season. Farms north of Cairo burn rice husks from the end of October through early November. The cloud of ash and smoke travels with the Nile towards the city, and that's what I smell now: the distance, the fields, the dreams of a country and people proud of the crops they grow, all relegated to incense, colouring the mornings and evenings when the humidity rises to carry the scent downstream. My grandmother's house is only a few streets away from the river. Here, the water and green dim to a dewiness that clings to my body, sharpening my sense of the border between my skin and the rest of the world. I feel trapped in this heat, aching to shed my outer layer.

The city's magic is in its elegance as a labyrinth. Wherever you are feels like its centre, Cairo having been built and rebuilt by countless empires, kingdoms, sultanates and regimes, each wanting to break away from the past by stating anew what counts most for its people. The centre where Teita's house stands was built at the end of the nineteenth century, when the Khedive thought to reimagine the capital as a Paris on the Nile. From the 1980s onwards, as its urban centres grew unbearably overcrowded, the city was again reinvented, casting off its ancient vestments to become a modern conqueror of the surrounding desert with new settlements like 6th of October City and New Cairo. Today it is at once sprawling and dense, like a musical note folding in on itself in a sea of echoes in which it's impossible to distinguish the first sound that started it all. The past is muffled by the noise of the present.

The country might claim to have outgrown its history, yet there is a continuous project of 'beautification' in the downtown area around Tahrir Square to maintain the image of the nation's former glory. Despite the city's attempts at decentralisation, all of its new settlements, suburbs and gated communities have highways, bridges and roads that lead back to the square. The capital has had many centres, but it only has one heart, and whenever the people burn with the desire for change, they always descend on the same place.

Tahrir is less than a kilometre north of here. During the protests, Teita told me, she could smell the tear gas wafting in the air with the people's cries for the collapse of the military regime. The gas deposited a stink in the walls of the house that has never left.

Teita's house is a concrete, industrial-style affair, one of imposing arches and recesses that recall the architecture of the Mamluks without indulging in the not-so-subtle extravagances of Arabs of times past. It looks as though time's fatigue rolled in slowly, dulling the cornicing details that would have held up the arches and the roof, wearing down the sharp edges, leaving behind a structure resembling a carved pebble.

My grandmother hoped to add stucco arabesque panels to the balconies, but 'gypsum is a thirsty material', and with the Nile drying up, the price was too considerable to justify.

'I'm sorry, it's out of my hands,' said the contractor, throwing them up in surrender.

'Don't worry,' Teita smiled, always prepared to mention the unmentionable. 'The boss said there would be sacrifices with the Renaissance Dam siphoning off our water.'

The contractor shrugged nervously, flustered by her comment. After that, he avoided talking to her directly and instead sent messages through his builders, reluctant to find himself tongue-tied in front of the madwoman.

The grooves in the rough surface of the house's raw-concrete walls collect dust. Given the water shortage, the Sufi institute deemed it halal to wipe the hands, face, forearms and feet with dust in lieu of wet ablutions. I remember feeling elated at our liberation from the shackles of finding a place to wash before prayer, clueless as to what this new freedom signified.

Leaving the checkpoint behind, I run into Salah, the street-sweeper, who's brushing his broom across the section of road that stands between me and Ramy's kiosk. He is wearing an orange uniform, his red cap pulled low over his eyes, which he's trying to determine whether to keep down in fearful humility or raise to greet the person walking past.

'As-salam 'aleikom, ya Salah,' I say wearily, hoping he'll pick up on the not-in-the-mood tone of my voice. If he starts talking, I could be here all night, and I need to go home and rest before tomorrow's journey.

'I was just wondering where all this radiant evening light was coming from,' Salah replies brightly. 'Of course, it's you, ya Shahed!' He pats my shoulder and picks up his broom to walk with me to the kiosk. 'We haven't seen you in weeks.'

'I've been busy studying,' I say.

Salah has hepatitis C and neglects to take his medication regularly, so every so often he ends up in hospital. If he's following me, he needs something.

'Ba'ol-lak, ya Shahed,' he begins. 'I know you just got back, and I don't want to bother you with this—'

'Ya 'amm Salah, we talked about this,' I interrupt. 'Just come to the Sufi institute, I'll take you from the gate myself and make sure the forms are filled out so you can get the money for your medication on time, instead of waiting around on the off chance that I'll pass by.'

'Ya Sheikh Shahed,' he says, clicking his tongue and trying to butter me up. The honorific works on some Sufis, but it isn't something I believe in. 'If I skip a day here to do that, what do you think would happen? The security boys and young police officers around here complain every day about the filth, just to keep me under their thumb. You know how these people are.'

'Mmm ...' I mumble noncommittally. It's an obvious trap to lure me into speaking against the uniforms. Salah is known to try to sell whatever information he can to the guards and officers stationed nearby. Someone overheard badmouthing the police isn't worth much, but someone with my family's history getting caught out ... This must be how he's been finding the money he needs in my absence.

'Can't you submit the paperwork for me?' he asks.

'I'll try,' I lie. I already tried, but the institute wouldn't process the papers without Salah's signature and thumbprint. They know that most people can't afford to make the trip and spend the day standing in line, and the fewer demands they get for financial assistance, the better a job they appear to be doing, the bigger the bonuses for the Chief Sufi and section heads of the trust.

The trees lining the street are bedecked with pale, dull leaves. Dust coats the parked cars, etched with graffiti featuring twisted military swords, a national flag with a rotisserie chicken in the place of the eagle, and scrawls telling army personnel of numerous ranks to fuck off.

Ramy is perching on a stool in front of the kiosk, waiting for the shift change at the police station one street down to bring him his next wave of customers. His back is stooped, his elbows on his knees, his breathing heavy as if he's just come from a long run. He's been managing the kiosk full-time ever since his father's health took a turn.

'I need to get something from here,' I tell Salah. 'My lighter's empty.'

'Tayyeb, we'll talk later,' he says, patting me on the back.

White gahannameya flowers cling to a branch over the kiosk, creased and dry, crackling audibly like embers struggling to stay alight with every passing breeze. Freshly fallen petals adorn Ramy's feet. He's been sitting here a while. In this heat, not even the bougainvillea will feel cool to the touch.

I blow a loud air-kiss. Ramy looks up and lazily waves his hand without shifting.

'How can you allow the neighbourhood to go this way, boss?' I tease, gesturing at the dust graffiti.

'I've tried to clean it, but it's pointless,' he says dejectedly. 'Tomorrow just brings more wind and dust and a fresh canvas.' His eyes dart from side to side as if to avoid looking at me. Something is on his mind.

I haven't seen Ramy since the last meeting of Kaffara, a resistance group with an impressive ability to get hold of banned books, smuggle official government papers and organise strikes. We convene weekly in a cramped apartment repurposed as a library. In case of emergency, a mobile phone is kept inside a locked drawer and switched on whenever someone is in. Furniture is sparse, save for a room filled with tables and old typewriters, their rollers bearing the dents of keystrokes of frustration, helplessness, grief and righteously indignant rage. The occasional sound of typing is muffled by the brass workshop downstairs. Aside from their use for taking minutes and making leaflets with information about ongoing strikes, planned protests and the names of imprisoned comrades, the typewriters sit idling. Ramy brings the printer from his kiosk to meetings. No uniform would question why, or where, he takes it when he closes shop. If they did, he would reply that it was his livelihood, and he needed to make sure not to lose it.

I can't ask him what's wrong directly. He would never give me a direct answer. His mind is a maze, not a corridor.

'Eshteri demaghak,' I say, nudging him to let the graffiti be.

'And when the police come by and ask why I haven't had the defamation removed? What will I tell them then, ya sheikh? Manzari yeb'a wehsh.'

I smile and can't help but glance at his hair. He bleached it earlier this year, but instead of taking the colour out as he'd hoped, the peroxide turned his tight curls a burnt orange. When I first saw the new shade, I half expected the brassy ringlets to fall out in my fingers. He would swat my hand away with a sharp slap whenever I caught hold of a lock.

'It's not on you,' I say about the graffiti. 'Besides, it's all mouthing off about the army. Police don't care about the army. You know what I mean.' I will myself to focus on his eyes, not the halo encircling his head.

He sighs and looks around to check no uniforms are around to hear us.

'Fahem, but I don't think the police see it that way. They're all uniforms in the end. 'Ana madani, w-'enta madani. The rest of us are all below them.'

If he's lashing out at the uniforms, soon he'll be complaining about the price of meat, the lack of job prospects for someone whose CV creatively dubs them an 'entrepreneur', the Nile drying up, and the inherent prejudices of dice that refuse to let him win at backgammon.

I flick a stray curl, willing him to react.

He gets off the stool. Shedding the gahannameya petals, he turns his back to me before squatting in front of some crates of milk cartons. He stretches his lanky figure forward and touches his fingers gently to the ribbed surface of the cardboard as he counts out loud. The cross tattoo on his wrist glows green in the afternoon light.

Watching over the kiosk is a photo of Ramy's uncle. He died twenty years ago in an attack by the army on demonstrators outside the state media headquarters.

'The Copts are shooting at our troops!' beamed state television into people's homes. 'They're rising against the Armed Forces that protected our revolution. They're trying to destroy this country. Is any group's cause dire enough to bring a nation to its knees? Do those who supported the revolution have nothing to say to the Copts? Be mindful of God and fear for your country. We must fight for our country!'

Pious, hot-headed Muslims heeded the call and arrived at the Maspero television building to defend their brothers in the army against the seditious Christians. Bodies of slaughtered protesters were tossed over the Corniche into the Nile. Naturally, the police would not arrest the military personnel responsible. The army and the police might not always see eye to eye, but better the devil you know.

Teita was working at her clinic when the Maspero Massacre happened. She had heard arguing in the waiting room and come out to find half her patients gone and the rest glued to the television set. Her nurse was on the phone, crying to someone on the other end. Teita messaged a doctor she knew at the Coptic Hospital to ask what she could do to help. A week later, her colleague wrote back: 'Sorry for the late reply, habibti. There were just too many of them.'

Teita didn't witness the sight of all those bodies piling up in the morgues, where they remained without being claimed, the living being unwilling to acquiesce to the false causes of death reported by the state's coroners. Bullet wounds became injuries from glass shrapnel; asphyxiation from tear gas turned into heart attacks; skull fractures from beatings were put down to motorcycle accidents, and the wearing of helmets and seatbelts made mandatory in response. The priests tried to convince the families of the dead to bury their kin quickly without performing proper autopsies, promising that the bishop would pray over their bodies, guaranteeing their place in a paradise much more generous than the world they had just departed.

Of course, I never knew any of this happened until Ramy told me. He explained that it was normal for a young Muslim living in today's world—an attendee of the Sufi institute, no less, and swimmer representing the Armed Forces besides—not to be privy to such 'sensitive' information.

Still crouching on the pavement, Ramy spreads the day's newspapers over some empty boxes and starts to pick out pebbles from the small pile that he keeps between the generator and the refrigerator. He pauses before reaching for each one, as if there were a right answer. Sometimes, I see him come out from behind the counter to rearrange or rotate them, concocting from the bronze-coloured stones a landscape of his own imagination.

'You're heading out tomorrow, aren't you?' he says with his back to me. He doesn't mention the Sufi saint Nizam, or the prison where he's being held, or the barracks that the army has entrusted me to escort him to in the Sinai, or the sermon I'm supposed to help him deliver to the soldiers there. The mission sounds like something a 'collaborator' would do, and it is, which is precisely why I volunteered when Major General Tala'at came to the Sufi institute looking for someone willing to take on the task. Being the Chief Sufi's assistant, I was offered the privilege first. Truth be told, given my family's history, I couldn't really have said no.

'When are you back?' Ramy asks.

'Friday night el-mafrood,' I say, ''inshallah.'

He glances over his shoulder. 'Can you message me when you get home?' He's turning two pebbles over and over in the palm of his right hand, and the clicking sound is soothing. It's as though he's summoned a voice from deep within the stones that can help him decide where to place them.

I raise my eyebrows at his indecision. 'Still looking for the perfect combination?'

'The news keeps changing as the country gets worse. If the papers stop lying, maybe I'll be able to make a decision. Maybe then I'll know what I'm betting on with each of these.' He holds up a pebble as if to prove his point.

The pebbles come from Saint Catherine's Monastery, built in the sixth century at the foot of Mount Sinai. Few people today are granted permission to travel to the region where it stands. In the company of the colonel who leads the national swim team, I am one of the privileged few, having travelled to the Sinai for swimming races. I feel guilty to have this dispensation, one of many afforded to me that Ramy can only hear about second-hand. When I returned from the holy site with the pebbles, he turned them over in his hand just as he's turning them now, looking for the hidden trick that would reveal the granite rooms I entered. He squeezed the first pebble between his thumb and forefinger, hoping it might give way to unveil a small compound of tight alleyways. He rubbed the second pebble in his palms, hoping the monastery's blue tiles—which look more Ottoman than Orthodox from the photos, he says— would spill out, tempering the unbearable heat of the city, giving him a lungful of mountain air filtered by rock, stone and clay. When he got to the third pebble, he lost hope. He clasped all the pebbles in one hand, feeling their weight, as if he were about to throw them against the wall behind his kiosk to see if they'd fall apart.

A few years on, the pebbles still haven't revealed any secrets.

'So?' he prods, rising to his feet and turning to face me. He straightens his back as he stands up, trying to appear taller, not that he needs to. I can still picture him looming over me on the first day we met, over on the other side of the road, underneath the trees.

'So what?' I ask.

'Will you message?'

'Of course, boss. Anything for you.'

I hold out my black lighter. He plucks it from my hand and leans back to grab a can of lighter fuel with a pinhole nozzle. A whistling hiss fills the silence. From somewhere beneath the whoosh, another sound reaches my ears, reverberating like wind rushing through a wooden hollow. It's the hudhud that stalks Teita's garden.

Ramy clicks the lighter a few times until he sees a flame rise. 'Your weapon,' he says, handing it back to me. I give him some change in return, and he takes it with one hand, transfers it to the other, then reaches over to slide it into my chest pocket, before turning to go inside the kiosk's tiny compartment.

I pick out two plastic-wrapped cheese sandwiches from the fridge and wave them in the air. 'Put them in the notta?'

He writes down what I owe next to my name, still breathing loudly and deeply. Maybe there's a new precinct commander. Every new commander drops by and threatens to shut down the kiosk if Ramy doesn't let him wet his beak a little. Most of Ramy's business comes from checkpoint guards, security officers at banks and embassies, and officials at the precinct. There's always a blue van parked somewhere nearby filled with boys eager to break faces and noses, their helmets too big for their heads, the tufts of puberty moustaches betraying their age. They look for all the comfort they can get in tea, hash, fermented milk and extra-salted cheese.

'Hey.' Ramy taps his fingers on a copy of *Al-Ahram*. 'Seen this?'

'Yeah, I heard,' I reply. He's pointing to photos of the Grand Ethiopian Renaissance Dam, which has been draining Egypt's lifeline for a decade or so. The structure was left vulnerable after an explosive attack a few days ago heated up the concrete. 'Blowing up the Renaissance Dam won't bring back our water,' the headline reads. If it wasn't the dam, where did they think the water was disappearing? The sun doesn't burn that bright.

'Looks weird, right?' Ramy says. 'I mean, all that water rushing through. They say it might even wipe out a few towns near Luxor and 'Aswan. Some of the islands there could be underwater by tomorrow. Apparently, our reservoirs can't handle the flow of water. For the first time since my great-grandfather's days, this city might actually witness the Nile flooding. Do you think it'll happen? I'd like to see that.'

'It does look weird.' I peer at the photo, which shows what looks like a leak in the dam's wall. The attack was enough to whip both countries into a panic. When I first learnt the news, I half expected Nizam's Friday sermon at the barracks would be cancelled, but of course, that would send the wrong message. The army can't show that it's scared.

'Ba'ol-lak,' Ramy says, bringing a water bottle out from under the counter. 'They told me to give this to you.' He handles it slowly and gently, as if sudden pressure on the plastic might set the petrol inside alight.

I take the bottle and prop my gym bag on my knee to put it away. Just more benzene to go with my benzene-bathed swimwear. When I'm done, I notice Ramy is still staring at the bottle's outline through the mesh. He has the same anxious, uncertain expression that he gets when he's sorting pebbles for the newspapers.

'What's it for?' he asks, and I can almost hear his voice breaking. In all the time I've known him, Ramy has had an incredible ability to speak when others would prefer silence.

His phone beeps an alert of the impending curfew. 'I have to get going,' I say, grateful for an escape. 'I need to rest a bit before tomorrow.' A small pop of air leaves Ramy's lips as he opens his mouth, but he doesn't say anything.

Leaving the kiosk, I give Salah the money I would have paid Ramy for my lighter refill. Even potential informers need to eat.

Salah kisses the note and presses it to his forehead, then repeats the actions twice more. 'God bless you and keep you.'

''Ameen, ya Salah.'

I look around, taking a moment. The trees' leaves are dim from the dust sticking to them. The whole country is waiting for a heavy rain to wash all the shit away.

*

Dusk settles, and the electricity goes out. The only light reaching my bedroom comes from the neighbours' window, which is partially obscured by the frayed silhouette of a figure on their balcony. Musa goes outside to smoke when he's visiting his parents. My curtains dull the shapes and sounds of the world beyond, leaving me suspended in the fog between wakefulness and sleep where everything real feels urgent.

My phone buzzes. It's a message from 'Araby, the driver accompanying me tomorrow to escort Nizam from prison to a military barracks in the Sinai where the saint has to give a Friday sermon.

'Good evening, Sheikh Shahed,' he says. This old 2010s brick phone of my mother's can only handle basic alphanumeric characters, so I'm lucky that 'Araby's messaging style is uncomplicated. 'Just confirming that I'll be waiting to collect you at the swimming pool in the morning, 'inshallah. I'll bring blankets, since we'll probably have to sleep in the car outside Segn 'Abu Za'bal tomorrow night.'

I don't fancy sleeping in a car outside a prison. There's a reason why 'Abu Za'bal is overcrowded; the Bahamut doesn't take much prodding to swallow people whole.

The ongoing communications shutdown means mobile networks are blocked and messages and calls require an active WiFi connection. The generator in Teita's house isn't running, so with the electricity down, my phone must have picked up Musa's parents' internet signal to receive 'Araby's message. I can hear the generator in their apartment block furiously pumping away. We depend on the 'Aswan Dam to provide us with electricity, but with the Nile drying up and the Ethiopian Dam further south devouring our dwindling water supply, power outages extend into long, stagnant stretches of darkness. My parents complain about the nightly blackouts and the generator's din whenever they're back in the country. Life abroad suits them better, I think.

'They know I smoke,' Musa said to me about his own parents when we first met. He explained that he came out to the balcony for the sake of their health. It wasn't worth risking it, given his mother's asthma and his father's pulmonary problems from years inhaling silica dust as an engineer in a cement factory, an industry infamous for shortening workers' lives, leaving them wheezing and gasping for breath.

I was struck by his nonchalance as he let that little piece of his history pour forth and float across the alleyway to my windowsill, where the book I was reading—a collection of poems by 'Abdel Rahman el-'Abnudi—was still open in front of me. My candle had a bad wick, so I preferred to burn it close to the window to stop it from smoking up the whole room. Ramy makes the candles himself. I've told him the cotton he uses is too thick, but he refuses to change it, even after I threatened to go elsewhere. 'It breaks my heart,' he said, pushing a bag of empty candle jars into my hands to call my bluff, 'but I understand.'

The light in Musa's apartment was behind him, and I couldn't really make out his features, except a toothy smile that he flashed often.

'Do you smoke?' he asked, extending a packet of cigarettes. If I had stretched my arm as far as possible, I wouldn't have been able to reach his hand.

'No, I don't.'

'Parents won't let you?' He wedged the packet back inside his jeans. The question was neither malicious nor teasing, making me smile. It was just an enquiry from someone used to living with other people as equals, someone who had outgrown all the juvenile concerns that make parents loom large.

'They're not usually about,' I replied, waving the book around vaguely.

'Mine are always here,' he said, pointing behind him with the lit cigarette. 'I come to visit them every Friday. I've never seen the lights on in your house, though.'

He settled onto the railing, his feet dangling over the dark void between us, leisurely splashing the air. I thought of my father sitting with me by the edge of the swimming pool, telling me to kick harder.

'Not at your window, at least,' he clarified, raising his eyes to meet mine. 'I thought the house was abandoned. Except for the garden. It's immaculate.'

'You're not far off,' I replied. 'I used to live here with my grandmother, Allah yerhamha. My parents live in Germany, and they don't come back to the country very often, but they still pay Teita's housekeeper—Umm Saber—and a gardener to come a few times a week to keep the house clean and the grounds tended, especially the sycamore and lemon trees. I'm not around here much these days, either. I usually stay at the khanqa—the Sufi dormitories—'

'I know what it is,' he laughed.

'Of course,' I said, patting my chest in acceptance of blame for any hurt I might have caused. I inherited the gesture from Teita. She often used it when coaxing me to finish my food—*blame me or hate me, but please eat.*

'My apologies,' I continued. 'But yes, it's easier to focus on my studies in the khanqa, so I don't come back here often.'

'Where are the lemon trees? I can smell them sometimes.' He waved the smoke away to clear a path for the citrussy odour and took a deep breath, his chest expanding briefly before giving way as he surrendered to a fit of coughs and laughter. 'I should really stop smoking,' he said, smiling broadly as he took a drag on his cigarette. 'Does it bear fruit?'

I nodded and pointed with the book to a corner of the garden enveloped in darkness except for a few slivers of light reflecting off the shiny leaves. The gardener wipes the dust from the plants by hand, whispering the names of saints, assigning guardian angels to those that need our prayers to survive the drought.

'Lemon tree is there,' I said, 'next to a wooden bench, which you probably can't see right now.' I held up an imaginary fruit between the tips of my fingers and kissed it emphatically. 'It bears sharply sour lemons, enough to make me grind my teeth whenever I make it into a drink.'

'Do you blend it with the peels, or without?' Musa asked.

'What's the point of the drink without the skin? Keeps it creamy.'

He laughed. 'Allah yenawwar, ya Shahed.'

The sound of my name on his lips disarmed me. I had almost let myself relax—one mask had fallen and another assumed its place—but now the calm turned to panic. How did he know my name? I felt deceived. He had uttered it with purpose, telling me, *I know you*.

I tried to get a better look at him, and as if to help me, he tilted his head slowly towards the window behind him and then back again. His profile came into sharp relief against the glow behind him, carving his features out of the shadows. Then, as if on cue, the building lit up brilliantly as electricity surged at full force through the wires not connected to the generator, setting off radios I didn't know were on and bringing back to life the streetlights between Musa's building and my own. My eyes were still on Musa's face. Even in the harsh, consistent electric light, I didn't recognise him from anywhere.

Squinting, he raised a hand to shield himself from the surprise luminescence, when the electricity went out again as suddenly as it had come. Groans emanated from the windows, born not of anger but of frustration, expressing a rupture in the reality people felt they were owed, one of many of our country's promised futures that hadn't come to pass. For a moment, the city had blinked open its heavy eyes, giving us a brief glimpse of what life would look like if the country were half as glorious as our president the Field Marshal insists it is.

'Do we know each other?' I asked finally, unable to place him.

'We were part of the same caravan at last year's Mawled celebrations,' he said. 'I accompanied you on the 'oud as you sang your prayers. My cousin Taha—you know Taha, long face and a baby afro—was on the drum.'

I shook my head.

'You have a beautiful voice. Taha made me join this Mawled because he knew you were going to be there, and he expected Nizam to be there too. He told me that you never join a hadra unless you know Nizam will be there. But you only had eyes for your Sheikh Nizam, of course.' A wink and a smile underlined his words. Nizam had yet to become a saint back then, but the spell he manages to cast on people is a miracle of its own. There are rumours that he can be in two places at once—unfounded, of course.

'I recognised you on the street a few weeks ago and almost stopped you,' Musa continued, 'but you had such a determined walk, so I thought you were in a rush. I saw you talking with the owner of the kiosk ... Ramy, I think? Anyway, I asked him your name. He looked at me strangely, and I can only imagine what he must have thought.'

I didn't have to imagine to know Ramy must have been thinking about my mother's history. I wondered why he hadn't mentioned that someone on the street had asked about me.

'Eventually, he told me you're called Shahed,' Musa said tentatively, sensing my unease. I still couldn't believe I'd survived this long in the city. It was only a matter of time before someone made the connection, and then what? Prison, or exile?

I remembered that Musa was a neighbour, meaning Ramy would be familiar with his face. The thought put me at ease. The last thing I wanted was to end up in prison, least of all for the sins of others.

Teita used to feel the same way. She blamed Mama when she was forced out of her job as a surgeon at the hospital and when she lost her lectureship at Mama's university. She blamed her for the police raid on her clinic, in which nothing was spared. Everything was taken, from the waiting room television to all of Teita's patients' folders. More than a few patients called her in the following days, reporting that the police had brought them in for questioning to ask if Teita had tried to recruit them into whatever anti-government coalition she belonged to, all because Mama was caught in a protest chanting, 'Yasqot, yasqot hokm el-'askar!'

'Don't worry if you don't remember me, by the way,' Musa said. 'When we were in the hadra, I looked like this.' He swiftly buttoned up his shirt, disappearing his wiry chest hair and a shield-like pendant that hung permanently around his neck, dropped his mouth open a fraction, arched his back into the slightest stoop and inhaled deeply as if preparing to roll through a brick wall. The whiff of violence and his sheer gluttony for air together painted an image of a man who felt that whatever he desired should be within reach.

'I'm sorry ...' I said, my memory un-jogged. I felt like an actor who'd forgotten what role they were playing, frantically scanning the script for any clue as to where they should go.

'It's fine,' he sighed, undoing his top buttons and letting his pendant breathe. He lifted his eyebrows to pull off his weary face and gazed into the darkness as if he were searching for something, before locking eyes with me again.

'So, Mama and Baba left you here and went off to live in paradise?' he laughed. 'And I thought my parents were cruel.'

'No,' I said, trying to muster a smile. 'They wanted me to go with them when they found a place to settle, but I felt like staying. I didn't want to leave Teita here, and I've never been comfortable outside of the country.' I wasn't aware of the truth of those words until I said them. I felt my chest heave at the thought of being away, then breathed a slow sigh of relief as I looked out on the sycamore tree growing between our balconies and smelt the sharpness of the lemon trees rising, brightening the night air.

From the corner of my eye, I imagined Teita moving across the grass, her feet landing heavily on the ground, her braided, silvery hair glowing in the dark as she took shears to the clump of mounting ivy that's been trying to choke the sycamore tree for as long as I've been alive. If it weren't for Teita, the sycamore wouldn't be here, and neither would I.

I didn't know Musa. If I did, I would have known I could tell him everything about my family history, what they did to Mama in prison, the state she was in when Teita found her there.

After her release, Teita tried to convince Mama to leave the country, to leave it all behind, but Mama couldn't do it. The passage of a few weeks and her dismissal from her degree programme soon convinced her. Mama's master's dissertation failed a censorship committee run by aging professors at a state university with all the prestige and aesthetics of a mid-twentieth-century fascist regime, complete with grand domes, fences around every patch of greenery and such meagre student allowance that Mama regularly had to pay out of pocket to print her research—all for nothing.

I was born in France, which was my parents' first choice among places to settle. Mama completed her master's in Paris, but she and Baba weren't granted the right to stay there once she was done. Mama couldn't explain the arrest on her record and failed to prove the 'systematic persecution' required to claim asylum. She and Baba came back here and briefly moved in with Teita, who had been living alone for a few years by then. They left me behind in her care as they hopped from country to country, a decision they reassured me was only due to the persisting infection in my right ear, which they worried would not withstand the cabin pressure of an airplane. The arrangement was a makeshift solution until they could make a more permanent escape. Baba never wanted to live in the country, so he was happy for any excuse to follow Mama out the door. In his words, people in Europe know how to live.

Within a few years, Mama and Baba got what they were coveting and were granted permanent residency in Germany. Teita was busy trimming the ivy suffocating her sycamore when Mama gave her the news: they could finally take me off Teita's hands, releasing her from her duties.

'I have all the time in the world,' Teita replied, gulping deeply as she snapped her garden shears, 'now that I can't work.' She watched the cutting words leave their mark on Mama, who was already burying her face in her hands to stifle her sobs. Pointing at me with the shears, Teita added, 'And the boy likes it here.'

Mama's suffering, her own job loss, both my parents' exile—all of it seemed so final in Teita's eyes. Life had gone by. Even the revolution had come and gone for nothing. Teita didn't mind that Mama protested—it even made her proud—but her arrest and exile were reminders that the army made victims of all protesters who dared dream of freedom. It made Teita realise that the life she had been living until then was illusory at best. Freedom had a price, and they had paid it, but what they got wasn't what they'd asked for. There could never be freedom as long as the men in khaki uniforms kept their boots firmly on people's necks. Teita wanted to outlive victimhood, not sit around waiting to grow old. Having me around helped.

My parents managed to leave, so singing their exile blues to someone I barely knew, who was still stuck here, seemed like it would be bad form.

Musa looked at me fixedly for a moment, as if waiting for me to move or change shape, and then said, 'Ebn balad. A child of this country, through and through.' He pounded his closed fist against the railing in a show of strength and nodded solemnly, half closing his eyes as if he did not need to see me. I couldn't tell if he was teasing or being sincere. In a flicker of the candlelight, his face softened again. 'If I could, I'd leave,' he added simply.

'Where would you go?' I asked, happy for the attention to be drawn away from me.

'Milano,' he replied, diligently rolling the letters off his tongue, making the name holy, as if it were a thing to be worshipped and savoured slowly. The sunlight and textures of the place were contained in his expression, like the word was an olive pit turning between his lips, tearing at whatever flesh still clung to it. 'Or Florence. I speak Italian, and my father has connections with architects in both places, so that could be my way in.' While that dream still held some flavour for him, the thought of other places besides this country ceased to nourish me years ago.

'Why haven't you gone yet?' I asked.

He sighed. 'My parents worry, that's all. When I was growing up, my father was off work for long stretches of time. Some days, he'd come home from the cement factory with bruises and sit there on the bathroom floor for hours. The factory was changing hands, and the new owners were trying to push out existing workers by cutting everyone's wages and withholding pay. One of the frontline workers committed suicide after being denied two pay cheques in a row. Then, early one morning when Baba and his co-workers had locked down the factory in protest, riot police descended on them to restore order with tear gas and batons. Baba was questioned but quickly released. After a few more years of protests and strikes, the factory was eventually taken over by the army, and Baba was kicked out. My mother was the breadwinner during those times. She's one of the owners of El-Souq restaurant downtown.'

'I know it,' I said. 'Baladi food, mostly, right?'

'Right. She would go to local farms and producers herself, which meant that sometimes—not often, but sometimes—she'd have to stay overnight at the farms, because of all this.' Musa gestured at the dark and whomever was behind the curfew. 'I remember hearing her talk on the phone to the other owners of El-Souq and her siblings, who'd tell her that a woman shouldn't do that, that they were proud of the work she did, but she shouldn't be away from her home like that. My father stayed out of it, but he worried about her and worried about us. If she gave up the restaurant, we would be thrown to the wind. So, he told anyone who needed to hear it that he always knew where his wife was. When people asked why he didn't go in my mother's place when there was a risk that she'd be stranded out there, he said that wasn't his problem, and that anyway, someone had to mind me. Hearing the words from his own mouth, and not wanting to emasculate a man whose wife was already the breadwinner even further, they shut up.'

'Is that why you want to leave?'

'Yes and no,' he said. 'I miss the country whenever I'm gone, so there must be something keeping me here besides my parents, but I can't tell what it is. People's faces, the strong brow everyone seems to have, the way we always laugh from the belly.' He shrugged. 'Can't tell you.'

'Reehet el-torab?' I asked.

'Could be.' He sighed. 'But what's the soil when you can't live as you wish? Haga 'araf. I have to prove I can be just like every other man in this country if I want the right to exist here at all.'

We were silent. The heat from the candle's crazed flame felt overpowering, and the smoke made me dizzy as I tried to focus on its ephemeral flight into the black nothingness separating my window and Musa's.

'I'm going now,' he said suddenly. It came out as more of a command than a statement.

By the time his window slid shut, I was back to unfurling lines of poetry like rays of sunlight bouncing off the seabed. Over the next few weeks, I sat at the same window, burning the same candle, next to the same book. Musa came out to his balcony like clockwork on Friday evenings, once an hour for three hours, but he didn't talk again. I hadn't learnt my script, but I realised it was my line. I just had to find the right words.

I sit up and stretch, feeling myself sinking again into the bed's softness as I try to rise. I think of the sharp cliff of Musa's shoulders, how his arms swing forward as if wrestling the air in front of him, giving him a slightly jagged walk.

Whenever we meet, whether it's at the Sufi café or by Ramy's kiosk outside the house, Musa always strides towards me till our toes are almost touching, his shoulders squared to face mine, before abruptly stopping in front of me and holding out his hand. Just as he puffed out his chest on the balcony, he leans into his walk with macho determination that would be parodic if he weren't so adept at pulling it off. He remains invisible until he wants to be seen, at which point all he has to do is stop and ask, 'ezzayak? He knows how to blend into the environment, an easy way to survive in the city. By contrast, as a Nubian, Nizam can't help but be visible, and that's why he's locked up in 'Abu Za'bal. And as a swimmer for the Armed Forces, I wear my visibility like a shield. What kind of trouble could someone like me cause?

Musa quit his job recently. He used to work as a site surveyor for a local architecture firm that began facilitating between an Emirati conglomerate and the Ministry of Culture and Tourism on an urban renovation project. The same Emirati firm 'developed' the Maspero Triangle, razing thousands upon thousands of homes in the urban slums of downtown Cairo to clear the way for hotels, shopping malls and offices. Musa's father grew up in one of those homes, not far from the television building, with his parents and seven siblings. As a child, Musa wandered through the rubble of the demolition collecting pieces of the debris—chunks of concrete, wood splinters, dirt, glass and cigarette butts—which he keeps to this day in a jar labelled 'my grandparents' house'.

He invited me to a talk at the Kaffara apartment, where he presented a zine he helped to produce about Cairo's fast-disappearing medieval cemeteries and necropolis. Musa's contribution to the issue placed photos of graffiti and scans of poems alongside architectural drawings of mausoleum facades, sketched in thick deliberate strokes that gave them an air of childishness. The zine was called *Tala'to Mayteen el-Balad Kollaha*, a reference to the unreasonable burden placed by the state on the people living in the necropolis and whose dead are buried there. *You've Even Evicted Our Dead*. To exhume a corpse is expensive. To hire a Sufi sheikh to transport it to another grave is also costly. Most have to accept that their dead will remain where they are even as their resting place is destroyed. As Musa says, 'Since when did a few dead bodies ever stop these people?'

*

It was only after she was arrested that my mother realised how unhappy she had been for most of her life.

Teita gifted her the name 'Hanan', which was widely viewed as an ironic choice, given my mother's lack of warmth and decidedly ungentle nature. Of course, for irony to have been the intent, my grandmother would have needed to look into Mama's future, and if that were the case, it would only mean Teita deserved her own reputation as a cruel, domineering person, who made a joke of what her daughter would grow up to feel most fragile about before she even had the chance to prove herself otherwise.

When Mama was arrested, she dropped her phone, denting the casing. That was twenty years ago. It was another November, and police had been picking off protesters by the Corniche as they left Tahrir Square. Mama had just delivered a carton of wound dressings, antiseptic fluid, inhalers and juice boxes to Masjid 'Omar Makram in an attempt to live up to her name. She had promised her mother that she wouldn't go down to Tahrir. As far as Teita knew, Hanan was at home with her husband. As far as Baba knew, she was with her mother, trying to keep her busy and away from the field hospitals. That was exactly where Teita wound up: tending to casualties being rushed in on motorcycles from a raging battle with the police on Mohamed Mahmoud Street, a few hundred metres from where her daughter was leaving the mosque.

Mama heard the explosions of tear-gas grenades—

bang

bang

—and decided that it was time to go home.

I stroke the phone's bruise and imagine my mother being pushed into a blue police van, steadying herself with one hand in the rough grip of an officer, the hidden device sliding perilously down her trouser leg as she raises her foot to clamber on board the vehicle. I see the young boy already seated in the van who notices her struggling and swiftly grabs the phone with his feet before the impact can rattle, hiding it in his slipper under the arch of his foot. He presents it to my mother once she has settled into the darkness and gentle jostling of the metal cage transporting them who-knows-where. Wiping the screen on his torn t-shirt, he apologises for his dirty feet, before asking whether she has enough credit for him to call his mother.

Mama is pregnant with me but isn't showing yet. When she said this to the police officer who dragged her to the van, he scanned her sceptically before replying, 'We'll find you a place to sit on the bench then. You've a long drive ahead of you.'

Every so often, the blackness in the van is interrupted by streetlights glaring through the small mesh window that hardly lets in enough oxygen for the people inside to breathe. With every brief flash of bright orange, I see the scene change in front of Mama's eyes, but when I try to picture her there, I see nothing. Not even her face, its nose gently rounded like a little piece of rolled dough, or her square jaw and high cheekbones, which give her an air of gravity, as though she were built of stacked bricks, drawing a wall between her and the rest of the world.

Mama told me herself that her mind at the time was blank. She sat in silence, simply waiting to see where she would end up. She was terrified of calling Baba, who had messaged her to say he hoped the wannabe revolutionaries' mindless actions wouldn't keep the fish he'd ordered for dinner from arriving warm. The thought of Teita's voice on the phone was equally terrifying; *the woman*, as Mama called her mother in moments when Teita inspired her fear and love, barely answered calls, and whenever she did, it was always to give Mama advice she hadn't asked for. She nodded to the boy, signalling that he could make his phone call.

Hearing his mother on the line, the boy's resolve to tell her about his situation failed at the last moment. 'Why would I be in Tahrir?' he laughed. 'I'm with my friends, we're going to the internet café. I'll be out for a while. I'm whispering because it's busy on the bus. Mama, I swear, it's all good.'

Nobody in the van made a sound. If the boy's mother could believe that he was safe, then maybe he was. Maybe they all were. Maybe arresting them was just a scare tactic—one that was working. Mama who wasn't yet Mama was scared. Her surroundings suddenly reflected what Teita referred to as 'Hanan's cold heart', a prison of someone else's creation in which it was impossible to dream of freedom.

The boy handed Mama her mobile back. She stroked the jagged dent in the casing, which her touch would gradually wear smooth over the following years. The new edge was still sharp, and she pressed her finger against it, hoping the searing sensation would wake her up and jolt her into calling for help. It didn't. Mama knew the reason why she had stayed silent while the boy lied to his mother was that she didn't know whether she had the strength to admit her situation either. She always found that she needed to merit saving before she could let herself be saved.

Baba had just started the espresso machine when Teita's keys clicked in the door lock the next day. She had left the field hospital at five in the morning, when the explosions of thunder and cracking of bullets from Mohamed Mahmoud Street had died down. Instead of going home and trying to sleep, she thought to pick up fresh fruit from a nearby stall and drop them off at her daughter's place. The wet season had come early in 'Aswan, so persimmons and dates had already arrived. They were bitter, she noted, but it was better than nothing. 'What's a winter without persimmons?' Teita asked the vendor as he placed two kilograms of the fruit into a black plastic bag, slick and slippery from his wet hands.

The first stretch of Mohamed Mahmoud was lined with shops and boarded-up fast-food restaurants. Further up, the street turns into a tunnel, with the polygonal brutalist concrete wall of the American University's library enclosing one side and the limewashed brick of the university campus rising on the other. Between these indifferent faces of the city, fifty people would die over three days. The character of the walls changed; once stoic, bitter and mundane, they became wilfully indifferent to the fire, the clang of metal pipes against cars, the *pop-p-pop* of tear gas, the blasts of shotguns. Whenever the city's labyrinth untangles itself into sheer, sharp lines, someone is bound to get brutalised.

Teita opened the door of Mama and Baba's apartment to the noise of the espresso machine rumbling like an engine on its last legs.

'Hana-an!' she called, her tongue wrapped tightly around my mother's name, conferring on it a customary extra syllable, for fear of what might happen to tenderness and warm hearts if left alone. 'Taʻali saʻdeeni,' she shouted, beseeching her daughter's help.

The wrinkles in Teita's hands were stained the colour of molasses from antiseptic—or was that dried blood? She tried scrubbing it off with a stone, but the stain only sank deeper into her skin, which seemed to have turned into a sponge. In the field hospital, there wasn't enough time to do more than apply tourniquets and wrap wounds in gauze; occasionally, bullets had to be dug out of people's shoulders, biceps, waists and thighs in order to staunch the bleeding. Yet the blood ran and didn't stop, pooling into bin bags and soaking through newspapers that doctors laid down on the table, leaving islands of red that darkened at the edges, until Teita's quick hands wiped the surface clean to place fresh layers down for the next patient.

Protesters ceased to be human and became landscapes of flesh. Teita's firm grip would produce thick, red rivers, but her lighter touches left only a burgundy handprint, the fine creases in her surgical glove faintly visible on their skin. Teita wondered how many people bore these marks of her care. How many would have them washed away by relatives in the morgue, and how many would get to wash them off themselves? Did those who survived see her handprints on their bodies in the mirror; did they press their own hands against the trace of hers to remember that someone thought they were worthy of saving? Did the kin of those who died see the marks and notice that in their last moments, their loved ones were held?

One man—who still hovered before Teita's eyes as she walked down the corridor in Mama's apartment—had climbed off the motorcycle he arrived on with no help and taken one step forward, before collapsing like a puppet whose strings had been cut. By the time Teita reached his crumpled body, the life had drained from his eyes. As she grabbed him by his soaking shirt, she caught the reflection of speeding emergency vehicles' headlights in the shimmering sheen of blackened blood.

Again and again, the bucket of oft-renewed water in which she washed her hands turned from clear to pink to—

bang

b-b-bang

—flowing so thickly between her fingers that it would coat her hand like a glove.

'Ma'lesh,' Teita whispered apologetically every time someone recoiled from the sting of her caramel-coloured antiseptic liquid, as though she, not the police snipers at the end of the darkened Mohamed Mahmoud Street, had been the one to cause the injury. Betadine mixed with blood, she noted, looked exactly like cherry wood whose grain was moved to run.

The churning grunts of the espresso machine grew louder as Teita approached the kitchen, and she wondered whether the sound was coming from inside her own head. When she entered, the first thing she saw was what remained of Baba's fish dinner: empty containers and greasy plates spread across the marble counters. It took a moment for her to notice Baba's hunched body in the corner, his head in his hands, like the spectre of the dead man from the night before.

Teita saw the persimmons rolling awkwardly on the floor before she realised that she'd dropped them.

'Hana-an!' she yelled again, as if kindness must be in the apartment, hiding.

The rolling sound of the espresso machine's motor stopped and was replaced with nothing but silence. Teita's strings were cut. She was just waiting for gravity to pull her down.

*

Once curfew is in effect, no one crosses the bridge between downtown and Zamalek. The checkpoint on Qasr el-Nil Bridge is impossible to pass, even with the forged letter from the Chief Sufi in my pocket. The only way across is by boat.

I train in Zamalek. I'm going to spend the night in the club's locker room, so I can be ready when 'Araby arrives to collect me at the pool in the morning.

My family has been part of the club for two generations. It is privately owned, but over time the Armed Forces have been pouring money into its facilities in exchange for entry into an *elite* institution. After a fire burnt the gymnasium down fourteen years ago, army contractors built the new building where the national team would train: steel I-beams rising like artefacts of themselves, a bare-boned skeletal structure that I can see through to the sky, like an open wound. The military paid for the team's travel to tournaments and sent colonels as their escorts to show that the whole country stands behind its athletes, and the waiters working the cafés on the club's grounds learnt how to properly salute. The club colours morphed into black, white and red. Except for when I'm at the Sufi institute, I wear an eagle pin on my mesh sports bag, which never seems to stop anyone from searching it.

I have only been criticised once for carrying the pin—and that was by Nizam.

He made the comment a year ago, on the day of his examination. Our tariqa had decided to put him forward to become a saint, a title he embraced fully, to my surprise. I had hoped he'd be above titles and shallow flattery, but it seems no one is immune. His acceptance of the honour threw me into a vicious rage, the intensity of which didn't last a day; after a baptism of benzene in the pool, I felt too tired to care, but the shape of anger was still swollen in my chest. The only reason I had considered joining this tariqa in the first place was Nizam's involvement in it. I knew the Sufis believed in saints, but I thought those were stories, metaphors, allegories; at worst, noise to fill the time between one tick of the clock and the next. Saints whisper prayers into the public's ears, pull people along on pilgrimage walks. Some are resurrected, though most die in the traditional way.

To show how much faith the army had in the longevity of Nizam's sainthood, a mausoleum was built in advance for the soon-to-be saint.

Musa called the move 'political'. Nizam had been a thorn in the army's side ever since he started petitioning the Sufi waqf to lower its lease rates for the sake of famers being driven off the land. The trust used to lease out agricultural land to just such salt-of-the-earth folk from the countryside, but now that the Armed Forces could drastically undercut the farmers' labour with a thousands-strong corps of soldiers, the waqf had raised the rates of its leases to rake in more profit. Unable to compete with the army's cheap labour and pay the waqf's extortionate rates, the farmers were evicted. Their plight was taken up by Nizam, and he had to be stopped from causing too much of a fuss. An arrangement was made in private, and soon after, Nizam was nominated to be a saint.

'The populace loves a religious socialist,' Musa explained, 'as long as the socialism stays in the mosque or the Sufi trust and doesn't affect the army's business.' I found the term 'populace' entertaining; it made the country sound like one homogeneous mass that could be moved and placed wherever it was needed, as if people had no will of their own.

As the Chief Sufi's assistant, I was required to attend the mausoleum's inauguration. Inside the central courtyard, I found myself surrounded by walls of sandstone and barred windows, with arched alcoves on three sides leading to separate chambers. A tasteful bit of construction—I couldn't believe it was contracted by the army. The military men were all sunglassed and suited in ceremonial attire, eagle-pinned and decorated like walking chandeliers. Two carried sebha beads, including Major General Tala'at, who thumbed them to keep count as he glorified God between chats with the other tan-clad men. The air was heavy with too much cologne.

I came across several generals, colonels and officers that I know through the swimming federation. They looked at the robes I was wearing and asked me how long I'd been under the Sufis' spell. When I shook hands with Colonel Khodeir, the swim team's director, the other rotab huddled together in a corner of the inner courtyard as if Sufism were catching. General Tala'at, however, grasped my hand with his calloused fingers, impressing the outline and scent of prayer beads on my palm. The imprint stayed with me when I returned to the circle of men reciting prayers, where I wished I didn't loom over the rest in stature and build so that I might disappear into the sea of white robes. I could feel all the uniforms' eyes on me, their faces sagging under the sun. The Sufi circle reeked of sweat and wet dog. I raised my cupped hands to my face in prayer to keep the stench away and was met with the cushiony odour of lavender oil fluttering up from my palms. The sweet perfume of the general's sebha. When even the piety of the rotab smelt fine, what chance did the Sufis have?

Nizam didn't attend. He sent his apologies in a letter to a state newspaper that was read out at the ceremony by General Tala'at, who stopped often mid-sentence to tell stories of the times he had met Nizam. The sebha kept moving, so I assumed his mind was elsewhere, counting virtues, favours owed, or seconds until he could leave.

As his mausoleum was being inaugurated—though it was yet to be properly consecrated by grief—Nizam had already begun his forty days of ritual solitude in the run-up to his sanctification. In the letter, he said the mausoleum didn't need him to be there in mind and body; all the place needed was his spirit, which was with us. General Tala'at cleverly spun this as evidence of heightened virtue, as opposed to what it truly was: the first of many indications of Nizam's firm stance against the people propelling him to this position of power.

Musa calls that wishful thinking, but I don't think so.

A blessing from the army isn't something you can refuse. That's why it surprised me when Nizam commented on my eagle pin. It was the first conversation we ever had, on the day of his sainthood examination. We happened to be entering the Sufi institute together. As I walked through the metal detector, the pin, which I never wore visibly on institute grounds, was in a tray among the other emptied contents of my pockets: keys, notebook, prayer book, phone.

'What's with the bird?' he asked me.

'What bird?'

'Your pet nesr there,' he pointed as I gathered my affairs.

The institute's security guards patted us both down. I was made to take off my footwear, despite wearing sandals. They didn't check Nizam's shoes. He stood to the side and looked around as he waited for me, his tall, lanky frame punctuated by a small gut that showed in the outline of his gallabeya. He seemed nervous. At one point he looked into the sun for a few seconds, his dark-brown skin creasing as he squinted, waiting for it to blink. Then his gaze resumed its wandering as though trying to place unfamiliar surroundings, picking up sparse trees, fake grass, parked cars. The institute is on an open university campus following the layout of a medieval Islamic quarter, complete with alleyways, squares with fountains—dry because of the drought—and deconstructed portals. Nizam seemed to shrink in the shadow of those immense columns that carry nothing, as if they were discovered and reassembled with no knowledge of their previous purpose. Maybe they just carry the sky and its ancient, eternal blue.

I was trying to formulate an answer that would impress Nizam as the guard kicked one of my sandals before stepping on the other and flipping it over with his shoe.

'You can go,' he told me, having sufficiently trampled my footwear, confident that I wouldn't fight back.

Pick your battles, I thought. Sandals didn't top the list.

I set the clasp firmly on the pin's tip, put it back in my pocket and walked away from the gate. Out of earshot of security, I confessed to Nizam that I represented the Armed Forces as a swimmer. The Sufi institute and the army exist in different worlds, and not many people on campus know that I compete. Somehow, though this was our first encounter with each other, I felt comfortable telling Nizam.

The Chief Sufi, my mentor, thought that I needed to grow out of such juvenile activities, saying I should dedicate my life, soul and energies—physical and spiritual—to the tariqa. I told him that my father had made similar comments. Baba used to find it endearing that I take after his own father in my love of swimming, but after Teita died, my poolside efforts became for him nothing more than a hopeless anchor keeping me in the country.

The Chief gave me his kindest smile. 'See? If it comes out of more than one mouth, it must be worth hearing, right?'

I continued to carry my pin, since on its own it didn't betray that I'd continued my extracurricular activities. And I knew, despite the ban on insignia of all kinds on institute grounds, that even the Chief himself couldn't tell someone to remove an eagle pin.

If anything, I thought the pin would be a bonding opportunity with Nizam.

'Do you need the eagle pin to swim?'

'It doesn't hurt,' I said, with an insinuating air of camaraderie, trying to draw on a shared understanding of how the times force us to blend in. My civilian wear only gets me through so many doors.

'Well, it hurts me,' he said. 'I feel aggravated just walking next to you knowing that you have it in your pocket. Like you're about to stab me in the back with it. If you're carrying it, wear it. Why else have it? Why hide it?'

'I'm just trying to follow institute rules.' His comments shouldn't have surprised me, but they put me on edge. I wasn't ready for sincerity. It was one of the rare moments when I have felt compelled to fill a silence, but I didn't know what to say. His pace quickened.

'Institute rules. I find things built to last to be evil,' Nizam said. 'Plastic, where does it end up? Monuments to victories, who was forced to lose? Your flag, do you raise it daily? Did you draw it as a child in school? Did you yell, "Long live the Arab Republic of Egypt"? Was the republic built to last? On whose back did you climb to fly the eagle? Do you need them prostrating for you to stand tall?'

'We have recycling centres for plastic now,' I said.

'Ah, there's hope for this country yet,' he said flatly.

Nizam had planned to spend his stint in solitude before his examination walking from Qena to Quseir along a hundred-and-something-kilometre stretch of road that many a saint and revered sheikh had walked before him. His holiness managed to disappear before he reached the craggy mountains, without leaving behind so much as a sebha as a token for the land. Ritual solitude included a vow of silence, and Nizam was arrested when he wouldn't respond to army officers at a checkpoint on the road. He hadn't warned General Talaʿat of his wanderings, which his friend would have supported if only he'd been told. Forty days of solitude turned into three months; although Nizam started speaking after forty days, it took the institute a further two months to find him and confirm his identity. It was only then that the officers authorised his release, finally satisfied that the Nubian man had not been presenting them with forged documents.

Nizam was given the option to postpone his confirmation, but, to no one's surprise, he preferred to get it over with quickly. After he accepted the nomination, there was never any doubt about whether he'd pass. In these circumstances, the only concern was that the examining sheikhs would be too lenient or too harsh in recognition of the hardship he had suffered, depending on whether they saw it as a test or a punishment.

'I'll be sitting behind the Chief Sufi today,' I told Nizam, leaning forward to keep pace with him.

'You're 'Abbas's boy?' he asked, covering his mouth to muffle his lisp as he said the Chief's name. 'Well, go on, 'ollena kam so'al. Give us a taste—nabza bass—of what I'll be facing in that room. I'm dying to be done with this. I'm so sick of having to prove myself in front of administrators. If they didn't have kids like you behind them, they wouldn't be where they are. Why do you do it?'

'Do what? Be the Chief's assistant?'

'Any of it. There's this, then swimming for the army ...'

I never know how to reply to these kinds of questions. After my parents left me with Teita, swimming had been the only way I could justify leaving the house for a few hours every day. The coach gave me a lane to myself, on condition that I plug my ears. I was half deaf at the time because of an infection in one ear, so he communicated the proviso by miming continuously before trying to reach over to do it himself. I slapped his hands away. I was ten and too old to be handled. He knew that.

Whenever I remember what happened next, a wave of panic still surges through me. One moment my feet were on the paving tiles, stepping lightly and carefully; the next, I was airborne. I didn't feel the coach's hands launch me in, and for a second, I thought I'd slipped. I threw my arms out as I fell away from the orange sky, the trees tilting off to the side, chairs and tables tumbling out of view. Then came the water, whiplashing my face and the length of my body. Everything stung, and I felt a pain in my right ear. My ribs and chest were scratched from where I landed on the plastic lane lines. But I didn't complain. I was in the water, and wasn't that what I wanted?

The coach wrote the workout on the ceramic tiles and gave me a watch to measure my sets. Below the water's surface, I felt restored. Here, the sound of thrashing arms and muffled shouts reached me like they used to when I could still hear. I wasn't wearing my goggles, so everything was blurred. I swam, indulging in my ability to move, feeling the rasp of my breath shaking the water. Orbs of air rose from my mouth and nose, appearing to me like a release of all the words I could no longer hear myself speak. It was the first time I noticed my thoughts could quieten, that the voice in my head was as distant here as the sound of the coach's whistle above water.

Why do you do any of it?

I couldn't see how it would be possible for anyone to pinpoint root causes in their life's trajectory, integrating the disparate, intangible, random forces competing to push them in one direction or another. The reasoning of the architect who designed this institute, by contrast, can be traced back to solid foundations mapped out with clinical exactitude. It's like something built by a program, with nothing of the personal about it—heartless, which is exactly what comforts me. Unlike a person's path in life, a place this artificial can be pulled apart and questioned.

It wasn't really the kind of thing I could tell someone about to be sanctified according to the institute's rigid protocol. But maybe that was why he asked me that question. If the institute could interrogate him, couldn't he interrogate me?

The answer, of course, is no. This country doesn't work that way.

Nizam headed straight for the library building, and together we climbed three flights of stairs to the examination hall. Brass plating on the battered door displayed geometric engravings resembling a hammer twisting in the wind, a detail copied from a Coptic saint's mausoleum by a disciple who believed she saw St Anba Hatre in her sleep. Saints who have walked various paths can percolate in the subconscious of the devout. *All inspiration is divine.*

The examination hadn't been publicised and was meant to be a quiet affair. Even so, a small gaggle of young disciples quickly crowded around us, eager to be close to the nominated saint. A

Sudanese student named Basma, who was also assisting one of the examiners, began speaking with Nizam in Nubi. Her smile with too many teeth contrasted sharply with his three missing incisors, the reason for his lisp. I don't understand Nubi, so I excused myself and walked away, greeting Fawzeya, who was preparing tea in the kitchenette.

As I took my seat in the hall behind Chief 'Abbas, I reached into my pocket and fumbled for the pin. My fingers grazed the edges of the eagle's wings, reassuringly still in place. I glanced over at Nizam, easily distinguished in the circle of robed sheikhs by his calico trousers and collarless shirt. Assistants didn't wear robes either, but the dress code didn't mention shoes.

'Going to the beach?' the Chief remarked wryly, raising an eyebrow at my sandals. The other sheikhs laughed, as did their assistants. Feeling exposed, I determined not to wiggle my toes lest they distract the examiners from divine inspiration.

The hall had no windows, only a domed shukhsheikha skylight, which framed a cloudless, unmoving patch of Mediterranean blue. As the proceedings began, the examiners seemed to melt into their chairs, pushing beads along their sebhas in what passed for intense concentration but was in fact mind-numbing boredom. Each examiner would ask Nizam a question, and after each answer was a debate that lasted for as long as it took for the sheikhs and the assistants feeding them information to exhaust their knowledge. There were long stretches of silence. Even the clicking of the beads petered out from time to time as the sheikhs dropped in and out of sleep. In the pauses in their pondering and gaps between their questions, I would look up and see the sky turn pink, then purple, then Prussian blue. It was the only perceptible indication of time's slow passage.

A few minutes in, most eyes were shut. I quickly forgot about my toes and tried to focus on my task of thinking up lines for the Chief. I couldn't help but stare in front of me at the naked crown of his head, which was almost always covered with a knitted skullcap. He got hair implants the moment he took the big office, and I could see baby hairs were starting to sprout.

Basma, an exceptional scholar, sat on the opposite side of the room, scribbling furiously. Her sheikh refused to let her whisper in his ear, fearing that her voice would make his mind wander, so anything she wanted to communicate to him had to be written down. Putting down her pen, she slipped a sheet to him across the mother-of-pearl tabletop. The sheikh picked it up with the tips of his fingers and glanced at it briefly before rolling it up with the other papers in his hand. Pointing the bundle at Nizam, he asked him to recite verses from the Qur'an that describe the rooh, specifically verses making no direct mention of spirits, souls or shadows. Basma rolled her eyes conspicuously and gripped her pen more tightly.

Nizam recited the sixth and seventh verses of Surat el-'Araf, and his lisp momentarily disappeared:

Fa lanas'alanna-llazeena 'orsila 'ileihim wa lanas'alanna-l-morsaleen.
Fa lanaqossanna 'aleihim bi 'ilmi-w-wa ma konna gha'ibeen.

It was Chief 'Abbas who asked him to defend his choice of verses, which meant I would have to find a counterargument.

Nizam responded, 'These verses deal in absences, specifically in the exchange of a message. A message might exist, but if its addressee is not present to receive it, it becomes meaningless. A message can be accepted or rejected, assuming a capacity for decision-making, that is, we have been endowed with some form of free will. "I've given you a gift, do with it as you please. My part is done."'

As I listened to Nizam, my own presence in the room started to feel accidental, as if I'd fallen from the narrow shaft of light above me and happened to land here. I found myself transported to a train station with the other attendees, where, recognising that we were all traveling alone, we decided to pass some time together as we waited for our respective trains. It seemed like the only place where we might possibly meet. I would never seek these people out—and yet, here I was. I couldn't shake the feeling that I had stomped on someone else's rising dreams to be here, deciding the fate of a saint-to-be who had already been deemed such by a higher power.

A plane streaked across the sky, its condensation line slicing the window in half. I couldn't follow its thread if I was going to follow the thread of Nizam's argument. His lisp had resurfaced after he finished his recitation and resumed normal speech. It was distracting, and I had to look at his lips to make out what he was saying.

Nizam's statement was well thought out, but it seemed like he was merely using the verses to support an argument, rather than drawing the argument out from the verses. That's the beauty of the text—it's malleable and has various meanings, even if sometimes it just means what it says. Nizam continued by expounding on the verses' importance in dialectical debates supposing the existence of a hypothetical receiver, which, he explained, formed the basis of Mulla Sadra's deconstructivism in the seventeenth century.

I'm familiar with this philosophy, so I knew how to counter Nizam's argument by using Sadra's own words on intuition to show that the giver and recipient could be the same person or manifest in the same physical body; the giver formulates the message into something meaningful, while the receiver is able to incorporate it into the physical world. I was proud of my ability to summon those lines. Being right or wrong in this room meant nothing, but Nizam would appreciate a good argument, and he would recognise my words on the Chief's tongue, even if he had never heard me speak before our chance meeting that morning. It would offset whatever he thought about my eagle pin and the poor case I had made for carrying it. Why had I felt the need to defend it? I'd been trying to prove that I was true to my nature, that my outside reflected what was inside, which, I hoped, was also the case with Nizam. But I had picked the wrong exterior to defend, and now I needed to show him my true colours. Challenging Nizam would mean challenging myself.

So, after carefully arranging my words in the right order, I leaned forward and whispered into Chief 'Abbas's ear, lowering my voice to a hushed tone out of a juvenile fear that my painstakingly constructed ideas would be overheard by one of the assistants and find their way to another examiner's lips. The Chief didn't react. I watched Nizam carry on with his speech. I tried again, this time speaking a little more slowly and audibly. The Chief made a comment about the versatility of the verses. I thought he must have not heard me.

'Laken ketabat Mulla Sadra—' I began, hazarding another attempt at passing on my message, but before I could say anything of use, the Chief reached behind him and squeezed my left knee. I remembered the eagle in my pocket and imagined stabbing his hairy knuckles.

The whole performance was unfolding to script, complete with hackneyed dialogue. I couldn't stand it. The Chief leaned forward, away from me, and nodded slowly, clinking his sebha beads to pass the time, lost in a swamp of his own thoughts, impervious to my charms and wiles. As more meaningless words were thrown around, my argument started to seem small and insignificant. I wondered what my reason had even been for coming up with it. Was I just spouting nonsense to make myself feel important among all these men? I had served 'Abbas in other examinations and used him like a ventriloquist uses a doll. When I led the Friday prayer, I often heard him sobbing behind me, while I'd cried just once in his congregation, and then only by exerting great effort and imagination. Maybe he didn't remember the way generals and other rotab shook my hand twice in appreciation of my achievements; if he did, he would surely have listened to me and relayed my words. Then I remembered this was the same man who told me that swimming was useless. I needed to control my anger; I was Teita's grandchild and Mama's son, so I already had a target on my back. Complaining about corruption would result in a very short conversation, at the end of which I would have to decide if I wanted to live in Germany or prison.

The Chief patted my knee again and pointed at the brass tea tray.

I got up slowly and walked over to the tray, looking down at my sandalled feet. I felt ridiculous, defeated. It stung even more because Nizam could speak so much better and more brilliantly, if only they pushed him. Or maybe not. His mind might be as shallow a stream as the minds of the examiners, which wouldn't even get my toes wet. But with the mausoleum built, the plot and monument erected, Nizam had to be built up to the size that the army had decreed. We all fell under his shadow, apparently.

Basma's sheikh, bored with the proceedings, started unfurling the bundle in his hand to look at what she had written, before placing the crumpled sheets on the ground next to his chair. I set the Chief's tea glass down on top of the pile of research I had prepared, watching the steam rise. I had tried to make myself indispensable, but the Chief and his office seemed fine without me.

'Is there any sugar?' the Chief whispered. A saint was manifesting before him, and so corporal were his concerns.

'No sugar,' I said.

He gave me back the glass and told me to take it to Fawzeya.

I left the room as Nizam was being asked whether working with clay all day required a different form of ritual purification from the dry ablutions with dust that were sanctioned in the drought. Without water to wash before prayer, the examiner said, worshippers were developing skin conditions.

My eyes took a moment to adjust to the light outside the hall, and I bumped into an assistant asleep on a chair.

'Are they almost done?' he asked drowsily.

'They're about to ask Nizam whether a green bee-eater really carries the soul of the dead to the next life.'

'Did you write that question?'

'Yeah. It'll save the world one day.'

'The world's already been saved, brother Shahed.'

'Of course, boss.'

Fawzeya was sitting in the kitchenette watching an old black-and-white film. Fez-wearing pashas were fighting off soldiers in the streets. After the death of one of the pashas' sons, passions ran high, and the popular rebellion against the army turned sour as people began to forget the greater good of the country. Compared to the performance going on inside the examination hall, the film felt both melodramatic and sincere.

I started washing up the Chief's tea glass in the sink.

'Leave it to me,' Fawzeya said, hoisting herself up. ''Akl ʿeishi, it's my job.'

'I won't tell anyone.'

She relaxed in her seat and looked back at the television. 'Have you seen this one before?'

'Yeah, it's a good one,' I nodded. The bridge to Zamalek came on screen, a pair of proud lions standing tall on both its ends. 'I live near there,' I said.

'Fancy boy,' she replied. 'I used to take public transport across that bridge. Your hair would turn white if you knew half the blood that's been shed there. I saw it. These old bones have broken more heads than you can imagine, you know. Now I've got arthritis, and the sheikh at Masjid el-Husein said I should help out the Sufis if I want to furnish my place in paradise. "A place where the bird of paradise will be born," he told me. So, I sit here and make you tea.'

'Taʿbeenek maʿana.'

She clicked her tongue. 'It's no bother, wallahi, ya beih.'

'Do you have any sugar?'

'Laʾ wallahi, it's all gone.'

'Great.'

By the time I got back, the sky above the shukhshaykha had turned a deep blue, and Nizam had unanimously been voted a saint.

'Shahed, take this, will you?' Nizam said to me. He was standing in the middle of the bulbous eight-headed beast that was the Sufi council and holding out a folded piece of paper. As I reached to take it, some of the beast's heads turned to look at me, but most remained focused on each other and their own conversations.

I removed the hairclip on the fold of the sheet and opened it to reveal Nizam's handwritten notes from the examination. In one corner was a line drawing of a battered wall with a door. He'd drawn a sketch of the scene from his point of view, the faces either abstract or disfigured. Above my head, he had written the word 'nesr'. *Eagle.*

'What do you want me to do with it?'

'Bin it, please.'

I left the room again, unable to stay a moment longer. I felt helpless and needed to ground myself with the weight of whatever I was carrying. I patted my pockets to look for the pin. It was right where it was supposed to be.

Fawzeya congratulated me on Nizam's ascension.

'It was all his own work and effort,' I said. 'The first sheikh without classical training to be given this honour. He'll be great for us and for the country.'

'Ya rabb, ya beih,' she said.

I held out the paper. 'Could you throw this away for me?'

'Is it yours?'

'Yeah, it's my notes.' No sooner had I spoken than the worry entered my mind that Fawzeya might keep the paper and try to learn in Nizam's own words what happened inside the room. I guessed that Fawzeya was illiterate, but I couldn't count on her not finding someone else to decipher the meaning hidden in the strokes. Each community has a keeper of secrets, someone who reads whatever others can't and relays whatever messages there are to be relayed. Then there was the word 'nesr' that Nizam had written above my head.

'Actually,' I said, pulling the paper back, 'I'll hold on to it.' I was feeling fragile and wanted to grasp the only piece of evidence that remained of my failure in that room.

'Good,' she said, releasing the wrinkled sheet from her calloused fingers. 'Even as a token. This is a big day for the nation. Shame it wasn't open to the rest of the disciples.'

'They couldn't risk a scene. I'm sure you've had to clean up the students' mess before. All the papers they throw into the circle.'

'No, I've never cleaned any of that up,' she said, clicking her tongue. 'It's the police or the army, wallahi, I can't tell the difference. They were in plainclothes, anyway, the ones who came and tidied everything away last time. You should've heard the way they talked to me. The point is, I'd take that paper with you.

'Don't blame the students for their passion,' she added. 'This is Nizam's gift. I can listen to him talk for hours. I can't always understand what he says, but I understand enough. I feel hopeful when his voice crawls into my ear, as though it's being carried by the wind ... I often find myself crying, overwhelmed by my own existence. Maybe that's why he deserves to become a saint ... he helps us see ourselves.'

I folded the piece of paper further, as if it might leak, and put it in my pocket.

Later, in my dorm, I dared to look at it again. Sitting on my prayer rug, I laid the note out in front of me. The odour of onions and garlic invaded my nostrils, probably the residue of Nizam's breakfast. I sniffed my own palm for comparison and only caught the whiff of chlorine seeping from my pores. My mouth tasted bitter, and I could feel a sticky layer of black tea clinging to my tongue. I still had some of my water ration left, but I knew I couldn't get up to drink without first settling the matter of Nizam's note. I didn't know what I was trying to get out of it, but I was sure something would surface if I only looked hard enough.

I was feeling angry enough to rip the paper to shreds, so I tried to pray, hoping to calm my nerves. Normally before praying, I find a moment of pause during which I can step outside of myself to commune with a light I can't see. Whatever doubts I may be carrying as I enter that moment have usually left me by the time I emerge; it's the only time I ever experience faith outside the water. When I lead a congregation in prayer, the waves of people at my back keep me afloat. They don't need to believe for me to find my own belief; if everyone in a mosque needed faith to pray, the religion would have died with the Messenger. All eyes are trained downwards on the point where forehead will meet floor in prostration, all ears trained on the sound of my recitation. Prayer is an invitation to be seen without being looked at, to be seen in solitude. Against all logic, prayers happen, and they are heard.

This time, however, the moment of clarification didn't materialise.

I returned to the note. Nizam didn't dot any of his letters, so it would take time to decrypt his writing. Arabic letters have been dotted since the early seventh century—a clever technology that ensured words on the page were unambiguous and clear cut, every sound hitting its mark. I pored over each character, trying to discriminate ta from tha, geem from kha, until finally, the essence of his mystifying symbols was revealed.

The eagle was one of the birds that travelled with the hudhud to look for Simorgh, their king. Like most of the flock, he resisted the journey. Below the miserable figure he had drawn of me, Nizam had scribbled a few lines from *Mantiq al-Tayr*, in which the nesr explains his reluctance to go. Why would he leave behind the reality he knew, asked the bird—a contented life of eating from the king's hand and performing at his court—for the sake of something invisible?

For Nizam, the surface was all there was to see. There was no such thing as putting on a nesr pin for appearances.

I'm close to Qasr el-Nil now, the same bridge that flashed

from the corner of my eye on Fawzeya's small screen while I washed the tea glass of a man busy deciding the fate of the country's soul. Tomorrow, 'Araby is driving me to be reunited with the imprisoned saint so I can take him to dispense more of his wisdom in a barracks in the desert.

I'll take the ferry across the water, and then there's just one more security checkpoint to pass to get to the pool. Checkpoints waste so much of my time that I always rush through the rest of the city, which feels to me like a scrambled mess of connected but unrelated streets. This bridge, though, is an art nouveau piece, a jewel on the river, adorned with lions. I would say they hark back to an African heritage, but the country inherited its fascination with majestic beasts from the French. Paris on the Nile. Where is the Nile now?

It smells like piss and hash on the Corniche, and something else—the rice ash is still burning. If the air were cooler, I could believe that it's November. But while night has camped out over the country, it's still roasting.

The bridge in the distance is cordoned off to hold back cars and pedestrians. I can make out a dark-blue van with metal-lattice windows and a guard standing by the backdoor. I remember seeing footage of soldiers flinging protesters off this bridge just twenty years ago. The water level is lower now; not even destroying the Renaissance Dam could bring it back. If thrown over today, the corpses would quickly break the surface of the water and become floating islands of rot. Some would wash away; others would wait for the water to rise again. Except that will never happen.

*

I jump the barrier between the Corniche and the steep-sloped craggy banks on the eastern side of the river. My ferry is down below, a rowing boat with a small outboard motor whose rotor turns lazily whenever a gust of wind picks up the smell of water, clear and fresh, celebrating the small joy of going on a trip. Overgrown thrush breaks through the soil on the slope, trembling and shaking at the slightest movement. I stop to consider my footing.

My eyes adjust slowly as I take my first steps down the slope, dislodging pebbles with my feet. I try not to look at the lights by the cordon on Qasr el-Nil Bridge. Even from a kilometre away, the glare would turn my vision into threadbare fabric, pierced with blind spots and little to hold the visible patches together, and I might trip. Faith isn't enough—I need my sight.

There are sleeping bodies everywhere. Dopers congregate here to smoke up and lay their worries down for a few hours. I don't smoke, but I understand the impulse sometimes—just to sit by the water and wander off. It would be rude to step over them, so I weave my way through the maze of bodies. I try not to look at the faces. It's too dark to discern features, but better not to risk—

—Hey, what're you looking at, boy?

—Watch out!

Sorry.

They used to gather further downstream, closer to the bridge, but the pay-to-enter promenade, built by the government to get rid of the boaters and pop-up cafés on the Corniche, makes that impossible now. This small stretch of the riverbank, between Garden City and the island of El Manial, is the only corner left where they can hide. If the promenade keeps stretching its fingers, people here will quickly find themselves pushed outside the city, which is exactly where the government wants them, out of sight.

Ramy comes here sometimes, or used to, before he started working nights. He helped me navigate the etiquette. Evenings on el-daffa el-sharqeya can end up shapeless if you don't know what you're looking for or how to get it. This is the place to come to bypass the communications blackout, if you need to make calls or get online without the risk of having an incriminating workaround installed on your phone. This is where to find people who can smuggle phones, money, food and medicine into prisons or pull strings to get you around bureaucratic dead ends. When we needed to find out where one of Kaffara's lawyers was taken after her arrest, Ramy suggested we ask here. Of course, everything costs money. This isn't a thoroughfare, and nothing in this country is free.

I accidentally kick a stone. It bounces a few times before being caught by someone who gently throws it back at my chest. I catch it and place it back on the ground. 'Leave it as you found it': that's the rule to live by here. Any evidence that remains in the daylight of your presence is evidence against you. People here are tolerated as long as they don't make themselves too obvious. That would be seen as a challenge, and the state always rises to challenges; the price of its security is blood. The safety of concealment brings its own risk—because how can you search for someone who goes missing if they were never here in the first place?

'This is what they do to us,' Mama told me. 'They force us to become invisible before they make us disappear.'

Orange dots sparkle brightly like fireflies, briefly illuminating moustaches and eyes before returning them to the darkness. Starlight burns away djinn, but these flaming points seem to stir up another kind of demon—one who takes the reigns and to whom the stoners cede control. With the police cordon visible not far away, everything seems riskier, pleasure more fleeting, more precious. We're reminded of whom we're hiding from, and his shadow looms large. I realise I'm holding my breath.

Breathe. There's no escaping these fumes.

Plumes of smoke rise like a fog and I walk through it all, moving past light after light without touching anyone. From above, I would never have found these bodies, primed to scatter and hide at the first hint of danger.

I can hear the low sound of running water now.

'El-meʿadeya menein?' I call quietly.

'Psst,' comes the response.

I try to locate where the voice is coming from while minding my step. 'Which way's the ferry?' I repeat.

'Psst. Men hena.'

I'm close enough now to hear the current. Here by the water, the murmurs of the people lying on the bank rise in a cacophony like a cloud of locusts.

A man grabs my arm. 'This way,' he beckons.

I let him lead me.

'Ma tekhaf-sh, easy. Here we are. There are only a few others so far, so we're waiting for more people to show up before we go. You in a hurry?'

'No,' I reply. I find a flat concrete surface and decide to sit down, if only to show how unhurried I am.

'It's been a slow night,' he tells me. 'If you want to get across more quickly, you might not want to wait.'

'I don't have the money to cross alone.'

'That's not the question.'

'I'll wait.' I lie back on the slope, apologising when I find someone's foot in the way. I shift slightly. It's hard to relax. I do my best. Closing my eyes makes me panic, so I try not to blink. Whispers ebb and flow, and I almost fall into a dream. The sound of the river tightens my chest and I imagine myself drowning. There probably isn't enough water to drown.

'Do you want anything while you wait, a smoke?'

'No,' I say.

There's a tap on my shoulder. 'Have you got a lighter?'

I pass my lighter to the hand. It clicks. I resist the impulse to look up and get a glimpse of the face.

'Thanks.' The lighter taps my shoulder.

I grab it and accidentally touch his fingers. Callouses and cavernous gashes, sharp and ancient.

'Mmm ... w-elli b-yehashshesh w-ma b-yehess-sh,' murmurs the man behind me contentedly, releasing a smoky sigh as he sinks into a daze.

My eyes close, and I don't feel like reopening them.

Drowning in water, water that drowns. It's not my fault—there's just more of it than there is of me.

'Nemt?'

'I'm awake,' I say, opening my eyes. I get up to climb on board the boat, expecting there to be more people by now, but apart from the boater, I only see two men, a woman and a young child. The men, almost indistinguishable in the low light, except that one wears a thick moustache, are carrying boxes and seem to be struggling, readjusting their handholds every few seconds to keep a firm grip. The child has blue eyes and a succinct valley below her lip and is shrouded in fabric in the woman's arms. Both woman and child are veiled, the woman wrapped in black robes, the girl in a blue scarf that recedes to reveal cropped hair and pierced ears. The blue of the scarf brings out more colour in the child's eyes than I care to see. I don't know if it's the darkness or if the kid has a flair for horror, but her eyes seem to grow wider to take me in.

'Are you fine with this?' the boatman asks.

'With what?' I ask.

He looks at the men with the boxes. 'You can stay here and I'll come back to get you,' he offers, 'but then you'll have to wait for another group. Otherwise, this load's ready to go, if you're willing to come along.'

'Wait, we've paid you enough to be taken across on our own. How much money are you looking for?' asks the man without the moustache.

'Just a greedy man,' says the woman.

'A wicked man,' the child adds, hissing at him and pointing

up two pencils held tightly in the miniature grip of her hand.

'I promised the boy he'd cross. I'm just giving him the option. He can say no.'

They turn to me.

'I need to get across soon,' I say. 'I mean, now ... is what I was hoping. So, it's fine, I'll cross with you, if that's okay.' I'm not sure why I've just agreed to cross the river with these anxious people who obviously see themselves as incendiary. I try to steady my voice. 'It's fine,' I repeat.

The men look at each other and then at the woman, who waves her hand in the air twice to usher them forward like she's chasing flies over a windowsill.

'All right,' she says. 'Yalla, nengez.'

As soon as the woman settles in near the bow, the child jumps out of her lap and wobbles barefoot around the edges of the vessel, as if she wants to meet the new adventure head on. When she's taken it all in, she returns and tugs the cloth that the woman was using to carry her, pulling out sheets of paper. She crouches on the floor and starts drawing, stealing frequent glances at the palm trees behind the sloped banks to transfer the image to paper, as if what she sees is about to change.

The two men and I help the boatman shove the vessel out and away from the slopes before climbing on board to join the woman and the child. Barely a star moves, which is reassuring. Everything is as it should be. Nothing out of the ordinary.

Just as we're about to set off, another man arrives looking to join our ride. He is wearing a beige sweater, black shoes and striped socks. His hair, long and wavy, is wet and slicked back. One informer who came along to Kaffara meetings used to dress similarly: standard-issue civilian clothes.

'There's no more space,' I tell him.

'I can see the boat, it's empty,' he protests.

I push off with the oar. 'I said no more space.'

'Is this your boat?' the driver asks me.

'No,' I reply. 'But I'm in a rush.'

I didn't trust how that man looked. I trust him even less now that I can see his silhouette trying to get a good look at me as more and more water separates us.

'You don't make the decisions here,' the boater continues. 'You don't know the politics of my making a living this way. Some people you don't say no to. I can't even go back now to let him on.' Angrily, he adds, 'I'll remember you.'

The driver busies himself gathering his rope near the side of the boat. I move away from him and sit at the bow with the woman and girl while the other two passengers take charge of the oars and start working us across the water. The woman looks at me uncertainly but doesn't move. There's nowhere else to go.

'Don't pay him any mind,' one of the men says, raising his eyebrow at the driver's back. 'Fadl,' he says, extending his right hand.

'Shahed,' I say, accepting the handshake.

'That's a good one,' Fadl says to the moustache. 'Wish I'd thought of a name like that.'

The moustache doesn't respond, and I sense his discomfort. He is still looking back at the riverbank and the silhouette of the keen, slick-haired voyager.

The girl has fixed her blue eyes on the distant light of the cordon, which seems to be drawing nearer too quickly for comfort. The kitsch rendition of a French bridge is alien here, wearing a suit that doesn't belong. It might look familiar now, but only for what it is: a cheap bit of trash, blissfully forgotten by the people from whom it was borrowed and christened by protests. That was the last time it felt new.

I follow the child's gaze and see the broadcasting building in the north, its circular facade, neat rows of evenly spaced windows, antenna stabbing the sky. *That's Maspero*, I want to say, *that's where they threw Ramy's uncle into the water*, but the words catch on my tongue.

Deep down I believe that, if they wanted to, the military could make the Nile flow in the opposite direction. The river would carry corpses south, rather than to the Delta and through to the Mediterranean Sea. The Blue Nile Falls would choke on the bodies. That'd show whoever thought to cut off our water. No, they'd probably get stuck somewhere between here and there. Who would win then?

There's no plaque commemorating any of the massacres the city's streets and riverbanks have witnessed. Only the uniformed dead count in this country—*they* were the real heroes of our revolution. But I have seen footage of their brutality. Watching a tape of the Battle of Mohamed Mahmoud in the library with other members of Kaffara made it seem less real. Television static from the original recording dissipates to reveal people running in panic from the loud booms of shotguns. A tyre is burning, the light interrupted by bodies emerging from the tunnel-like street. There's a sound rising and falling in the background like crashing waves—the cheers of protesters celebrating in Tahrir, just outside the frame. The chants are a balm, the tide lapping at the shore, as if the voices crying out for *Bread! Freedom! Social justice!* could wash the martyrs' blood off the pavements, heal their wounds and raise them from their graves.

A young woman dressed in baggy clothes is coughing her lungs out in the arms of an older man. He shoves an inhaler between her teeth and yells, 'Hold your breath!' before plunging the cylinder down to release the acrid medicine. She looks as if she's about to be sick as the solution rolls over her tongue and into her throat. The cough subsides and the woman walks off-screen, stage right. *Her hair is too short. That isn't Mama.*

We replayed the video so many times that the pain became predictable, numbed. I lost all interest in the actions of the protesters and focused instead on mundane details in the shot: limewash chipping off one of the walls, a poster on a lamppost, which I looked for afterwards in case it was still there—it wasn't—the uneven paving stones that were torn up to be used as ammunition against the dark. On the fifth viewing, the woman turned into a hollow shell, like animatronics in a theme park, acting out a scene to teach me something that I wasn't quite getting. For the first time since meeting my Kaffara family, I felt like we were seeing things differently.

'It was a true tragedy,' Musa lamented. 'But though massacres like this should never happen, reprisals are only to be expected.' The other members nodded along, as if what he had said made any sense.

This particular massacre was the revenge of a police force that felt frustrated and undermined by the Armed Forces, who had rolled into the city pretending to be the saviours of the revolution when in fact they were there to make sure it failed. Police officers found guilty of torturing protesters were imprisoned, but the army was immune from even the slightest criticism. When the police felt powerless, they lashed out, and the army had to allow them these minor tantrums. I would have preferred to believe the fake death certificates attributing the fatalities to road accidents than accept this truth. The alternative would mean admitting that this country makes deaths like this routine.

I knew what the risks of joining Kaffara were from Teita's stories. Death has never been something I've been afraid of. The only possible redemption I can imagine for those bodies that went over the railing is a revolution to turn their deaths into sacrifice. Then, all we'd have to do to enjoy whatever success we managed to scrape is pretend they gave their lives willingly for the cause.

Mama and Teita glimpsed the paradise that I still long for. They saw the best and the worst of the country. Teita couldn't live with the loss of paradise, while Mama traded her history for a paradise in Europe. Grief of that kind has a price. Part of me hopes that I never find anything so heinous that I have to look away, because to witness is to be powerful, to witness is to expose, to witness is to imagine an end to cruelties endured and the possibility of leaving suffering behind. It's a way of saying,

'The past has passed, and it doesn't have to come to pass again.'

The girl appears next to me and shows me her drawing. 'I'm not done,' she says, 'but this is it so far.'

'It's pretty,' I say. She's drawn a side view of the bridge, the smoke rising from the people gathered on the bank and enveloping the soldiers above in fog, and the boat with us inside, including an outsize representation of herself, drawing the scene.

The child is recklessly indifferent to the dangers in her surroundings—uniforms above, water below. She presses her fingers to her lips, silently shushing herself, and leans over the side of the boat, grabbing her guardian by the gallabeya to stop herself from toppling over. The woman keeps her eyes fixed on the lights at the bridge. She wants to know the very moment it happens, the moment when they see us or hear us. If the child's fingers loosen and she slips away, there will be a splash, and that would mean the end of us all.

Twenty minutes pass, and we're still on the water. I start to think that we've always been here. The moment's ease weighs heavily on me. We're all so vulnerable because of the others' presence. For as long as we're on the boat, our fates are intertwined.

I hear sounds of water: the river lapping at the sides of the boat, oars breaking the surface, droplets streaming up and splashing down.

The child is still leaning over the edge of the boat. One arm clutches her mother's robe while the other stretches down, trying to reach her reflection. On the water's surface, her mirror image reaches up towards her, trying to break free.

We are all prisoners of past horrors. Their shadows and faces flutter down below. For a moment, I see the square face and prominent brow of Ramy's uncle rippling beneath us. The boat sways from the ghosts' fury at what they experienced, at our still having to sneak around the city twenty years later. *Why are we still trapped here? Why are you still out there? Isn't this over yet?*

I look over my side of the boat and glimpse my own face.

Touching my nose, I'm surprised to see my reflection keep time with me. I long for the comfort of the Kaffara apartment, where we think up hypothetical ways of changing the future without having to face the reality of any of this. Either we jump off and meet our destiny head on, or we reach out to it in perpetuity, waiting for the dreaded moment when the boat rocks, a grip loosens, and a gallabeya's hem slips through fingers. *Splash.*

I worry there will be consequences for not allowing that man to board. He might have been in the police, or a dealer whose payment is free passage, and now, in retaliation, we could find police on the other side. *I have to have faith*, I tell myself, trying to quell the rising panic. *This isn't how this ends*, though it would be fitting. Life could end at any moment and it'd be fitting. On a borrowed bridge, in a side street, or on a rowing boat.

*

Teita had been standing outside the precinct for an hour when the lawyer showed up.

The temperature had dropped unexpectedly the night before, so Teita was wearing a heavy scarf with blue and gold arabesque patterns around her shoulders. She had brought an extra blanket, just in case the police refused to release Hanan and made her stay another night in an overcrowded cell with bare concrete walls that absorbed the day's humidity and slowly released it into the prisoners' weary bones. *If she's going to be kept there, then at least she'll be warm*, Teita thought to herself, glancing at the black plastic bag on the ground. Inside were a few sandwiches, crisps, juice cartons, biscuits and wafers, which Teita now regretted packing, since it implied that she was expecting Hanan to stay longer in jail.

The first thing the lawyer, a man in his late twenties with acne scars that had never healed, said when he arrived was, 'We're going to get her out, ya doktora.' This put Teita even more on edge.

'How do you know that?' she asked, though it was clear she wasn't expecting an answer. Hope was a toxin; she would rather deal with the ugliness of reality than be disappointed. As much as it hurt Teita to admit it, she was angry at Hanan for putting herself at risk, not by going down to the square, but by leaving the protests on her own, without a friend.

There was a still an hour to go before Hanan's questioning. The lawyer, experienced in dealing with the police, had said they should arrive earlier than the appointed time to stop the officials from trying to rush the process through with no one around. He brought Teita a wooden stool that he kept in the boot of his car for whenever he was made to wait. Teita refused the seat and carried on pacing in agitation, but instead of wearing her down, this gave her the air of being unstoppable, urged by her own helplessness to keep moving even when there was nothing to do but wait.

Baba showed up fifteen minutes before the scheduled interrogation. He was dressed in a shirt and jeans with a coat that wasn't too flashy. Unlike much of the country's elite, Baba didn't come from old money; he was one of the disdained nouveaux riches who had just started to make his way up the social ladder. Mama's arrest was his failure—proof that looking the part wasn't the same as having the armour afforded by privilege.

''Ezzayek, ya tante,' Baba said, kissing Teita on both cheeks. She scarcely reacted, turning her head almost imperceptibly with each kiss.

Baba had gone down to the square with Mama on the Friday of Anger at the beginning of the year, but only because the whole country was out and there was nothing else to do. Try as he might, he never understood why Hanan carried on protesting afterwards—even after the president's fall. How did she find the time, alongside her master's degree and research job at the think tank? A few evenings a week, she would go out with her friends to heavy-metal concerts at El-Saqia, exhibition openings and shisha cafés to talk politics. Baba watched her move in an instant from haggling with the butcher over meat prices to discussions about everything from Pan-Africanism as a way to throw off the yoke of the euro and the dollar, to the sudden disappearance of mad cow disease, to what point there was in a sign reading 'Cleanliness is Next to Godliness' on a wall where blood was still encrusted between the ceramic tiles. She was constantly being dragged into the same mind-numbing and inane chatter—except to her, it wasn't just chatter. When Mama was arrested, Baba realised there was a possibility he didn't know the woman he had married at all. She had never been as safe as she seemed. In his eyes, she should have heeded the danger and contented herself with what she had. It was time to be realistic. The dream was over.

Baba looked at Teita's plastic bag and remembered that he was supposed to bring a change of clothes for Mama. The lawyer had mentioned it the day before; it was something families were often asked to provide. Neither Teita nor the lawyer said a word about his empty hands. If Baba had said anything, Teita would have told him that all she cared about was getting her dear Hanan out of this horrible precinct.

'How long have you been waiting?' Baba asked Teita. 'If I'd known you were getting here earlier, I would've come.'

'It's okay, ya habibi,' she said. 'I couldn't sleep anyway, and I brought a book to read in the car while I waited.'

'Yalla,' said the lawyer, raising his arm to usher them up the precinct's steps.

They were stopped inside to have their identities and Teita's plastic bag checked. After passing through security, they were left standing a while in front of an old desk before the officer behind it finally looked up to address them.

'We talked yesterday,' the lawyer began. 'I'm here to pick up my client.'

'What's the name?' said the officer.

The lawyer produced a photocopy of Mama's identity card. As the officer lifted it for inspection, Teita clenched her fist around the carrier bag handles, digging her nails into her palm.

'Who are you?' the officer asked, looking up at Baba.

'Hanan's husband,' Baba answered. His words seemed to come out too loudly, and he worried that he had revealed his desperation to have Mama back just so he wouldn't feel so weak. *Why would she put herself in danger like that*, he thought, reaching for his wallet to extract his ID again.

Lazily chewing a piece of gum, the officer turned Baba's card over a few times before placing it on top of the photocopy of Mama's ID.

'Where's the marriage certificate?' he asked briskly, folding his hands together.

Baba winced as if he had been walking on coal. Turning his

back to the desk, he buried his face in his hands. *The fucking marriage certificate!* He and Mama hadn't updated their ID cards since getting married, so unless she carried her marriage certificate around—which, obviously, she didn't—Mama was still read as single in the eyes of the government.

Teita stepped in to try to salvage the situation. 'We can get it,' she said confidently. Turning to Baba, she whispered so sharply that every word seemed to cut his ears, 'Do you have a scan of it? Anything?'

'Nothing,' came his terse reply. He felt even more helpless than before. 'But I can go and get it,' he assured the officer.

'You can, but there's no point in coming back,' the officer replied. 'She's not here.' He passed the photocopy and Baba's card back across the desk. The sound of paper against the uneven grain of worn wood scratched in Teita's mind. She shook her head in disbelief.

'We ... we spoke to you yesterday,' she started, her voice halting out of concern and confusion. 'You told us to come back today.'

'She's no longer here,' the officer said, not looking at Teita but again addressing Baba.

'Where was she moved?' Baba protested, trying to overcome the building feeling of having failed to protect his wife by not filling out his paperwork. 'Why weren't we informed?'

'Informed?' cried the officer, raising his voice. 'I'm informing you right now. There's nothing for you here. She's been transferred to the military police—they're conducting their own investigations into prostitution in the square.'

*

When we reach the other side, I jump out of the boat, pulling it by the line so that it stays tucked against the concrete long enough for the woman and child to climb out. The moustached man shakes my hand and thanks me—I don't know what for, but I squeeze his hand back and give him a pat on the shoulder.

'I'll be seeing you, Shahed,' he says. I murmur my agreement and hand him the dock line, leaving the men to unload their boxes. Then I take the cobbled steps up the bank and jump the fence at the end to make my way onto the road.

I know the guards at the next checkpoint, which is right by the perimeter of the sports club. Half the club's land is taken up by a horse track that dates back to the British colonial times, when the people last had a king to overthrow. Now with the military, what is there for the country to conquer? They're here *to protect us.*

My parents once took me to watch one of the horse races, not from the stands but from the sidelines, where we were pelted with clumps of dust and mud. I saw the slight, slender jockeys beating the animals with a wild fury. From the way they gritted their teeth, it seemed like they were hurting themselves.

My mother said, 'You really have to muster up that kind of cruelty on your own before you can unleash it into the world. That's why they grit their teeth.'

My father agreed, but he added that it takes a lot of work to be a jockey. 'Riding a beast at that speed isn't easy,' he said. Even then, I could tell he was missing something. Teita told me that Baba only sees half of what's around him and ignores what he doesn't like. Don't be like him, she warned.

At night, with the lights out, the horse track is transformed into a dark plane where shadows race to and fro. In the absence of wind, the dirt retains the footprints of track-and-field teams rampaging barefoot through the hippodrome like a many-headed beast. They have weak backs and can't lift their knees. No grace.

I jump down from the pavement onto the grooved road and follow it ahead, watching the rhythm of my shadow extending and falling back under the streetlights, until I arrive at the checkpoint.

'As-salam 'aleikom,' I say, lowering my eyes.

Men in armour and helmets, dangling rifles from straps around their necks, respond in chorus. '*Aleikom as-salam, 'aleikom as-salam, 'aleikom as-salam.*

Magdy, an ex-army officer turned private security guard, calls me by my name. He asks where I'm off to this late, and I flash my forged letter from the Chief Sufi. It's all part of our routine. My role is citizen, his is flippant security personnel, except this play is all about subversion; we're acting for an audience submerged in the darkness, avoiding the front rows—this is immersive theatre, and no one wants to get splashed with confetti.

'Face is almost healed up,' he tells me.

'Yeah,' I reply. 'I'm starting to feel like myself again.'

'You look like yourself too.' He pulls my chin and turns my head to look at my nose. 'Lucky Khalil didn't break it. He's a big man.'

My fingers curl into a ball without closing into a fist. That would look aggressive. I'm docile, easy-going, with a cold heart that wouldn't let a drop of blood because it all rushes to my skin. I'd never cringe at another man's probing touch—that would admit either revulsion or attraction. I'm soft stone, and I feel nothing.

Keeping hold of my chin, Magdy swivels my face towards another of the men, who's wearing tan trousers and a chequered shirt and sitting on a stool nearby, turning over pieces of charcoal in a shisha made from an abandoned Fanta can.

'Can you believe this is what swimmers do to each other in the pool?' Magdy asks him. 'Apparently, this is just from this kid's regular training.' He turns my chin back to face him. 'It's healing quite well.'

Violence is an integral part of swimming. It's the only way the other athletes can get over the fact that we spend hours in each other's company barely clothed. If we touch each other, it's always to assert strength; otherwise, what would it say about us as men of this country? Khalil—one of the other swimmers—let a stray arm fly into my goggles when we were practising race starts. Ten swimmers in one lane makes for a tight squeeze, and we all thrash as hard as we can through the water to get away from the rest. His swimmer's kiss took a week to fade.

Magdy pulls me so close that I can see my reflection in his shiny brown eyes. Each of his irises is encircled by a thin ring of white, which I feel like brushing away or clawing out. Long eyelashes. His nose is bulbous and lined with scratches from a young baby putting tiny sharp fingernails to good use, fighting the good fight.

Magdy's people are the reason I smell of petrol. A few weeks ago, this checkpoint stopped the pool technicians from passing through and confiscated their equipment and chlorine canisters. The new crew started using benzene to purify the water. No-smoking signs were installed by the pool, though a few older club members, who always have an empty lane reserved for them, continued to light up. Water can't catch fire, the coach assured us. I suspect that it can. When I first smelt petrol, I thought something had gone terribly wrong with my nose, but the coach insisted that my nose was fine, if slightly off centre. One of the swimmers, an optometry student, announced that long-term inhalation of benzene can cause brain damage and rashes. If I scratch my skin, I bleed. I give fingernails as wide a berth as I can.

'But you've still got circles around your eyes,' says Magdy. 'Got to let the swelling from Khalil's punch breathe a little.'

'Must be the goggles,' I say. 'They put too much pressure on my eyes. It's affecting my vision, I think. Or rather, the headaches they give me affect my vision.'

'Maybe it's just a lack of sleep.' He releases my chin, and my hands relax. 'Lines all across your face,' he continues. 'Inflamed capillaries, purple blood vessels. That's not good. Probably the insomnia you've been telling me about. It's a real medical issue. Don't ignore it. Your team wouldn't appreciate that. Your results won't lie. Don't forget that the country's prestige is in your very capable hands.' He takes my hands and lays them palm up. 'These could move oceans, probably.' He traces the lines to read my fortune. 'When the other officer here told me that someone broke your face, I couldn't believe it. I can't believe it now, and I'm looking at you. Did your father see your face in this shape? A prayer callus on your forehead would've pissed him off less, probably.'

I've known Magdy since I was a kid. I've always managed to smile when he plays the part, but his tone now is different. When I was younger, before the era of communications shutdowns, Magdy would text me whenever I took a taxi home from the club to ask if I'd made it back safe. He'd sign off his messages with 'Your uncle Magdy'. Since my parents were away for months at a time, my father employed him to provide security for me. An extra pair of eyes never hurt. When I started walking or riding my bike to the club, Magdy stopped getting paid. I still give him a few pounds from time to time. He means well.

He takes the fake letter from the Chief Sufi out of my hand and starts reading.

'I'm sorry, but we have to take extra measures now and actually read the documents people show us. Part of our duty.' Then, he whispers, 'I think Chequered Shirt over there wants to replace me. He's police.' I nod to show that I understand.

I look at the gun on Magdy's waist. His jacket hangs loosely and doesn't conceal it. It's not like my father's gun. This one has blunted square edges, and it's not as clean as Baba's, which Mama polishes whenever she thinks Baba and I aren't at home. When I once caught her cross-legged on the ground with all the pieces of the gun laid out on a towel in her lap, she showed me how to dismantle, clean and assemble it. I sat down beside her wearing my gallabeya, and she draped the towel over my knees. I felt the weight of the weapon's parts piling up, but I couldn't remember all the steps. She made me do it three times.

'If anything ever happens and you need it,' she said, bringing out the box where Baba keeps the gun, 'take this and run.' She showed me where the box's key is hidden on a string inside their bedside lamp. 'Go inside the cupboard, and open the box slowly. It's important that you hide first. Protect yourself.'

Along with the gun, the box contains a selection of old family photographs. Mama pointed excitedly at a picture of my grandmother holding me in the diamond halo of her arms. 'You know, she showed me how to do this,' she said, nodding at the gun that lay half assembled in my lap. 'I was also seventeen when my mama taught me. Funny how some patterns repeat themselves, isn't it? Reassuring.' I looked at the photo in Mama's hand. I couldn't see Teita's face. She was busy looking at me.

Teita had just died. 'Umm Saber and I buried her. My grandmother's siblings, some of whom I recognised from photos, attended the funeral. I had never met any of them before, and given that some of the men wore police uniforms and the others dark suits and sunglasses, I understood why. One of the men in suits—a major general, Teita's older brother—shuffled along the carpet to sit next to me. He knew my name and passed on his best to my parents before asking whether Teita ever mentioned him. I simply said, 'Yes, General,' which made him smile without giving too much away.

When Mama was arrested, Teita had called her older brother to ask if he would intervene on Hanan's behalf. 'It's complicated to get dissenters out of prison now, habibti,' he'd said. 'Back in January or February, when all these protests first started, I would have said it was possible, but now ... Just pray for her, sister.' Teita replied that he wasn't her brother and never spoke to him again.

'She never forgave me,' he said to me. *No, she didn't*, I thought. If he had helped them, maybe Mama would be in the country now, but the general hadn't been willing to risk his position for some wannabe revolutionary, even if she was his niece. In his eyes, Hanan needed to be controlled, and if her mother wasn't going to discipline her, then prison would.

He insisted on holding Teita's funeral immediately, saying that an unburied body was torture for the soul. But while Teita waited in a hearse outside the mosque for her funerary prayers to be announced, all I could think about was Mama's soul, and what it must feel like for her not to be there.

'Here, keep looking through them,' said Mama. She handed me the box of photos and swiftly began putting the gun back together herself. Dripping gun oil left grease stains on the towel. Metal slid and snapped into place. 'It's too light,' she tutted, clicking a screwdriver to the trigger. 'No one should ever be in a rush when they have to make this kind of decision.' Passing me the gun, she instructed me to stow it in the box and hide the key.

'Where is your father?' she groaned, standing up. 'I don't like him driving around with those friends of his. Rotab, rotab, rotab, and all of them trouble. I swear, that's the only reason he brings us back to this country.' By 'us', she meant the two of them.

She started to walk away, muttering quietly to herself. I called after her, and she stopped to lean against the door frame, watching me as I flipped through more of Teita's photos.

'Do you ever wish you could have got revenge ... I mean, on your uncle?' I asked quietly. 'For letting them take you to jail and do what they did to you, when he could have stopped it?'

Mama shook her head and sat down. 'What good would it do? There's no going back to my life before it happened, and if I carried on holding a grudge against him, it would only take away from my life since. He's just one more small man in a country full of small men.'

'Is Baba one of them?' I asked tentatively, even though my real question was, *am I?*

'No one's perfect. Your father isn't perfect, zayy ba'eyat el-nas.' Her reply rolled off her tongue almost too quickly, as if she had repeated it so many times that it was an instinct.

I only ever go back to the box to look for more photos. I ignore the gun. I've always known I would never be able to fire one, and I feel sick if I even try to hold it. I can't stand the thought of violence, especially when it's so close to home.

Mama did make it to the 'aza' that the general organised in Masjid 'Omar Makram. I'd seen her eyes darting around as we walked to the mosque, trying to catch fate sneaking up on her, looking to spot the blue van before it could disappear her again. We arrived there safely. As the Qur'an played in the background, prayer books of du'a's were passed around with the name of the recently departed on the first page. A sadaqa garya, to help furnish Teita's place in paradise. It's the same one I carry now.

Around me I see ghosts rising from the shadows, from the night, from stories of states in havoc, tales of this country in revolution. Photos like the one Teita took of the mosque morgue show me that terrible times have passed. On my bad days—when the electricity goes out and the shower runs dry and I can't swim and can't work—I remember that the terrible times are still going.

That Magdy is in front of me reading my letter renders the farce more real, which makes it more ridiculous. The idea of something like this actually happening is unbelievable.

But it is happening.

'To whom it may concern ... Safe passage for the bearer of this letter ... this student ... a follower of our path ... fellow of men who feel the fear ... pietist?' Magdy looks up. 'What's a pietist?'

'Like a monkish person.'

'Mmm ... I see.' He scans the rest of the letter and starts nodding, having spotted what he's looking for.

The Chief would never write a letter like this. It's an excruciating text to hear out loud, like something straight out of the ancient courts. I followed a template and typed it out myself. All I needed was 'Abbas's signature, which was easy enough to copy. The Chief is rarely in his office, and time-sensitive paperwork sometimes has to be signed off without him. Sufis are all about appearances.

'Your father got us dinner last time he was in the country, a few weeks ago,' Magdy smiles. 'For everyone here, actually.'

'Ragl gada',' Chequered Shirt adds.

'He's a great man,' says Magdy, trying to outdo Chequered Shirt. 'We miss him. These days, the only way to get you to stop and give your uncle Magdy a moment is to interrogate you when you're passing through.' He turns to Chequered Shirt. 'I've known this kid since he was this big,' he says, raising his hand to the level of his belly button. 'Can you believe that?'

Maybe people like Magdy are never really born, I think. No, it'd be too easy to imagine demons as the root of all evil. Magdy is capable of it all by himself.

A sly smile turns the corner of his mouth. He asks for my ID to cross-reference its number with the one written on his paper. His eyes dart quickly between the two rows of digits. I'm unable to pull my gaze away from his lips, which smack repeatedly while he reads as though mouthing a code that would lose its magic if he were to utter it aloud.

I tried speaking to the other guards, the uniformed ones, on my way home once. It was just a stray remark, something mundane about how crowded it was that day. I didn't get a reply. Magdy told me not to engage with them, pointing to his temple and then pointing at the guards. 'They aren't worth the trouble, homa 'ala 'edeehom,' he said, looking at their vacant faces as if scanning distant landscapes. Pious faces with hallowed expressions, meek faces with hollow expressions, mythical faces with unnameable expressions, roman faces with roman expressions, empty faces with no expressions. These were the faces I grew up seeing every day, and when I find myself alone—on a mountain, in prayer, in the water—theirs are the faces I still see.

Now, though, I avoid turning my head towards them, but they pull my eyes back and show up in my peripheral vision—vessels where life has the potential to dwell, like a bathroom sink full of spiders, vulnerable to rainfall and a change of season. They only form first impressions of me. One of them looks at my feet, then up at my face, then back down at my sandals. I wiggle my toes. He looks dazed and distant. *'Ala 'edeehom*. Half of these guys probably can't use their weapons.

A week ago, halfway through a training session, dull booming sounds pulsated through the water. At first I thought it was my own breath. Outside, a kid had thrown a firecracker into a bin on the street corner. Two officers dropped their weapons at the sound, and a third shot at the bin, yelling, 'I got him!' We left the pool prepared to see a corpse on the road.

The troublemaker was taken to a nearby police van, where security boys were smoking hash—the only way to get through each day's monotony. They passed joints to the boy's lips as he sat back in handcuffs, until his parents arrived, begging to get him back.

'Really,' his mother wept, 'he's a decent lad.'

'That doesn't mean he didn't do anything wrong,' Magdy replied.

The kid was flying.

'They must have beat him,' his father cried.

'You're taking him as we found him,' Chequered Shirt said.

'Yenfa' 'aradi el-shabab?' the father asked.

Magdy nodded his consent, and the boy's parents set about giving small notes to each of the soldiers, who pocketed the cash without looking at it or saying a word. Thanking Magdy, the parents beckoned for their son to come out of the van. He stumbled down in a daze. The guards keep a bucket in the van for tending to their bodily needs when they're on duty, and they leave its lid open to let the stench out whenever an arrestee is inside.

Magdy is still glancing back and forth between my ID card and his sheet of paper. I wonder whose line it is next. Then, he looks up at me.

'Do you want some tea?'

'No, teslam,' I reply. 'I need to run.'

Usually, I like listening to Magdy's rants. He has something interesting to say most of the time. Whenever he talks about the revolutionary years and how he helped round up the old guard, to whom he was always merciful, he calls me a 'child of the revolution'. It's a common enough name that a rebel group has adopted it, so whenever he says the phrase now, it's as much a threat as a term of endearment.

I realised that I had grown older in his eyes when he started telling me stories. 'You wouldn't believe the shit I've heard people come out with,' he said once. 'One of the presidential palace guards admitted to me, almost bragging, how much he enjoyed hanging protesters by the arms with their entire weight pulling on ropes tied around their wrists. Their actual methods, eh ... unimaginative. But disgusting. There's no place for people like that guard in this new country of ours.'

My father told me, with the pride of someone privy to secret information, that it was people like Magdy who used to shove sticks up prisoners' arses and tighten wires around their pricks till they went numb. But then, my father also taught me that, as a child of the revolution, I should know how to treat people from the old guard. Meet them on their level.

'Swimming for the country will keep you going, but only up to a point,' he said. 'You'll have to put up with it all, and with people like Magdy, decency is what wins the battle.' He was right, but who's to tell who's decent? I don't think I am. In fact, I'm certain I'm not. I take people for what they are and don't think they can do better. I'll be the first to admit that I meet Magdy on his level, but there's nothing decent about it.

I spread out my fingers as far they go, imagining tearing the webbing between them, then relax. The guards smoking at the concrete barrier are laughing, immersed in the darkness of their own world. Streetlights shake and flicker; the blackout is coming, and soon we'll be plunged into real darkness. The trembling light sends shivers through the acacia tree's sword-leaves in the absence of any wind. The air doesn't move much here, except to lift up the dust and remind me that I'm still in the city, that I still smell like petrol, that the van is occupied by a guest of Magdy's and the stench-bucket is unlidded. You can't wave away the stink, so the odours mix together until I can't tell them apart. That's the real tragedy of this never-ending heatwave: the air doesn't circulate these days. Instead, it settles in small clumps, so every neighbourhood has its own atmosphere. Around Teita's house, there are trees. Green trees, tall trees, mulberry trees with veiny trunks, as if their roots are attempting to ascend to life above ground. It's mulberry roots that tear out paving and break apart asphalt, carrying the souls of the living and the dead. They have to be cut so they can grow with a new season. The government treats the people as it treats the trees, trimming us back every year.

I've never come across a past that I've wanted to revisit, but carrying around Teita's Polaroid of the mosque morgue makes me enter that time again. Seeing the bodies laid out with blocks of ice on their chests, cold currents rushing to her nose and undercutting the smell of rotting flesh, Teita felt overwhelmed. Now, she's gone, and I'm the one who has to revive her memories. Hearing men like Magdy and Baba talk, I realise that people have always known that scenes like that existed. I don't know how they live with that knowledge, other than to ignore it, block it out, push it into the background. Baba's meandering around Magdy's chequered past tells me one thing: even if he knows this country is unliveable, he'll never change it, because he still views Magdy as capable of keeping some other evil in check with his boot on its neck.

A hint of breeze passes through and picks up the scent of jasmine. I can smell it now. It sweetens the dust, and my body is torn apart from the ecstasy of smelling something not of the city. Even the subtle undertones of shit can't snuff it out. I relish these moments of life. A spoon clinks in Chequered Shirt's tea glass, and not even his music can drown out the sound. People drink tea in suffering and in joy. I can't tell which of the two this is. I leave the door open to possibilities.

'Ah, to be you,' Magdy sighs. 'We can't all go off who-knows-where into the night to do who-knows-what the way you do. Ever since you got booted from the national team, and I'm only reading what it says between the lines of this letter of yours—here, you can have it back—you've been lying awake and considering your life, and you've realised for the first time that you have options. It's a shame—ripe fruits start to rot, you know. Granted, it is unseasonably warm at the moment, and you can't be blamed for that. It's the end of the world, after all.

'You're like my son,' he says finally. 'You know that, don't you?'

'How did you know I'm no longer on the national team?'

He points his chin towards the paper in my hand. 'It says so right there. They're replacing you, just like Chequered Shirt will soon be replacing me.'

I weigh the letter in my hand. I wrote these words myself; nothing here would betray me. Magdy must have heard about this from my coach or a gossipy teammate. *It's just a misunderstanding*, I almost say. Then I remember there's no point explaining myself. He's winding me up, pointing out all the eyes hiding in the dark and keeping a watch on me.

'Go and shake his hand before you leave,' says Magdy, nodding to Chequered Shirt. 'He'll appreciate it, and soon enough, he'll be the man you need to know around here.'

He sighs mournfully. 'All this now, when my son's in hospital. Doctors say he'll be an invalid. I'll have to keep being the breadwinner. Ah ... to be of you and yours, and of your generation.

My daughters work as well, and bless them, they send us some money—as a token, nothing more—every month. Strong women. I told them, "Keep the money for yourselves. You never know what tomorrow will bring."

'They're not going to be like me. They'll be better. You should see how many suitors I have to refuse for them. But when they do get married, I'm not going to accept anyone of a lower rank than us. A clean-cut young man like yourself ... But there's mischief in your eyes tonight. You're about to cause trouble, aren't you?'

Accepting Magdy's parting handshake, I pocket the letter and cross the cordon. At the turning that leads to the club, I look back and notice that he's wearing a new pair of boots. *This guy still has some self-respect*, I think, *who knew?*

With Magdy in the boots, the only place for anyone else is under them. Appearances can be deceptive, but they look clean. I could see myself wearing a pair like that, though never in this weather.

I can't believe it's this hot in November.

*

Cold, she thought. The bare concrete floor of the cell was cold.

When she and Baba moved to France, Mama tried to follow her therapist's advice to keep her eyes open whenever thoughts from *that time* came to her and to record herself as she searched for words to describe how she felt.

The glass panel in her therapist's small office was covered with black card, which let through a sliver of luminescence whenever anyone walked past the motion sensor lighting in the hallway.

High on the wall near the ceiling was a bare bulb controlled by an electric switch that was somewhere else. The light switch near the door of the cell produced nothing but an empty cluck *sound that seemed to emanate from elsewhere. She was surprised to hear a voice yell* stop that! *from behind the door when she fiddled with it.*

Then there was the intermittent light that had sneaked through the mesh window of the van, lighting up the face of the young boy who had hidden her phone.

Hilal, as in crescent moon, she explained to the therapist, as if the meaning of the boy's name gave another layer of meaning to her story.

The therapist explained that focusing on minute details from the moments before a traumatic event was the brain's way of trying to integrate a narrative in which crucial parts were missing. His voice was weary, which made her feel ashamed. She was focusing on the wrong thing. Her vision of the events was *askew*.

Mama usually tried to keep the days when she had therapy free, but today she was meeting a researcher who wanted to collaborate with her on a paper.

She arrived at the café and saw him propped against the

wall outside, facing the sun. He was holding a cup of coffee, which made her think he had been there for a while. *One of those 'researchers' who hangs out at cafés all day to use the WiFi, hoping to save money on heating bills and flirt with the staff*, she thought to herself, channelling Baba, who would be furious if he knew this pseudo-intellectual was the reason why he had to stay home on a sunny day in Paris to look after me.

The researcher, a twenty-something Alexandrian, smiled when he saw her. He was around her own age, but he struck her as being of a younger generation.

'Hanan?' he asked, already extending his hand. He bowed forward slightly as she accepted it and she found herself automatically doing the same, laughing at the exaggerated decorum they were showing each other, and a little startled by the firmness of his grip.

'Djaber,' he said. 'Thank you so much for meeting me,' he added quickly. 'I can imagine you must be very busy. C'est trop gentil.'

The French at the end of his sentence tripped her up, and she could only muster a meek 'merci' in response. The word came out in an embarrassingly baladi accent: *mercy*.

They had to keep their heads bowed as they entered the windowless room where the deposed president's image loomed over them. A group of soldiers was milling in the corner, talking and laughing. She heard a screech like a chair being dragged across the floor from a video playing on one of their phones. It was the sound of a person screaming, distorted by audio compression into something inhuman.

A secretary in a corporal's uniform was writing at a desk. Beside his ledger was a mug of pens, its broken handle glued back in place. Above him was the portrait of the man whose presidency had been overthrown by the people nine months before.

Her head was bowed when she walked in, so she hadn't noticed it. Then, she heard a woman's voice—excuse me, sir—*breaking* *around the edges, as if it hurt to speak—*I just want to ask, what's his *portrait doing here?*

She lifted her head slightly, trying to glimpse the woman out of the corner of her eye. An outstretched finger was pointing up at a golden frame on the wall, where she caught sight of his face against a background white as snow, wearing that familiar, dignified smile.

'What fucking business of yours is it if his photo is up there?'

A corporal had emerged from the group in the corner, while the other soldiers stayed huddled around the phone, which was now playing hip-hop on low volume so their superior wouldn't hear. She would learn that the corporal was called Ibrahim. He paced up and down behind the line of women and barked till their bodies turned rigid.

'Howa 'agebna 'ehna! And he's still our fucking president, got it?'

She looked down at her feet, avoiding eye contact with the soldiers. Ibrahim shoved her forward, but she stepped back into her place in the line, trying to disappear, wanting to ask for help, for mercy, but knowing that those words held no sway here.

'Nemti, ya sharmoota?' *the corporal sneered, jabbing a drill bit into the back of her neck.* 'What are you so afraid of? If you did nothing wrong, you have nothing to fear.'

*

I lie back in the deckchair at the pool and watch waves of pigeons circling, leaping and diving above me.

Earlier, while I was swimming, it worried me that I couldn't see the pigeons. I suppose it would be hard for anyone to see them, since they absorb all the light that comes their way, and there isn't much of it at dawn. Streaks of pink and orange brighten the clouds now; there are no shadows. The parasol that's open by the pool has loose strips of fabric hanging from its metal frame, so I can only imagine the insect-like figure it would cast on the ground in daylight.

Those restless black spots animate the air. If not for them, I wouldn't believe there was any air left.

I raise my hand and see vapour rising from my arms. I bring my hand closer to my face till its edges blur and can see that it's shaking, though only slightly. Fair enough, given the effort I just exerted. I move my hand slowly away till its contours become more defined and look at it with one eye closed, then the other. My right eye is worse.

I'm worried my vision is going. At first, I thought it was the migraines, but after I broke my nose, the headaches started to push right inside my brain. It might just be all the stress. Thinking about migraines can sometimes induce one, which is why I've been spending more time in the water. The benzene has nothing to do with it. Benzene is a fact of life. Migraines aren't, and we shouldn't have to live with them.

The tips of my fingers are still tingling from having been in needlessly warmed pool water. Blood percolating and bubbling under my skin can only be a good thing, though—a sign that an honest effort was made.

Colonel Khodeir told me that letting a little blood might relieve my body. 'Make a few shallow cuts into these veins here'—he flicked my temples, a look of seriousness stapled in his brows—'and let it bleed a little. That will relieve any migraines that are triggered by a rush of blood.'

In a brightly lit bathroom, my father showed me how it's done. I thought I should let him teach me something, anything, so I'd have a skill or a trick to remember him by. He laid down a towel next to the sink and spread out an array of sparkling metal instruments with sharp, tapered edges, like robotic insects anticipating life.

Thick red streams ran down from Baba's temple to his cheek to his chin before falling in sluggish drops onto the marble countertop. I trained my eyes on his fingers holding the apparatus, the manicured cuticles and curls of blonde hair over his knuckles. I remember glancing in the mirror and feeling like I'd accidentally met the eyes of people in an adjacent room, so I looked away and focused on the man towering above me. I'm a foot taller than Baba, but in my memory he takes on gigantic proportions, with hands big enough to crush heads and lift cars. I never saw much of him, and I have to imagine him somehow. I don't know what expression I wore when I gazed back at him, but whatever it was made Baba smile reassuringly. 'There's no pain in it,' he said.

His smile brought crow's feet, which carved channels for the blood to flow straight into his eyes. A hiss, a blink, strands of blood stretching between his eyelashes. He washed it away quickly, overturning the towel and sending the tools tumbling into the sink. Discordant notes rang out as they clashed and met in the basin, flightless birds singing their death with bloody beaks. He washed the instruments and dried them, leaving his face wet to cool. The tools went into a small travel bag for toiletries, which I put back on the top shelf for him.

Baba is close to sixty and has never needed glasses. Germany sounds less stressful than here, though. What I lack in age, I make up for in eternal dread of where I'll be at the end of each day.

Exhale. I still have that tense feeling in my chest from trying to suck in more oxygen than the atmosphere contains. The warm air smells stale today, like it's been left out for too long.

Everything went to plan last night. I made it to the club and into the locker room, stowed my bag in my locker with the bottle of petrol stashed inside, laid down a training mat on the wooden benches, covered myself in my robe and quickly fell into a deep sleep. I thought I'd be more anxious, but tiredness prevailed.

At one point, I heard the technicians outside and caught the smell of chlorine. The night crew must have bought new chlorine tanks or paid to retrieve the ones that were confiscated a few weeks ago. *Maybe there's hope for this country yet*, I thought, falling back asleep.

I massage both veins and feel my blood pulsing. I won't get a migraine today. I can always see these things coming early on.

Pigeons keep soaring and plunging above me. The vague scent of jasmine pushes through the night. It never stays past the early morning, but a little has been kept aside just for me. *Exhale.* My muscles relax, and I sink further into the deckchair. I'm too tired to resist gravity. The sky shrinks away and darkness seeps into my peripheral vision. I'm still asleep.

I see a page of text. Clear lines. Sharp strokes. Deft movements. Chicken-wing arms. Water breaking. White caps. My hands move to follow the lines across the page when I read. My whole body does the same when I'm swimming, following the line on the ceramic tiles of the pool's floor. For some reason, I never have the heart to stop at the wall. Each time I get there, the world turns upside down for a second; I see sky, ceiling, sun or spotlights and come back to find there's even more line, as if a never-ending labyrinth is unravelling beneath me with every tumble turn. I simply swim through it, pulled forward by some draught, following in the wake of a ghostly apparition that streaked through the water before I jumped in. Sometimes I catch up with my apparition; sometimes the line stretches further between us.

But I'm human, I have limits.

Whoever created the concept of the line stretching from one end of the pool to the other had a gift. It's an unnecessary thing, practically speaking, because the swimmer's direction and orientation are already implied by the pool's lanes. The line is just a distraction. It stops short of meeting the wall, and the swimmer fills in the gap in the labyrinth; with every flip, I commit more of myself and find out how much farther I can push. While it could go on that way, a labyrinth that never ends would have no point. If I'm ever to stop at the wall, the ghost has to disappear before I get there, leaving me with nothing to keep chasing.

Of course, none of this occurs to me when I'm in the pool. Now, as I ready myself for a trip to the Sinai, it strikes me that I've always confused the arid desert with the landscape underwater, where nothing can grow without a struggle. Benzene, chlorine, salt. I've never been in a body of water that wasn't toxic somehow.

The last time I went to the Sinai, I drew the gaze of a Palestinian swimmer with exceptionally broad shoulders and a legendary broken wing. In the recovery portion of his stroke, when his arm breaks through the surface and reaches forward to pull water back, Hakeem's wrist goes limp. It's a fault he never sought to correct, since he worries about compromising his natural abilities.

We met last month at a regional open-water race that was taking place in the desert on our side of the border with Palestine—in Armed Forces' territory. A local Bedouin tribe, the Ghawalis of the Tarabeen, helped to coordinate attendees' safe passage from the capital to the beach to deter vendettas that other Bedouin might have against the military. It was a peacemaking mission between the tribes and the army, a fact I didn't know until I climbed on board the bus to the race site and found it full of soldiers, most with soft adolescent fuzz above their lips and terror in their eyes.

'Don't talk to them,' warned Colonel Khodeir. 'Just focus on your race. They're here to keep you safe.' *Safe from what?* I wanted to ask, but that would be a naïve question. In this country, it's better to be silent than appear naïve.

We hit the road before curfew lifted. My teammates and I stared nervously out the windows at the novel view of country houses emerging from the morning mist, shrouded in an early orange sun. The scene changed as we drove on, and by the time the city was two hours behind us, all there was to see was an endless expanse of desert. My heart stirred with the sand, aching for a return to something primeval.

When we arrived, the beach was buzzing with frantic activity. The Bedouin had put out dining tables and erected three small pavilions, one of which housed a special array of cushioned chairs and shisha pipes for the federation officials, higher-ranked rotab and elders of the Ghawali tribe dressed in gallabeya and turban. Rank-and-file soldiers ran around with sieves of bright-red coals to refill the shishas of their seniors. Buoys were pulled out to the water to line the racecourse. A little way off was a mess tent, where a group of men in loose shirts and slacks walked about barefoot, stirring large pots of rice and roasting fish on an open grill.

The fabric of the tent blowing in the wind made me think of Teita's Polaroid. I saw the soldiers from the bus and imagined their young bodies torn and bloodied, their flesh piled on tables or wrapped in white shrouds, like Teita when we put her in the ground. The smell of burning fish scales and the popping sound of heat breaking meat made me nauseous. I wondered if the soldiers had ever seen death, and for the first time, I felt sorry for them. If they died today, they would be alone, their remains given up to the sand or the wind.

Hakeem came and sat down next to me on the beach, dragging me from my reverie. He dug his heels into the sand, reminding me of the way I trailed my feet to slow down my bike as a child.

'This is exactly what I needed,' he said, piling up sand over the bumps where his feet were buried. Looking up at me, he asked, 'Did you travel here from Cairo?'

'Yes,' I replied, noticing his gaze had shifted to one of the groups of soldiers.

'You guys almost look ready to cross the Bar Lev Line,' he continued. 'I've seen films about Khitat Badr and the heroism of your forces back in '73. How against all odds you managed to outwit the enemy that October morning, and in Ramadan, no less.' He clicked his tongue and smiled. 'If I hadn't grown up in Ramallah, I'd have thought you liberated us.'

'Is that where you travelled from today, Ramallah?'

'No,' he said, lifting his feet and watching sand pour off his toes and flutter in the breeze. 'I was in Gaza, visiting my grandparents.'

He reached into his pocket and pulled out a brown paper bag, which had inside a cucumber, a cardboard box of goat's cheese and two tomatoes with skin so red and taut that they were ready to decay.

'Do you have a knife?' he asked, straining his fingers to try and tear through the cardboard. I shook my head. Hakeem laid the bag down with his meal on top of it before running to the mess tent. Returning with a steak knife, he leaned over and hacked slowly at the cardboard box, careful not to let the contents leak out of the packaging. When he was done, he proceeded to cut the tomatoes and cucumbers into thick slices.

'Sammi be-'eedak,' he said, nodding towards the food.

'Teslam,' I replied, reaching for a slice of cucumber.

'This is all I used to eat as a child, especially when I stayed with my grandparents in the summer. To this day, Geddo gives me two tomatoes, a cucumber and cheese whenever I travel for a race. "How else will you win?" he says.'

He turned to look at me. 'When I told him your federation was going to feed me, you know what he said?'

'What?' I asked, biting into the cucumber. Its thick skin broke in a flood of sweetness, transporting me to summer days when Teita would point the garden hose in the air so I could run around in a shower of rain when such mercy seemed unimaginable.

'El-Masri ye'asmak fi lo'metak, el-'askar yesra'ha w-ye'telak,' Hakeem said, standing up. He marched back to the mess tent to return the knife, his feet sinking into the sand with every step.

Break bread with an Egyptian and you invite the army to tear the morsel from your throat.

For a moment I wasn't sure if I should be offended. I watched over my shoulder as he handed the knife to a young soldier who was busy cutting pieces of baladi bread in half with scissors. I swallowed down the last morsel of my cucumber slice quickly so that it was still soothingly cold when it reached my throat.

'Your grandfather sounds like he's got it figured out,' I said as Hakeem settled back down on the sand.

'What's that supposed to mean?' he asked, cinching his eyebrows as he waited for me to reveal my hand.

'Nothing,' I said. 'I've just never heard that saying before.'

'Geddo's an artist.' He bit into a tomato slice smeared with cheese and chased it with a slice of cucumber. 'He also warned me not to tell my grandma that I was coming here today.'

'Why?' I asked.

'Sitti wouldn't have been happy about my coming to race with motabe'een zayeekom.'

Of course. While the coloniser raised three walls to hem Palestinians in, it was our president the Field Marshal who completed their sequestration by sealing off the passages near Rafah.

'So, why did you come?' I asked.

'I wasn't given a choice. Apparently, my permit to leave Gaza and get back home to Ramallah isn't valid anymore. The swimming federation said they could get me out of Gaza if I came here to race, and that from here, I can make it back to Ramallah in the winter. Nezam, fein wednak, ya Goha?' He sketched the absurd route in the air and shook his head.

'Ta'rees,' I added, cursing the Armed Forces.

'Koll,' he replied, pushing the bag of food towards me.

Colonel Khodeir called me over to a freshly laid table in the dining pavilion. He told me to bring my friend to sit and eat and served me a plate of fool medammes and eggs. A cloud of smoke wafted from the direction of the mess tent, coloured with sharp aromas of sage, lemon and thyme that overpowered the smell of burning flesh. The sky was clear: no birds, no clouds, just an unbroken spread of blue meeting a deep azure horizon. There were no whitecaps on the water, which was calm but for an occasional gust of wind.

A banner above the VIP tent displayed the name of the Ghawali tribe and an image of the great nesr. Perched at the side of the pavilion was a deep earthenware jar next to some smaller jars for decanting.

'Zamzam water,' declared the president of the swimming federation, General Ra'fat. 'Straight from the well in Mecca.'

The swimmers were invited to drink from the water as a blessing to give them strength. General Ra'fat dipped his hands into the amphora and took a loud slurp, letting the water that was left fall back into the zeir. When I grabbed a decanting jar, he clicked his tongue and said, 'With your hands.' I put the jar back and cupped my hands in the water, muttered a prayer, then drank. The liquid tasted metallic and rolled over my tongue thickly.

When Hakeem tried to fill a plastic bottle with the Zamzam water, a private snatched it out of his hands. 'Leave some for the rest of us,' he said.

Hakeem was of Bedouin descent. His tribe, the 'Azazma, had a history of conflict with the Ghawalis, but after decades of fighting, they had found peace. While he was here, Hakeem was under the Ghawalis' protection; the tribe leader attending the race, 'Abu Sitta, knew Hakeem's family and promised to keep him safe from the generals and soldiers. When the private provoked Hakeem, 'Abu Sitta simply smiled, waving his hand as if stirring water: *let it pass.* Hakeem poured the water back into the zeir.

I had no doubt that I would beat Hakeem in the race. He had learnt to swim in open water, so he never measured the distances he covered. Despite the romantic image of a swimmer driven by pure love of the sea, someone with no idea of how far they've swum could never beat a swimmer who knows the length of a metre. It's the distance between my left shoulder blade and the fingertips of my right hand when I spread my wings. At peak fitness, my stroke can propel me just short of two metres forward. My arms move quickly. My wrist doesn't stray.

On the starting line, I pressed my toes lightly into the sand as a light surf of warm water lapped at my feet. A countdown was playing over the loudspeakers. I felt like a pillar of salt, anxious and ready to dissolve at the touch of water. My heart was beating in my throat, and I sensed Hakeem tensing up next to me. My stomach was empty, and I felt weak yet sharp, as though possessed of faith.

'Abu Sitta fired the starting shot from his rifle. The first movement unfurled. Instinct kicked in—the only thing I've ever been able to count on. I leapt into the water and the surface disappeared. The taste of salt. No black line to follow. All I could hear was the washing-machine sound of arms beating the water in a frenzy. Large groups make me panic; in the city we describe them as fawda, and while that's exactly how an open-water race looks from the outside, order quickly finds its way to the front of the madness. The group grows an edge as the lead swimmers dictate direction and pace, and like a flock of birds, the assemblage assumes the v-position.

All I can remember from the race is the sight of Hakeem's seemingly static feet in front of me. Rolling sheets of water flowed back from his hands and off his toes, which curled at times as if trying to hold on to the waves. I swam in his wake. That flutter of water from another swimmer's feet floats a pleasure like no other. Jellyfish lit our way, and around them the natural blue dropped dark and clear. Salt water burned my lips and cooled my sunburnt skin.

Once the distance was covered, all the strokes counted, the final sprint sprinted, I stood up and walked out of the sea.

The sand was warm beneath my sinking soles. Barely able to stand, I knelt down in prayer, panting, trying to calm my breath, thanking all the higher powers present. I watched the race that I left behind me continue to unfold. Hakeem came a distant second. I lost myself in staring at the crags around us, thinking about General Ra'fat's gift to us of blessed water when any water these days was a blessing. A minute had passed before someone came to shake me from my trance and congratulate me, covering me with a towel even though it was too warm for one.

Hakeem was disqualified. A false start.

I tried to remember if he took the front at the initial sprint. He didn't. He had sped up and passed me four hundred metres in, so if he was disqualified, I should have been as well.

Then there was the question of the knife Hakeem had borrowed from one of the privates to slice the food his grandfather had packed for him.

'Where is it?' Colonel Khodeir wanted to know.

'I gave it back,' Hakeem said, and I corroborated.

'Did you actually see him give it back?' Khodeir asked me, and I attested that I had.

They weren't convinced and commenced searching him, emptying the contents of the paper bag—a stub of the cucumber we shared and the rest of the cheese—to find nothing.

By making peace, the Ghawalis forfeited their right to say a word about injustice, giving the army free rein to do as they please without consequence. But I didn't go to the race on a peace-making mission. The federation disqualified Hakeem because they could, and I protested the disqualification because I could, and because it was the least I could do as a witness to injustice, peace be damned.

Hakeem was given a penalty that kept him off the podium, and Khodeir barely looked my way for the rest of the day. On the drive back, he put me at the back of the bus, telling me to stay out of sight of the rotab. 'It's best if they forget you,' he told me.

But I don't want them to forget me.

When Nizam and I arrive at the military barracks, I'm going to douse myself in petrol and set myself alight.

When the uniforms paint themselves as saviours, they make the rebels into terrorists. We've tried the slow, democratic approach to change before. Twenty years ago, while voters were arguing about constitutional amendments, the army killed Ramy's uncle. A month later, all of Mama's cries and Teita's pleas couldn't stop the horrors that were wrought inside that jail.

I want to show that if I'm a terrorist, it makes the state into the killers. The soldiers in the barracks will find themselves powerless to stop my death, since they were never meant to save me in the first place. I'm their enemy, and when I burn alive, it's their enemy who dies. If they want to avenge my death, they'll have to aim their rifles at their own hearts and pull the trigger.

I remember a thought from this morning's workout: *I can't go on, I must go on*. The words are hopelessly tangled in flashes of water and lapping arms, the sun above me burning itself to a completely different colour, my fingers tingling then, tingling still. Drops are already drying on my skin in the windless November heat, the chlorine leaving behind blotches that divide my body into lesser segments. All I need is a good shower to scrub off the stains and the smell, and then I'll be whole again, then I'll become myself.

I would usually have attracted a cat or two by now, fearless urban strays licking eagerly at the chlorinated water on my skin. There's been a recent spate of dead cats on the city's pavements, found with vacant sockets and chunks of flesh missing and the static sound of buzzing flies emanating from their gaping, cavernous mouths. I realise the cats won't show up just as I become aware that I've been waiting for them. Time is slipping away from me. I need to get on with the day. Sometimes, fear helps.

The clock reads 06:03. The sky has lightened with the rising sun, but the pigeons are still circling, still fretful. I look around a moment longer at the swimming pool, taking in how it swallows purple light that refracts in infinite directions, the rays only overlapping in the dark black-green of the deep end. The light pushes into the corners and reveals that the audience is gone. There was nothing lurking in the dark last night, no ghosts rising from the shadows by the checkpoint. The black line on the floor of the pool hides no horizon and no secrets, so all I have to do is keep following it.

But some lines just lead to a dead end.

On my last trip to the federation's offices, a line in my folder was highlighted. I wouldn't be paid for the race I won in the Sinai, for reasons 'Unknown'. Withheld pay only meant one thing: the cost of keeping me on the national team surpassed my worth. I had proven to be trouble, just as history had predicted. No one was going to fire me, but I could count my days of swimming for the country over. This is what comes of quiet diplomacy, when people protest meekly without disrupting, asking politely for whatever reforms can be spared.

Even if the national team won't call on me, the club will always keep me on. But the performance of swimming with the team no longer appeals to me. I've come to realise that the infinite freedom I feel in the water is enough to make it deadly, because it sets a standard that the rest of the world can never meet. It lasts only as long as it takes for my skin to dry while I sit in my deckchair throne and watch the birds, until someone else comes to burst my fragile bubble.

Teita brought me to Sufism because she believed in life after death. If she didn't believe in it, she wouldn't have been able to carry on going in a world that denied her life. It's been eighteen years since the army took over the presidency, promising not to serve more than two terms, swearing that they didn't want the burden of leadership and would give it up as soon as they could. They never will—if they let go of power, they'll be held accountable. I'm left with no choice but to bring accountability to them.

'You'll have to learn to speak their language if you're going to live here,' Baba told me when Teita died and I insisted on staying in the country. It's taken me a few years, but I've finally learnt their language. I'll speak to them with a fire that they can't ignore.

Pigeons shake the trees now and a rat jumps out and into the bushes. There used to be a dovecote on top of the locker room. It was torn down because the population grew and overflowed into the ventilation ducts. The smell of rot filled the lockers and the club members feared an outbreak of disease. Some say disease already broke out and that's why the pigeons and the cats are dying. I don't believe any of it.

My teammates start to pour in through the gate and gather by the pool. I look at their faces and anger blooms inside me.

They see me now, and I must leave.

*

'He cries too much,' Baba told Mama when she entered the door. 'He only just managed to sleep half an hour ago.'

Baba rubbed his eyes in an exaggerated expression of exhaustion and stretched his limbs until his elbow and shoulder *p-popped*, before *c-cracking* his neck with both hands, as if it didn't belong to him.

'You shouldn't do that, ya habibi ya baba,' Mama said frustratedly, a faded smile on her lips. The sound used to disgust and delight her when they first started dating, but time and distance dulled its effect. *The sound of heads cracking. The sound of a pipe hitting another. Glass crunching underfoot, ancient sound-pebbles turning in the waves, wearing each other down into dull nothingness. Metal tools in a basin.*

Baba pressed his chest against the wall and twisted his back as if trying to unscrew himself at the waist. She walked past him into the small living room and saw me sleeping on the floor, my head propped up on a pillow.

The east-facing window of the living room looked out onto a street. Café-goers were sitting outdoors and chattering over the constant din of car horns. There was a cheap shawarma place nearby that Baba ordered food from most nights because Mama couldn't cook, couldn't eat, couldn't sleep. Baba would often wonder where his wife disappeared to every other day. As he watched her watching me sleep from the doorway, he saw her disappear again before his very eyes. Collapsing on the couch, Mama drew a baby-blue crocheted quilt around her exhausted bones and faded out of the room.

Baba squatted down next to me and found my breathing was still steady. He rolled an index finger over my nose, rounded just like Mama's. Behind him on the sofa, Mama stared ahead, but she couldn't see him. She was sleeping with her eyes open again, her lips moving to make sounds that weren't coming to her.

'Did you eat?' she murmured. The wave of the words on her breath crashed against the cramped apartment's lime-green walls and died. Baba waited to see if she would notice his lack of response and ask the question again. He got his answer from the sound of her lungs drawing deep breaths, as if she'd been submerged and had just resurfaced, starved for air.

Then, as if it took all her strength to summon the words, she exhaled,

'Can you please close the curtains?'

'Take off your clothes,' ordered a low voice.

She touched the bloody sleeve of her hoodie to her nose. She was thirsty. Chapped and cracking, the skin of her bottom lip had split open, baring soft, swollen flesh encased in crusted blood. Her nose had been bleeding too, but there were no fresh droplets on her sleeve where she'd dabbed it, so it must have stopped. The veiled woman with the low voice told her that she also got nosebleeds from the dry, dusty air inside El-Hikesteb.

She removed the jacket that she was wearing over her hoodie and stepped forward, her arms away from her waist, ready to be patted down. Even this slight motion pained her. Her whole body was a bruise. The day before, she had looked at her stomach and seen her skin peeling, raw and reddened around the burnt, black patches where the guards had prodded her with bare wires that made her writhe in pain, the muscles in her throat unclamping only enough for her to groan.

The room had a window that looked onto the corridor outside, where soldiers were walking back and forth. She could hear their boots squeaking on the tiled flooring. There was a faint smell of ammonia and bleach, like in hospitals. In the corner of the room, a mop was standing in a bucket that she couldn't look inside from here. That she didn't want to look inside.

A few men laughed from behind the glass. The veiled woman was saying something that she couldn't make out.

'Excuse me?' Her blood was pumping loudly inside her head. 'I

didn't hear you.' She pressed her palm against her ear to allay the ringing.

'I said, all your clothes,' repeated the woman, raising her voice this time. *'The doctor will be here in a moment.'*

'What for?' she asked the woman, though she already knew the answer.

The door opened right on cue. It was a man in a khaki shirt, his sleeves rolled up to his elbows, his shoes scratched at the tips but polished.

'He's going to perform a check-up on you.'

'No,' she said flatly. *'You mean a check-up to see what the soldiers did to us?'* She pulled back her sleeve to reveal an inky bruise surrounded by streaks of red where the electrical wire had run across her skin. *'What about this?'* she asked, lifting her shirt to bare her back. Dark patches where the clubs landed, where boots kicked her when she had tried to curl up on the ground. A gouge from the drill bit.

Ibrahim, the young soldier, walked into the room, yelling.

'Ba'ol-lek 'eih, ya te'la'i, ya h-agi 'aneekek,' he threatened. He was standing toe to toe with her. She didn't cower when he raised his palm and brought it down on her face because she didn't expect anything would be able to stop the beating. Her body gave way despite her, thudding against the cold ceramic already smeared with blood from her nose. Ibrahim put his boot on her neck and pushed down. I will never leave here, *she thought*. I will never be able to leave.

Suddenly, the choking was over. She could hear the plod of his footsteps receding as she felt her breath return.

She pulled herself up unsteadily, coughing as she rose to her feet. *'Please,'* she spluttered, wiping the blood that dribbled from her mouth with her spattered sleeve. She started again,

'Can you please close the curtains?'

The man in khaki and the men in the corridor watched her as she undressed. Other soldiers gave the scene through the window only a passing glance and walked on past, inured to what was taking place. She no longer believed these were humans. How could they be?

She lay down on the cot. The doctor dragged over a stool and sat down at her feet, rummaging through the tools in the metal basin beside him. She wondered how many people he had used them on.

Her hands leapt to her mouth when she felt his touch.

'What's your name, dear?' he asked.

Sobs erupted from her chest before she could reply.

*

Grabbing my bag from the locker room, I leave just as the swim team is starting to crowd in. I wave at Khalil, who asks whose soul I'm rushing off to save. I smile and turn around to give him the middle finger. They're all Sufis too, so I never take offence. In fact, I don't think I know a single person that I'd count as an enemy.

'Araby is bumming a cigarette off a security guard outside the pool's gates. When I think about last night and all the obstacles that might have stopped me from being here on time, I'm almost grateful to see his face. It's the colour of baked bricks, and just as furrowed.

'Sabaho,' he says.

'Menawwar, ya 'Araby.'

'You're all sweet talk. I never believe it. Especially from a Sufi.'

'Can't blame you there.'

'How was training?' he asks, extending his hand to take my gym bag. 'Did you train today? I just saw the rest of the team go into the pool.'

'I started earlier.'

'I could've waited if you wanted to train with your boys.'

We start making our way to the car.

'Do you still need to drop your stuff off at the khanqa before we head off?' he asks, leading us along a corridor of trees that winds towards the horse track.

'No, best we get going.'

'You sure you want to take this with you?' He holds up my bag, feeling its weight.

'That bag you're holding has got Khayyam's missing manuscript inside. A rare books dealer gave it to me last night, and I'm not letting it out my sight.' It's a gag that I pull out with 'Araby when I want to evade his questions.

He laughs. 'You know I couldn't bear to spend another day so close to the text only for it to slip through our fingers again.'

'It won't this time, I promise.'

'Araby stops in front of an angular car with beige licence plates, both emblazoned with the national eagle. *Not one of the Sufi institute's cars*, I think. It's an old Lada. The army has a fascination with this model, which looks like a child's drawing—a trapezium plonked on top of a rectangle—as being a relic of a glorious past. When President Sadat opened the country and freed its market sixty years ago, the Lada was one of the first cars to be imported en masse while remaining affordable. The licence plates on the car we'll be driving mean 'non-civilian'. It's the perfect union of capitalism and militarism.

'Where'd you get this?' I ask.

'I had to go pick it up this morning. It's what you have to drive if you want to get to where we're going.'

I look around to try to discern if there's a reason why he's speaking so elliptically. Long-distance runners fly past us on their way around the hippodrome, kicking up dust. They're dressed for November weather, despite the unseasonable warmth, in leggings that would show the outline of their genitals if not for the running shorts worn over them. A barefoot boy wearing a half-buttoned shirt and denim shorts leads a horse to a rider, who is waiting with her helmet on. She asks him why the horse is limping, to which the boy replies that it isn't. I can tell there's something off about the horse's gait, and I don't know anything about them.

The sky is empty except for a few condensation trails left behind by planes. The passengers on those flights are no more unknown to me than the minds of the runners, the stableboy, the horse and even 'Araby. When I scrubbed away the chemical stains from my morning swim, I also washed off whatever peace I found there. Or maybe I'm just remembering my swim as peaceful now that it's over. It doesn't matter either way.

'Araby opens the boot to load my swimming bag, but I gesture for him to wait.

'You go warm up the car,' I say. 'I need to take my wet gear out of that first so it doesn't suffocate and start smelling of damp. Don't want the manuscript turning into mush.'

He hops in the driver's seat and starts the engine. I pull the bottle of petrol out of my bag and line it up among the plastic bottles of mineral water ʿAraby has packed in the boot, tearing off the label in the process so I can tell it apart from the rest. *It will be safe here*, I tell myself, starting to feel anxious as I slam the door of the boot.

Heat spills out of the car when I open the passenger door. It's a bare-bones military vehicle, with a radio and nothing else. No air-conditioning.

'A blank slate,' says ʿAraby. 'Drives like a dream, though. So, back to the khanqa first?'

'We're heading straight to ʾAbu Zaʿbal. I told you already.'

'Of course.' He waves his hand to brush away the demons in his head.

'We've got a long day ahead of us,' I say. It seems like a justification for my haste, but there's another subtext that I can't voice directly. *I need you awake and alert, ʿAraby. I can't hold your hand.*

'It'll be fine,' he says as I buckle myself in. 'Ready?'

'Tawakkalna ʿalallah.'

The sloped riverbanks are empty now, except for a few plastic bags and dozing baladi dogs. The Nile is still, the reflection of buildings crisp in its stagnant water.

Whenever ʿAraby drives, he waves obsequiously to every uniform on the road, gripping his licence and the car's registration tightly between trembling fingers. Today, he barely slows the car at the checkpoint on Qasr el-Nil Bridge. The Lada's beige licence plates will grant us passage. ʿAraby taps his forefinger impatiently on the wheel as we approach, lifts the same finger to acknowledge the uniforms, and breezes past the barricades with nothing more than a lazy salute from the policeman on duty. I would have felt better if they had stopped us and searched the car. It might have convinced me of there being a chance that the Armed Forces weren't above the law. Instead, the police at the checkpoint avert their gaze as we pass. They know full well that witnessing any behaviour of the army is a sure way to end up with a target on your back.

An army vehicle transmits the will of a power greater than any individual. We're headed to a prison to find a sheikh who's lost his mind, and we've been given this car to rush us to our destination. Why would anyone stop us? Even if they wanted to foil our plans, it would do no good to hold up a car like ours, since for that to work, its passengers would need to possess some sort of agency or free will. We do not. 'Araby works for the Sufi institute, and I'm a disciple. The only reason he's doing this is to get paid. I'm doing this because they want me to try to win back their favour, and I can't let them make me invisible. Soon, I'll reach the end of the line.

'Our way is green,' says 'Araby.

*

EL-BAB EL-THANI

We head out of the city and join a freeway flanked by arcades of palm trees and planes of sparse green. Half-dressed buildings are visible in the distance, standing to attention in ordered files in their uniforms of bare concrete and red brick: an affordable housing project that became too expensive to finish. The Ministry of Youth and Sport considered buying it up to turn it into permanent athletes' residences, but the thought of how much water they'd have to supply to the complex just to keep us all hydrated made them abandon the whole affair. Nothing is worth that cost.

Other drivers slow down as we pass, either turning to look at us or forcedly fixing their eyes on the road ahead. The sky is clear. The sun is ordinary.

I haven't left the city by car since I was a child. In my adult life, I've only ever known this road from the vantage point of the federation minibuses that take us to and from swimming races. My memories are of teammates screaming, fingers surfing the wind rushing past outside the window, music blaring from handheld speakers, crisp packets passed between buses by hand across a canyon of asphalt and rolling waves of heat. Once, close to where we are now, a chant kicked off on my bus and spread through the convoy. A boy in the row in front of me was the first to start singing and clapping. He was enthusiastically joined by others until the chorus shook the seats and windows: *Segn ʾAbu Zaʿbal! Segn ʾAbu Zaʿbal!* It felt like my eardrums might burst. The tune was carried on the dusty air to the next bus, whose passengers picked up the words and shouted them even more loudly.

I stuck my head out the window and looked at the athletes across from us, their mouths open, voices tuned down an octave, palms striking the side of their bus—our mirror image. We were on safari. Scanning the horizon, I tried to catch sight of the prison from the chant, but it didn't appear. I didn't know then about all the prisoners who were gassed in the back of a police van and met their deaths at its gates.

I fixed a smile on my face and hummed along to the chant, trying to harmonise with the rattling of the engine. For the first time, I felt ashamed of Mama and Teita. They were both in the opposite camp to everyone travelling with me on that bus: young boys who would join military academies or become doctors in military hospitals. As men they would invent new ranks for themselves so as never to feel smaller than the *true* military rotab, like our team director and federation president, who earned their titles by stomping down the revolutionaries who tried to topple these monolithic structures twenty years ago.

'Araby rolls the window up just as I notice the putrid smell of shit and dug-up earth. The freeway is crossing over a cluster of dark-grey gridded buildings filled in with bare red bricks: a slum that I remember from childhood. The correct term is 'informal housing', as opposed to formal housing meant for people of a different quality, people like me. Up ahead, the road is skirted on both sides by long adobe pathways leading to shuttered farmhouses. One house's barred window has been pulled out with a chunk of the wall, offering a view into the life of the place. Metal rebars criss-cross a room strewn with rubble and broken furniture. I try to imagine how uncluttered and orderly it must have looked when people lived there.

The car swerves suddenly, narrowly missing the mangled corpse of a dog with a punctured stomach. 'Araby steers sharply and we dance briefly in mid-air, hands raised, prepared for collision.

'Ma'lesh,' he apologises. 'Didn't want to run over it.'

'You did the right thing,' I reply, wincing at the mess of skid marks running through the dog's blood and innards.

There are children sitting on the concrete barrier separating the freeway from the slums. A young girl and boy stand on the roadside with packets of tissues and bottles of tainted water, waving them at our car as we pass.

'Sons and daughters of beggars,' 'Araby mutters under his breath.

As he signals to leave the freeway at the next exit, I reach down to put my shoes back on, questioning whether I need to go close-toed. I'm not sure whether today calls for a business look over the comfort of sandals.

'Araby taps my arm with the back of his hand. Ring striking muscle. I look up and see he's smiling. He lifts his index finger to point up at the view through the windscreen, then returns to tapping on the steering wheel. Ring striking rubber. I can almost hear the chanting: *Segn 'Abu Za'bal, Segn 'Abu Za'bal*. Horror rushes towards me as fast as we're rushing towards the horror.

'Hamdellah 'ala-s-salama,' says 'Araby. 'We made it.'

''Alf hamdellah,' I reply mechanically.

In the shadow of the looming prison walls, the world seems to be crashing down. The whole of 'Abu Za'bal is slightly sunken into the ground; the feeling of threat is strictly topographic in nature. Before there was a prison here, 'Abu Za'bal was the site of another kind of industrial complex, one of chemical plants and cement companies. The low-altitude land was chosen for the factories so the filth they produced wouldn't seep out into the city. Eventually, shit flowed in instead. The rain turns 'Abu Za'bal's slum alleys and prison cells alike into a giant cesspool. Today's residents must be thankful for the drought.

Until a few years ago, the prison here was like any other incarceration centre, but the Armed Forces had their sights set on the industrial town growing up on 'Abu Za'bal's back. They began by slowly taking over the manufacturers, buying out companies and parachuting in retired generals to fill administrator positions, all while using the eagle's wing to draw a veil over what was going on inside the factories. One of these was the cement factory where Musa's father used to work as an engineer. It fell under the state's control when members of the board informed on the father-and-son team running the company, landing them with *terrorism* charges. The company's stock price plummeted after the founders' arrest, and the Armed Forces swept up as many shares as they could. Eventually, when there was no more reason to hide the reality of what was happening, they started to push out the factory workers, reducing and withholding their wages and threatening them with imprisonment on *terrorism* charges if they resisted. After one of the workers died by suicide after not being paid, the others locked themselves in the plant for three days, carrying on the production line, even negotiating ways of sending out deliveries of cement, so that prices wouldn't rise for contractors and workers because of their protest. The name of the rebranded company on the packaging was blacked out and replaced with the words, 'We don't trade your needs for ours; thank you for supporting us.'

Early one morning, when the factory workers were ladling out slow-cooked fava beans, Musa's father flicked the switch of the kettle and saw it click back immediately into the off position. He tried again. Nothing. He turned to his comrades, all risking their skin for each other's jobs, and asked whether there was a power outage.

'My phone was charging around dawn,' said a young man whose family had been working in the factory for generations.

A blast reached their ears, followed by the chiming cacophony of glass breaking and a clatter of metal rolling across the factory's uneven cement floor. A window shattered above a table and rained sharp shards down on the workers, who leapt quickly to their feet, hoping to wake up from their nightmare. *We held the light in our hands ...*, someone sang, as riot police revved their engines behind the factory's metal door—

bang

bang

More factories fell quickly into the mouth of the hungry state, until finally, a few years ago, the interior ministry and security forces invaded and swallowed the town whole. Overnight, 'Abu Za'bal's factory workers, electricians, carpenters, mechanics, metalsmiths and café owners all found themselves inside prison walls for the crime of living and working in a town that the ruling Armed Forces deemed worthy of attention. Paid labour was replaced by the slave labour of prisoners, profit margins increased, and construction materials and chemicals became cheaper. The price was our blind eye towards the reality of life for people inside.

We drive under the freeway, and the hum of the Lada's motor ricochets off the roof of the underpass and rings back to us, making our small car sound like a speeding train headed for collision. The prison faces the outside world with beige-and-red walls that seem like they're leaning outwards. Lotuses are painted on the capitals of pilasters—decorative columns that bear no load. It shows what kind of foundation this civilisation possesses. It's a country on life support, hooking itself up to fake tubes to keep its cheeks lush, but what's the use? Not even the Nile flows anymore.

This is what Mama has been running away from all her life, and I'm heading straight for it. I'm volunteering to enter prison, confident that I'll find my way back out. They can't suspect me of being in Kaffara, or I wouldn't have made it this far. And I have the nesr and its beige licence plate protecting me.

'There's a no-man's land behind that wall,' says 'Araby as we approach. He tells me this to reassure me that we won't find ourselves inside the prison before our eyes have had the chance to absorb it, but it's also his way of proving himself useful, showing me that he knows something I don't. Just inside the walls, before the entrance to the prison proper, buses ferry people to the slum only half a mile away; the ten-minute walk under an eternal exposed sun would make anyone curse before they were even close enough to smell the filth of the ghetto. Sunken land makes it difficult to remove waste. Why would they build the prison in a literal hole?

It excites me when I realise the expanse of no-man's land is an invitation. Rather than emphasising the distance between the prison and what lies outside, beyond the freeway and the farmhouses, it admits to an insecurity of the government's police force that I've long suspected: they can't differentiate between the people inside the prison and the people outside. As the saying goes, if a city has a prison, it is a prison.

'Araby slows down to look at a line of people queuing outside the walls. Some are holding their kids; others carry food, blankets, folders. Others still can barely carry their own weight. Teita used to stand outside gates like these, waiting for any word or signal that would tell her that her daughter was alive.

'Stop watching them,' I tell him. 'Let's get to the gate.'

'Just seeing if I recognise anyone,' he grins. 'It's a joke,' he adds quickly.

The leaning walls, informal housing and no-man's land together give the whole complex the effect of a labyrinth, albeit a straightforward one. It's a maze with only one route and no diversions, either the result of a trick or the path to one. A gravitational force is slowly pulling the car inwards, as though reeling us in on a fishing line. There's no point in fighting it—it's not a battle of wills. Living in this country, I've come to value the power in submission. *Save your strength for the fights that count*, Teita told me. I've been saving my energy for years and I'm bursting at the seams, anxious to get inside these walls, grab Nizam and leave for the barracks.

A young guard wearing a fitted uniform is standing by a black-and-white metal barrier. 'Araby hits the brake, remembering suddenly that he's in control of the car. The guard pinches an imaginary key and twists. 'Araby obeys and switches off the engine before rolling the window down. The guard leans over and places a hand on the Lada's roof.

'What are you here for?' Peppermint chewing gum, slack jaw, bored eyes. Focused, but bored.

'Araby fishes around in the glove compartment and pulls out two folded sheets of paper. A nesr shows through faintly from the letterhead on each. 'Which one is it?' he asks me, shaking the papers in my direction.

I open both letters and read them quickly. One authorises us to enter the town, but not the prison; the other has tomorrow's date and prophesies a future in which we arrive at the grounds of an army battalion in the Sinai with Sheikh Nizam in tow. Nizam's kunya is written alongside a foreign word that it doesn't belong with, and I realise that his official name is different from what he calls himself publicly.

'Is it there?' 'Araby asks me. I hand him the appropriate letter and see his hand tremble as he takes it and passes it to the guard. I realise he wasn't shaking the sheets at me, and there's no wind making them flutter either—just an inner tempest sending ripples to the surface. I'm not the only one terrified of this situation.

'Get out the car,' the guard orders us.

Prisoners and non-prisoners all look the same to them, so they stopped trying to differentiate. Saves them the embarrassment of being wrong.

We've only been driving for an hour or so, but my legs feel stiff. I've been clenching them. I put on my coat to have something to hide in and stand in front of the car with 'Araby. The guard gets in the driver's seat and begins his search, running his hands over every part of the machine.

'Khawal ebn metnaka,' 'Araby curses. 'Bet he doesn't even wash his hands. Hey, officer!' he calls. The guard looks over the dashboard with his hands on the steering wheel. 'Araby hesitates, then says, 'Don't make a mess.'

'I'm not going to mess with your livelihood, ya 'ammi. Don't you worry. Gotta do this, though. See that camera on top of the gate? They're watching me.' His fingers feel around for a button. 'How do you open the boot in this ancient car?'

'Araby walks around to the back of the Lada. 'The old-fashioned way,' he replies, jingling his keys.

The guard jumps out of the vehicle with one hand on his gun and snatches the keys from 'Araby. 'Go and stand in front of the car with the boy,' he commands. There's a note of weariness in his voice alongside his irritation. It's a convincing show for the cameras.

'Araby raises his hands dumbly and bows his head as he takes his place next to me. I'm holding my breath.

'Just let the man do his job,' I tell 'Araby. 'Why provoke him?'

The bottle of petrol is inside the boot, so I don't want the search to be too thorough. I know I could still back out of tomorrow's plan without risking anything, which makes me more convinced that it would be wrong to give up now. Taking the path of least resistance means choosing to keep things as they are, and life can't go on like this. I can think of no greater tragedy for the country's future than the idea that ten years from now, this could all have stayed the same.

The last time I saw Musa, he told me not to go through with the plan. He said that if every revolutionary went chasing after death, there'd be no victory to celebrate. 'You can't hold on to liberation when you're dead.' *But death is the only thing these uniforms respect*, I wanted to reply. Even Teita's brother only showed up after she died.

'It's this macho attitude of the army that's got you thinking this way,' Musa argued. 'Men see glory in dying when they can't live life on their own terms. But if you've got a problem with the way the country works, change it.' The people tried that two decades ago, and here we are. The slow work isn't doing it. The Chief Sufi can tap my knee to quiet me; the army pushes me off the podium and out of the swim team as soon as I dare to challenge them. There's no changing this system from the inside. It has to go.

I try not to think about Mama and what I know goes on behind prison walls. The country's intelligence and security forces don't hold back, and they aren't secretive about their punishment methods. I scan the guard's face for signs of a capacity to torture. I think he would surprise me. What wouldn't this man do to break the monotony of everyday life?

The people waiting outside the prison look tortured in a different way: dusty faces, battered souls, trails of tears burning paths from their eyes to their chins. Teita's face swims stubbornly in front of my eyes. There are fewer people standing here now than there used to be. In the past, 'Abu Za'bal's gates would be crowded by supporters of the political prisoners and activists inside, but after repeated waves of arrests, which cost Kaffara several of our members, Musa decided that it wasn't working. 'If we carry on like this,' he explained, 'there won't be anyone left to go and stand outside the prison.'

I hear a woman pleading with a guard. She's looking for her youngest son and was told by his friend that he was taken to 'Abu Za'bal. The two boys were arrested together, but while his friend got out, her son is still missing. The guard arguing with her looks like he's scarcely left his teens himself. He calls the woman 'mama' in a show of his respect for elders while impatiently insisting that her boy isn't here. She yells back that she knows he is, and I feel embarrassed for looking at her, so I return my focus to our own guard and our own predicament.

Our guard calls me over. I'm still not breathing. *Exhale.*

'Didn't I tell the kid to come over?' the guard shouts when he sees 'Araby take a step towards him. 'Stay over there and watch over your car and your livelihood, ya 'ammi.'

'Araby takes a seat on the Lada's bonnet facing the prison. I go around to the back, where the guard is standing with my mesh gym bag.

'What's in this?' he asks. 'Smells like petrol.'

'It's benzene. From my swimming pool.' I reach inside the bag and pull out my flippers and goggles. 'They ran out of chlorine and had to use benzene to sterilise the water.'

'That sounds unhealthy,' observes the guard. *We wouldn't have had to do it if it weren't for people like you*, I want to say.

'You sure you don't have anything else in here giving off that smell?' His hand roots around inside the bag and emerges with my speedo. 'Is this yours?' he roars in delight. Holding it up in both hands, he waves it at the guard who dismissed the aggrieved mother—now relegated to a stool, where she's waiting with a young man who I'm startled to see bears an uncanny resemblance to one of the boys from the pool's missing chlorine crew—and exclaims, 'Look at this! Is this like the one you wear?'

'Get your hands off that,' yells the other guard. 'You've no idea where it's been. I can smell it from here.'

Our guard ignores him. 'Is there enough space in here for both balls?' he cackles.

I hold out my hand to take the swimsuit back.

'Call yourself a woman's name,' he says, 'and then I'll give it back to you.' He dangles the speedo in the air tauntingly. 'What's your name?' he grins. 'What's your name?'

'Say Fatma,' the other guard calls over. 'That's his mother's name. It's the only way you'll get him to shut up. Respect our guests, Yasser.'

Yasser drops the speedo on the ground as though he's suddenly bored. I crouch down to pick it up as he moves on to inspect Nizam's gallabeya, plastic-wrapped, still fresh from the laundry. I entertain the idea of striking back at him, but it seems like an unlikely prospect. I've never participated in competitions of macho posturing. The reason I stick to the pool is that water makes everyone slick, a hostile material that bundles us together in our colourful swimsuits. Hostility from the guard feels just as natural. If I need to be on my knees picking up my speedo for him to stand tall, that's a measure of his smallness, not mine. Submitting to his authority means I'm refusing to play his game.

Yasser unfolds the blankets that 'Araby brought for us to spend the night in the car and finds the water bottles underneath.

'Mineral water, ya dalaʿ, ya dalaʿ,' he sings. 'Can I have one? It will make my day a lot easier. Consider it a way to bless your arrival into our sanctuary. Quench the thirst of those protecting you.'

He holds out his hand as I take out a bottle for him. 'I'll need two,' he says. 'One for drinking, the other for tea and such.' I pull out another by the neck and give him both. With the water bottles under his arm, he gives the boot a final rummage and briefly picks up the petrol, but it's clear he's already lost interest.

'Go on through,' he says, handing back the car keys. 'The khabeer will meet you at the border of the town to be your guide.'

My mind is still catching up as we get back inside the Lada. ʿAraby starts the engine, and I start at the sound. Yasser moves aside the steel barricade, and we drive through in silence, raising a cloud of dust.

Two young boys appear on the road, shuttling a wheelbarrow full of rusted scrap metal. They peer into our car as they rush past us with a curiosity usually reserved for babies and pets—we are recognisable, but with unknowable intentions. It dawns on me that I have never felt lost in the city, however hard it can be to navigate. Now, though, I am on the shores of a new world, of which I know very little and to which my only connection is someone I'm supposed to extricate from inside. When I pull him out, will water flood in to fill the space he used to occupy? Will his scent depart with him, or will it stay here like jasmine at dawn, or benzene in the boot? Will he even want to leave?

The last question took shape early this morning when I was in the pool, and I answered it then. *If he's lost, he'll want to be found.*

At the town's entrance, a white sheet welcomes visitors in red painted letters. Below the sign, the khabeer of the ghetto makes no attempt to acknowledge our arrival. He simply stands and looks at us, wiping his bald head with a handkerchief. Under an awning beside him are two earthenware amphoras on metal stands. Tin cups are tied to the jars' handles with a bit of twine. One of the handles is broken, with nothing left but a stub drawing the promise of a curve that's long gone. The pottery is sweating, even in the shade. The khabeer dips a cup into one of the zeirs and drinks a few sips before letting the cup drop. There's a violent wobble in his gait. Stiff hips, perhaps, or a limb that's shorter than the other, or a limp from a fracture that didn't heal right. No missing legs or missing feet—I can see all his toes in his flip-flops. Maybe I can wear my sandals.

The car is so close now that we can see the crucifix on his chest. The khabeer waves his handkerchief sharply, motioning to us to follow him as he turns around and teeters under the sign and into the ghetto. Even with the windows up, I catch the sweet, citrussy fragrance of decomposing waste.

Two minutes into the labyrinth and the concrete walls and no-man's land are out of sight. The town's narrow passageways feel several degrees cooler than the outside world, and several degrees apart from it. Satellite dishes sprout from windows and rooftops, and garlic, lentils and ammonia waft through the air. I saw clouds in the sky on our approach, but here, the density of buildings allows for only one colour at a time overhead: slate or blue, never both. It already feels like I'm drowning, and I haven't yet left the car.

As we follow the khabeer onwards, people from the town move lazily into our path. I notice 'Araby is perspiring heavily, despite the shade, as though he's pushing the car forward himself.

'They'll get out of the way,' calls the khabeer over his shoulder. His wobble takes up more space than he does, and he bumps people aside to clear the road. No one seems to mind.

'I'm staying with the Lada till we get out of this place,' says 'Araby, nudging the car forward. His foot hovers over the brake pedal, ready for the ebb and flow of the sea of people around us.

'They'll think we don't trust them.'

'I don't trust them,' he retorts. 'And this car's my livelihood, 'akl 'eishi. You've got nothing to lose if you go out there.'

'I've got nothing to gain either. I've been sent here just like you.'

'Mish nafs el-faseela, ya boss,' he says. 'We come from different places.'

He's right. If anything happened to me here, someone would come looking for me. 'Araby's family would join the queue of people outside, hoping to find a sympathetic ear and a stool for when their strength ran out from standing and screaming in the sun.

I can sense 'Araby fighting back the urge to utter what's really on his mind out of a fear of my stony response. I don't mean to seem cold, but I must be giving off that impression. It could be panic. Or that I don't know how I feel about being here.

'You know they're not Muslim, right?' he blurts.

I close my eyes as his words crawl into my ear and down my spine till I feel them them trembling through my hands.

'Wow, look at those teeth clench,' he laughs. 'Loosen that jaw, ya Shahed. You don't want to bite off your tongue now. What would a sheikh do if he couldn't preach? I just meant to say—'

''Araby,' I breathe, 'I know what you meant to say. We've got a long journey ahead of us, and I can't handle your heinous bigoted shit right now.'

I'm surprised to hear the words come out of my mouth, though I have a feeling that today will be a day of surprises. I can tell 'Araby is nervous. He feels outnumbered and doesn't know what to make of the crosses he sees around him: the khabeer's necklace, the tattoo on his wrist, graffiti on the buildings. There's a mural of saintly faces above the words 'MARTYRS OF MASPERO'. It's illegal to talk about this history, but everyone here is already in prison. Ramy stares out at me from the faces of the icons; I see his honey-coloured eyes, his square scar, his peroxide-bleached locks, and I feel ashamed. I try to remember Ramy's uncle's photograph in the kiosk to see if he made it onto the mural, but all the square-jawed faces are too fair. Either they took liberties with the depiction, or he isn't here.

'W-lazem yohotto sooret el-gaban,' 'Araby frowns, pointing disdainfully to a portrait of a Coptic businessman who ran a wildly unsuccessful presidential campaign a few years ago. 'Just like every other Christian in this country, as soon as the tide turned, he ran off to count his coins in Europe. I hear he has a huge mansion in London with gold bars stuffed inside the walls.'

If 'Araby wants to feel pride about having stayed in the country, he need only remind himself that he has stayed out, at least, of places like this. I wonder what 'Araby's presidential candidacy would look like.

'What are we even doing here?' he asks me.

'Trying to find the magzoob,' I reply, hoping the religious term for Nizam's holiness will win him over. Or it could give him another target to rage against. 'Araby rejects icons in all their forms: spiritual awakening doesn't keep his family fed, and neither do revolutions. He has accepted poverty as a reality, but he'll never make his peace with life. Anyone who tells him they have divine answers is selling him something he isn't buying—spooning him poisoned honey, as Teita would say.

He fidgets in the seat next to me. 'And what's Nizam doing here?'

'What are any of these people doing here?' I ask rhetorically.

'They deserve to be here.'

'For doing what?'

'Terrible things.'

'Like what?'

'They're enemies of the state. Killers, thieves, beggars. They might not even be Sufis, Shahed. What would we do then?' he asks, laughing at his own joke.

'All these people? It's as packed in here as Mu'izz Street.'

'More like the alleyway I was raised in. I left for a reason.'

He slams the brake, and I throw my hands out to stop myself from crashing into the dashboard. The Lada screeches to a stop in front of the khabeer, who has stopped walking. He bangs twice on the bonnet and gestures to 'Araby to park where he is, then hobbles to my door and knocks on the window with his ring. I see that he's grown out the fingernail on his right pinkie, just like 'Araby.

'Ghasheem,' mutters 'Araby, shaking his head and leaning over my lap to inspect the window for damage.

The khabeer is blocking my door. I want to ask him to move out the way, but he's already busy in conversation with someone, talking animatedly about some kind of disaster in one of the town's other neighbourhoods. He feels the door brush him as I open it a crack and backs away to give me some room without turning away from the woman. I step out under a patch of blue sky to the smell of warm dust and rotting fruit.

We're parked outside a single-storey structure that stands out as squat and half finished even among the other bare buildings. A mismatched smattering of venetian blinds and latticed mashrabeya screens have been cobbled together to protect the inside from the outside. One window is covered with a woven wool blanket dripping with water: air-conditioning. The word 'HOSPITAL' is painted in red over the doorway in the same lettering as the sign that greets the town's visitors.

The khabeer is speaking to a short woman with broad shoulders who wraps her head covering in the same way as the Bedouin men in the Sinai. Her face is sagging, her skin tanned and melting in the sun, lines drawn from eyes to chin. I try not to listen to their conversation, assuming I won't understand and not wanting to intervene in the workings of a place that seems to operate on a different internal rhythm to what I'm used to. I offer the khabeer a handshake, which he accepts without a second's interruption to their dialogue, but when I turn to greet the woman, they stop talking. Looking me up and down, she eventually extends a doubtful hand from under the scarf around her shoulders. I fumble clumsily and struggle to clasp it before I realise it's a prosthetic.

'Don't tear it off,' she says. 'It's become loose from all the work I've been doing.'

'Noura's been clearing away raksh from where a flash flood hit the other side of town,' the khabeer explains to me. 'How much longer will it take?' he asks, turning back to her.

'At least till tomorrow,' Noura replies. 'The suppliers couldn't get through and had to turn back, but they left everything by the tunnels in plastic-wrapped bundles and sprayed them with a scent to keep the jackals away. We can climb over the raksh to get any supplies that we need vitally, but I'd rather move the debris and figure something out.'

'Maybe allow some men to go through and help with the lifting—'

'Last time your men walked through my neighbourhood, they caused trouble, and we had to teach them a lesson. If you want that to happen again—and this time I swear we'll burn them alive and cut you off completely—then let's have them. Let's have them. They used to say that a strong woman in this country is worth a hundred men. So, how many men have you got, ya khabeer? Show us how big you are. Or is this all a show for the boy? Send them over. We'll bury them under the rocks out there and let the jackals have at them. We need fertiliser anyway, and it'll save us from having to order it from the balad.'

'If you don't clear the raksh and get us our supplies tomorrow, then I won't be able to call them off,' the khabeer says.

'You from Masr?' Noura addresses me suddenly.

'Yes,' I nod. 'I've come here for ... for Sheikh Nizam.'

'Nizam? Did you bring anything for us?' she asks.

'Like what?'

She turns and speaks to the khabeer in a dialect I can't understand. I catch only a few snatches: '*how long will the foreigner be staying*', '*works for the government*'.

'Noura's just teasing,' the khabeer assures me. 'She wasn't like this when she moved here. I remember when she used to be Ms Noura. Her father owned land just outside 'Abu Zaʽbal.'

'And now I own nothing, but I help people,' Noura says to me. '*My* people. We have to, while your government just waits around for us to ask for aid and then forms committees to investigate what's wrong with us. "Why can't they just help themselves?" Well, that's what we're doing. What does your Sufi committee do? Is it just gallabeyas instead of suits and brass plates, or do they actually get anything done? I'd say I have a few favours to ask, but what's the point? I might be in here but I still know proper manners, and if I were visiting people who I expected to show me hospitality, I'd know to bring them something.'

'Khalas, ya Noura, that's enough,' the khabeer scolds. 'He's only young.'

'He needs to learn. He's not on the right side and he doesn't even know it.'

'When are you leaving?' the khabeer asks me.

'We leave tomorrow with Nizam. He should be back here by tomorrow night.'

'Keep him,' Noura says. 'We don't want him. He's a useless excuse for a man. If you didn't bring anything with you, then you're just like him, and the least you can do for us is take him away. We can smell his perfume all the way from our neighbourhood. Incense won't clean this place out, you know. May we never witness such an evil as that man again.'

'You're in the same pr-prison?' I stutter, regretting my choice of words before they've even left my mouth.

'We're in a different n-n-neighbourhood,' she replies.

'You're ruthless, ya ʽammeti,' says the khabeer. He turns to me. 'He's struggling. Nizam, I mean. Being here is getting to him. He's in the ward for political prisoners, and some of his fellow inmates still have backing in the city, so Nizam is lucky enough to get a bit of time outside every day. When he first got here, he used to plant things in the dirt patch, but the birds and crows ate everything he tried to grow. And the guards didn't allow him this indulgence long. "We have to conserve water," they told him, before burning the plot. "The Nile is drying up, and those who waste water are brothers of the devil, ya sheikh."'

The khabeer shakes his head and purses his lips in a show of compassion. 'This is the way things go in prison. Nizam doesn't give sermons for Friday prayers and isn't allowed any writing implements. He just walks around the enclosure, staring at his feet.

'But it's incredible, he's been here just over a month, and in that time the government has suddenly remembered we exist. We're getting a new pump for our septic tank, and the flour they give us to make bread isn't filled with bugs and cockroaches anymore. I say we keep Nizam. Good things come of having him here.'

'Like the long line of people trying to sneak in to see him,' says Noura.

'What kind of people?' I ask.

'Poor people who believe in his power as a saint,' says the khabeer, looking back at Noura when he realises that he cut her off.

'Speak, boss,' she nods.

The khabeer continues. 'They believe that he's gaining some kind of mystical power since he's spending more time suffering. Apparently, he wasn't doing enough of that outside.' He smiles, satisfied with his last comment. 'Nubians don't do well in prison, you know.'

'We know he still gets his fee for being a saint, and what a saint he is,' says Noura, curling her lip. 'Even the few men in high office who do wind up in here don't go to prison in the way we do. I'm sure he'll come up with a good poem about this whole thing, distilling the experience to its purest essence. Do you see anything pure here?' She gestures with her head at our surroundings and lets out a dreary laugh. 'Maybe your hands. Will you clap for him? I hope so. Would be a shame for the money spent bigging him up to go to waste. Really, they should've spent it on this place. Look around, they locked us in here with death during the pestilence more than a decade ago, and they haven't opened the doors since. But we didn't all die, as you can see.'

'I've only had the chance to speak to Nizam once,' says the khabeer. 'I was accompanying him into the town for a meeting with an officer, who drove here to visit him in a car with licence plates just like yours. I remember Nizam was relaxed on his way to see the rotba and merrily rolled cigarettes as he strolled along. It was almost as though he didn't notice all the hardship and suffering in the streets around him, or he didn't care. Just as Noura said, he doesn't even go to prison like everyone else. He seemed to think people like that rotba were on his side.'

The khabeer shakes his head. 'People look up to Nizam here, as they do in the rest of the country. I asked him if he could help us at all by appealing to the rotba and letting him know about the daily miseries of life in this town. With Nizam's intervention, maybe the rotba would see to it that we were provided with construction equipment and materials, so we could build a proper medical clinic and rebuild some of the houses that collapsed during the last earthquake.

'Nizam said he didn't have that kind of influence and that, truth be told, he didn't think it would make a difference if he did. He told me the rotba wouldn't care about the plight of people here, and that our real concern should be what would happen if an army officer did take an interest in the town's issues. The Armed Forces are nothing if not respectful of the police's right to a semblance of power, and while the army controls 'Abu Zaʻbal's factories, the police control the gates and the streets. If the army were to muscle in on the police's dominion, Nizam said, then the people here would be bound to them forever. That was why he believed it was better for some people to suffer out of sight; the shade was its own mercy.

'What he was saying was: *this is freedom.*' The khabeer pointed around at the half-built, bare brick buildings and the growing piles of rubbish baking in the heat. 'It might look like freedom to him after being in prison and seeing his plot burn, but he should know better. Prison grinds you down to nothing, like a tahoona.' He presses his palms together, twisting and squeezing them against each other. 'With every rotation of the mill, with every time you come back here, you become smaller. For some reason, your man has shrunk himself down, and I believe the reason is that rotba he saw.'

I'm beginning to see that the people who hate Nizam despise him for not being what they were promised he would be—a saint, a prophet, a saviour. They still have faith in the idea that the government could mend its ways and keep its word to support every child of the country. If Nizam can't intercede with their oppressor and deliver them to freedom, then he crushes that hope.

'But I thought you said Nizam helped you fix things up,' I say.

'He helped the prison fix things up,' says the khabeer.

'Now we're forced to smuggle in our own resources through tunnels just so we can supply the town with all its necessities,' Noura adds.

A young woman is pushing an elderly woman in a wheelchair out of the hospital, taking care to steer clear of the wood offcuts scattered by the doorway. A few men stop to help her, but Noura holds up her hand and tells them that the woman is handling it. I think of how empty the no-man's land looked and how chaotic this feels in comparison. The buildings here are run down and doing their best to stay erect. Steel rebars poke up from the hospital, not trying to hold up the sky but letting it sink slowly on top of them. I worry that if the shuffling feet, machinery and chatter go quiet, I'll hear the low, agonising moan of metal twisting and bricks crumbling. If they're putting in this much effort to keep the town afloat, maybe they're just as much slaves to appearances as Sufis, only missing the pristine gallabeyas. *Just let it all fall*, I want to say. But where would be the dignity in that? Is dignity of any use in a place like this? Maybe it's less about dignity and more about survival.

I ask Noura whether smuggling the supplies is dangerous.

'What will they do if they catch us?' she says. 'We already live inside a prison. And I believe—don't ask me why, I can't explain it, but my heart and head know it—they would never mix the people in the town with the prisoners in the cells.'

'They don't want a revolt,' I say.

Noura bites her tongue. She has no reason to trust me. 'Nizam being let out of prison to spend the night in town with you has already got people talking,' she says hesitantly. 'They feel like it could be the start of something.'

I've heard that in some rural parts of the country, time is conceived of as a series of different places rather than different moments. If I were an optimistic person, I'd think that these people were transforming the place where they live because they want something different to happen, something far away from the turn of the mill that grinds people down into smaller pieces.

A man is throwing pieces of wood up to a pair of arms sticking out of a first-floor window. He smiles at the hands when they reach outside, waiting to pull the pieces of wood through. The wood then reappears on the rooftop, where more scaffolding is being raised.

''Ash, ya 'Abdu,' the khabeer greets the man throwing up the wood.

''Ash, ya kbeer,' says 'Abdu in a voice as automatic as the rest of his body. He doesn't look to see if each piece of wood has been caught before he launches the next one. I wonder whether he'd notice if it weren't, and what he'd do if it fell back down.

'Ya Sheikh Shahed,' calls 'Araby from the car. He's rolled the window down and is leaning over the empty passenger seat to talk to me. I don't like that he called me 'Sheikh', which he thinks will elevate me among present company, but it's done now. I like to feel strong, but it seems like my strength only exists to wield over other people.

'Sheikh 'ala nafsak,' Noura mutters.

I felt strong this morning when I was swimming. My body went through practised motions that only stirred the water around me. When I got out of the pool, water filled my place and erased all impressions on its surface of my presence, regaining a sense of composure and calm.

'Araby is still sweating. He looks worriedly at the people who've gathered around us.

'I'm going to drive to the gates and wait for you there,' he tells me. 'We can sleep in the car tonight.'

'I think I'll spend the night here,' I reply. 'If that's possible, I mean.'

'It's possible,' the khabeer nods.

'You go ahead,' I say to 'Araby. He checks that I won't need anything from the car before rolling up the window and locking the door.

'Go for a loop around the hospital and it'll take you back,' the khabeer tells him. 'The road out of town looks smaller when you're leaving than on the way in, so keep an eye out. Otherwise, you'll just wind up back here with us laughing at you.'

'Shokran, ya kbeer, but I'll find my way.'

As 'Araby drives off, a few people walk past us carrying a large tub of boiling water that smells of salt and lye. 'Who are the tourists?' they stop and ask the khabeer.

'They're here for some inspiration,' he laughs, turning to me as if I'm in on the joke. We join in with his laughter as the Lada rolls past, and a promise is kept. 'Araby manages a smile and waves, a one-man procession. An omen of good things to come and go, come around again and then leave. He gets a second chance and manages to leave. I stay.

*

The khabeer knocks on the door of Nizam's flat, which rattles not just after every rap but endlessly after, betraying its fragility. He descends two steps of the staircase, prepared for flight, leaving me on the landing in front of the door. I see Nizam's silhouette behind it and realise the material isn't opaque. It's recycled glass, recovered from who knows how many windows, vases, door panels, religious icons, heated and compressed together to form a stained-glass pattern that shows no definite image, washed over with dyes, etched with the prints of fingers and palm lines from where people pressed against it with their hands. Nizam opens the door, which falls back rather than turning on a hinge, giving me the impression that he emerges from colour. I'm nervous.

He's looking down as if a sword is hanging above his neck, ready to drop. I can't see his eyes but can feel them, like sunlight, washing over my feet. I went for sandals in the end, abandoning all decorum. He looks at my calico trousers, rolled up over the ankles so they don't drag. He must have expected these trousers because his eyes don't shake. My belt has been tightened beyond its original construction; I added the requisite holes myself in my room at the khanqa. My shirt is examined next—he expected it to be better ironed, but he doesn't know that it spent the night crumpled in my gym bag, because I slept in the locker room. His eyes are now at my navel and I start to see the hollowed sockets, glimmers of light reflecting off the final drops of water in a deep well.

He starts suspecting that they've sent someone he didn't expect, which reassures me: my stomach is taut and the shirt hangs loosely enough around my waist that I don't look like a ruminating bookish Sufi. But for Nizam, this is also cause for nervousness—his eyes widen, and the water's surface stirs as if shaken by wind. I must be some sort of spy. He's about to die. The thought startles him. Only then does he realise that he averted his eyes upon opening the door to give death a chance to take him without his knowing. Even in his prison cell, where most people who come knocking have the right to invade his space, he looks or calls out, yet he opened this door so thoughtlessly. The army has built him a mausoleum, but he still believes he will be surprised by death. The fear preoccupies his mind so much that he doesn't think to react to it. His eyes carry on moving up, faster now. My shirt is fastened to the penultimate button, and the whole way up he just sees its colour, which reminds him of rope. Then my chin. He doesn't really see my face and is beyond fear now. He thinks he's already dead. He wants to be out of this prison and this life.

'As-salam 'aleikom, ya Shahed,' he says, and before I can respond, he pulls me in with the embrace of a drowning man. My arms wrap tightly around him. His gallabeya smells of stale sweat and wet dog and has the coarse feel of being inexpertly handwashed and half dried over and over in a small cell that doesn't get much light or air. He's lost weight. His muscles seem to be the only thing keeping his skin from peeling back over his bones.

The khabeer continues to climb down the stairs, loudly shuffling his feet. When the front door of the building bangs closed, Nizam turns and walks back through the coloured door. I follow him, but he's already at the far end of the room by a window covered with a stained buttonless shirt. He stands behind the shirt and looks out onto the street as though he's forgotten I'm still here.

I stand in the middle of the room and try to take in the space. The place has been done up by someone. The kitchenette area is clear and defined, tiled with broken ceramic and mortar filling the awkward gaps. I can see cracks; the heat must've got to it, so it didn't get the chance to dry out slowly. Nothing's unfinished, just undone. There's a mattress on the floor and a long plank beside it. Rugs, towels, blankets and sheets are piled on a chair. There are heaps of broken bricks in a corner, bits of rotten wood, the honeyed smell of sawdust.

'This is one of the workshops,' Nizam says from behind the shirt. 'They're letting me stay here so you and I can meet. I'm on furlough from the prison from today until tomorrow night.'

There's a small square table with a secret inner compartment, but the lifting top is scratched and askew; I see the shadow underneath. I walk towards it.

'You can stay here, of course. I heard you asking the so-called khabeer outside, so you can stay here. You'll have a time of it. Something to add to your list of achievements, for whenever you have to find a proper job outside of swimming and the Sufi institute. Can't be an assistant forever, right?'

I try to remember what I said to the khabeer outside, but the whole day has been a haze. I know I can't have strayed from the official line, which is that I'm here to help Nizam. I wouldn't ever say anything against him because I know very well that any indiscretion could be used against me. That's a weapon anyone could dangle in front of me forever to force me to dance to their tune.

His hiding behind the shirt makes me want to hide. He retrieves a pouch from his breast pocket, rolls a cigarette, and calls over his shoulder, 'Do you smoke?'

'Why not?' I reply. I sit at the desk and run my hands over the surface. Not a bit of dust. He places the pouch and liquorice rolling paper on the tabletop, and I set about rolling my first cigarette.

'I don't smoke,' I admit, peeling out a blackened paper and laying what looks to me to be too much tobacco on it.

'It's a disgusting habit,' he says dismissively. He overturns the pile of material from the other chair and brings it to the desk. 'Ruining the body that's given to you as a gift, that the government nurtures.' His cigarette hangs lazily between two fingers, and his left hand nestles in the palm of his right. With the second, he moves the first; fingers move to move fingers.

'Especially given the investment they put in you, not to mention all the effort that you've put into building yourself up to be the formidable *man* that you are.'

I can never measure up to the men serving in our Armed Forces, though, so what's the point? But I can't say that. Not even to Nizam.

The paper sticks to my hands before I can adequately roll it together. I remember walking out of a shower in the locker room as steam thickened the air and stuck to my body and the tiles. I was in a state of undress, with not even the speedo that the guard fondled preserving my modesty.

My coach told me to cover my loins when showering with teammates.

'They're like your brothers,' he said. 'Only peasants do what you're doing.' When I asked what the problem was, joking that it wasn't anything they wouldn't have seen before, he simply asked, 'Is there something you want to tell us?'

I looked down and saw droplets of water sticking to my body, my belly button, my hands hanging loosely at my side, hair flowing from my navel to the instrument he was trying to ignore. I knew what he was implying. My brothers were just around the corner, but the tiles threw their laughter everywhere.

I bend over to lick the liquorice paper without daring to lift it from the desk, worried that it will disintegrate.

Nizam looks at the result and smiles. 'Are you happy with that? May I sit?'

'*Please*, make yourself at home.'

'Too kind.' He lifts his gallabeya slightly to give his knees room to roam and sits down, rocking back and forth in his seat. 'It's a sturdy one,' he comments, patting the chair. 'Didn't expect that.'

'Putting up a good fight. Best be kind to it.'

'Oh, definitely. It's why I've been on my hunger strike. Just so it doesn't have to carry too much weight.'

'Are you not eating?' I ask, suddenly horrified at the spectacle of him smoking. I try to imagine how far off kilter the world must be to him now with all the fumes of tobacco and sawdust in the air.

'It's only the second day,' he says. 'Don't worry about it.' He nods to my cigarette again. 'Are you happy with that?'

It's filled with air pockets and bears dents from where I tried to spread the tobacco after the paper was already stuck in place. 'It looks like a twig,' I say.

'It does,' he nods, slipping his own cigarette in his mouth. 'May I roll you one?'

'If it wouldn't be a bother.'

'It would be my pleasure,' he says, already reaching for the twig, 'especially for a brother who's come all this way to see me. Where is it you've come from today?'

'The city.'

'Must look its ugliest right about now.' He tears the black paper and pours the tobacco out on the tabletop. 'Honestly, why in God's name would they leave us the daytime to conduct our good business? I feel infinitely more religious with the sun at my back and would rather take it slow when it burns bright. I'm crepuscular—night time gets me all wound up and I can't sit still. But the day? Take me to the nearest mosque and hide me inside. Let me lean lazily against a wall and watch the courtyard soak up all the light as I count down the hours till the marble flooring is cool enough to walk over to leave my sanctuary. Even the smell of mouldy carpets wouldn't keep me away.

'The smell of people, though—that deters me. Keeps me huddled in a corner trying to cover my face rather than hear all the comments about my skin. I've never had a conversation in a mosque without the other person mentioning 'Antara bin Shaddad's blackness. I used to pretend I didn't know who 'Antara was sometimes just to hear which version of the poet-warrior's story they'd deal me.' Nizam smiles and shakes his head. 'But what's the use? One must practise patience, even when it isn't easy. Even with tyrants.'

'I'm aware,' I say. 'Patience with tyranny' used to be the Brotherhood's explanation for burying their heads in the sand when it came to the Armed Forces.

'You grew up in the south, right?' I ask, trying to sound curious, which I am. Nizam's history is a mystery, and the government has tried to keep it that way. You can't protest about what you don't know.

'Yes,' he says, extending the word as if he's throwing lines of sound in every direction, fishing for whatever will bite. 'A small island. South of the reservoir, but before the 'Aswan Dam. I haven't been back in a while, though. It's always sunny there—cool in the early evenings but warm at night, because after sunset, the ground releases all the heat it's stored during the day. I'd go to bed cold and wake up sweating in my sheets. The windows would be fogged over by daybreak, and the room became a sauna.'

He pauses in contemplation, his eyes resting on the mound of tobacco that he emptied out of my sad cigarette. 'Only thing I miss about it is Lake Nasser, really,' he says. 'Used to go fishing there for days and nights on end. Just me and a few others in a small boat. My mother used to come along from time to time. I believe she still goes fishing, but just off the island now. Our people can't go to the lake anymore, because of ... you know.'

The Armed Forces have always kept an iron grip on the Nubians' ability to move through their territory. It's become even worse ever since Nubian farmland was taken over for the army's 'subsidised' vegetables—subsidised because of the slave labour of young conscripts from different governorates who are sent by the army to work the land. With nowhere to escape, these troops must submit to every abuse and humiliation meted out on them by the officers who fancy themselves pashas overseeing the farms. There have been more than a few whispers of suicides that Kaffara has managed to trace around the country, but the bodies don't turn up, or if they do, they're found hundreds of kilometres away and it's impossible to prove a causal link.

'Lake Nasser has motorboats patrolling it now,' Nizam continues, 'as well as sentry points all along the coast. It reminds me of the artificial enclosures they build in zoos. It's all desert around the lake. Anyone who hadn't seen it would never believe a lake existed in all that emptiness. There's not a blade of grass around, even though it's fresh water. A couple of trees, skinny and young. The lake looks out of place, even sinister. I had to drink the water myself to believe it wouldn't kill me.'

'Did you go poaching crocodiles?' I tease.

'No, never touched them. Poaching crocodiles is against the law, and I never wanted to get into trouble,' he replies, with no trace of irony. 'When I was sixteen, my friends and I would go out on boats, mostly to fish, but for the stated reason of making sure there were no poachers about killing the poor beasts. We never saw crocodiles, but at night we imagined we did. The sky would be blanketed with stars, and I'd see thousands of eyes blinking out at us from the dark waters below. The only disturbance was the slight rocking of the boat whenever anyone moved inside the hull, though we tried to stay still as far as we could. Any movement in the water—unless it was from a fishing line, lure or fish—we attributed to crocodiles. It was dark, so it was impossible to know for sure. Poachers would hunt and skin them, then take the rotting flesh with them to clean up the scene of the crime. They stirred the sand to hide any trace of blood, but we could always tell it was there. And there'd be vultures circling the spot where the animal was dragged out of the water.' Nizam draws rings in the air with his cigarette, leaving whirls of smoke hanging above the table.

'It's a good thing that we never saw any poachers. We were never armed with more than knives and sticks—for the fish, which we'd dry in strips on the wood and subsist on for as long as we were out there; that's why I've always been skinny—so we'd have been powerless to stop them if we had found them. God help us if we'd come across a crocodile. We just thought our presence on the lake would deter poachers. The crocodiles were shy, lurking in the water, waiting for a weary, sleep-deprived head. Some nights, when everyone else was asleep, I'd imagine something banging against the boat. I wouldn't dare look over the side for fear of seeing something looking back up at me. Eventually—I can't remember when exactly—we realised the poachers were too good at their jobs, and there was nothing left to poach, or nothing left to protect.

'I've only seen crocodiles in the city zoo, so whenever I think of the lake, the city and the zoo come to mind. You could never patrol the whole lake or even see its edge, and it's the same with the city. But in the zoo, there are just a few metres between the animals and the horizon at the edge of their enclosure. It puts a limit on all the possibility that life could hold, if there were only space to put it. Tsk.' He moves his hand as though batting away a fly trying to land on his face. The smoke is stirred into shapelessness, then carries on hanging in the air like a mangled dream.

'When were you last there?' I ask.

'It's been a moment. I don't get to go anywhere, anymore.' He pulls out a new sliver of liquorice paper for my cigarette. 'We do have a tree in the enclosure in front of the political prisoners' ward. I'm only allowed out there to pray, with the rest of the inmates standing in their own enclosures behind me.'

'I'm surprised they still allow you to do that.' I don't mention that the khabeer said Nizam was too preoccupied to give sermons. They already seem to have a very shaky peace.

'It's a true pleasure, really. Nothing like feeling yourself supported by all those murmurs behind you. Half of them don't know how to pray. I think they do it because it means standing together in line, and no one wants to miss out on a chance to bring order to chaos. Everyone becomes part of a bigger whole. It's one of the few moments of peace we get to enjoy, and the only time anyone listens to me anymore.'

'Do you have your own prayer mat?' I think of my own mat and all the times I've slept on its soft maroons and blues, an island of my own, a castaway in my own room.

'No, just a jute canvas, and even that's a perk of being a political prisoner. The others have to get dirt on their blue uniforms and foreheads. The administration probably takes note of those marks to keep track of who's showing up regularly. Hard to stop people from praying behind you, though, and I think the guards and the interior minister want me to keep up my image as a saint who's being dignified by suffering.'

He pauses and retrieves the tobacco pouch from his pocket as if he wants to move on from what he's talking about, but he can't hold back from another musing. 'Infinite patience for wrongdoing,' he says, staring at the pouch. 'That's what we need. Any revolt results in loss of life.' He has the demeanour of an administrator tallying profits and losses.

I watch him laying tobacco on the paper and see that I used too little. He puts the pouch back in his breast pocket before moving on to the next step.

'How's your level of patience going?' I ask.

'I've got all the time in the world now, or at least however long I have until I leave it.'

As he rolls the paper, Nizam's own cigarette hangs from his mouth like a torch, bobbing up and down with the movement of his hands. He puffs on it to keep the flame going, and his chest rises impressively with each breath, not because he's inhaling deeply, but because his body looks so thin and frail that any expansion seems monumental. For a second, I imagine Musa hiding beneath Nizam's skin, remembering the first time I met him. *You only had eyes for your Sheikh Nizam*, he said.

'You've grown thin,' I say. 'Less meat on those bones.'

He puts down my unfinished cigarette. It unfurls on the table like an offering.

'Your blood runs thick in your veins, brother,' he says. 'Come to gawk at the suffering?' He spits out smoke with the words and his breath chases after. 'To feel close to the misery? To feel holy?'

I can see the points of his shoulders like a protective claw on his back. He is heaving, and I worry he'll snap from trying to draw a breath that his body can't handle. He isn't looking at me so much as through me, his eyes fixed on my chest as if he's lost his sight. I'm at just as much of a loss as he is.

'The weight loss is from before I found myself in prison, ya Shahed,' he says finally.

Tomorrow night after our job is done, I will not be returning home. That thought crashes down with its own load of terror. But while for me life will not go back to how it was, for Nizam, it might be years of the same.

'I've found people always call me by my name to make a point,' I say. 'Or right before trouble arrives.' It's best not to assume any intimacy with this man.

'I've found the same to be true,' he says, picking up the paper with its load of tobacco and bringing it to his lips, 'which is why I've never responded when people have called me by my name.' A glob of spittle falls onto the desk when he licks the paper. His mouth is watery from drinking fluids to fill his stomach on his hunger strike. He wipes the droplet away with one hand and gives me the cigarette with the other. 'He can ignore us mortals when we call out. Why aren't we given the same dispensation?'

My hand pauses mid-air while reaching for the cigarette. 'That's blasphemous,' I say, feigning indignation. 'What if these walls have ears?'

'Oh, come on,' Nizam scoffs. 'There's no one listening in. The disappointing truth is that no one cares about us in here. We're out of sight and out of mind. Be honest: if you hadn't been sent here, would you have visited me on your own?'

My elbow hits the table and I'm no longer reaching for the cigarette, but I leave my hand hanging in some sort of gesture that proves my intent to bridge the gap between Nizam and myself.

'How could I have gone about doing that?' I ask.

'True,' says Nizam, shrugging and pushing the cigarette into my hand in one motion.

I twist it in my fingers to look at it. Smooth, evenly paced tobacco, no wrinkles. I put it in my shirt's breast pocket and pat it in place. 'I'll keep it for later.'

'You'll probably find it again in a few years. It'll serve as a nice reminder of this time we're spending together. When you light it, say a prayer for me, will you? Like all those people who stand outside the prison walls. Oh yes, word has reached me about them. Some days they start yelling and I can almost hear them. They know they can't send me letters because I'm not allowed any materials for writing, so they set their prayers alight and send flaming balls of paper flying into the prison. Somehow they've deluded themselves into thinking I can reconstitute messages from ashes.'

He laughs as he says this, but I can't help but feel a bit of a sting. I used to be one of those people who believed in him. I sat through his endless examination hoping to witness his ascension. All I got was his fall from grace.

'I got delivered bags of ash by the prisoners who had to clean it up and the guards who put up with the smell. What a waste. I'd kill for a fresh sheet. That cell will probably stink of burnt paper forever now. My cellmates hate me for it. But the pilgrims continue to visit me as though I'm some sort of shrine. Apparently, they tried to visit my mausoleum, but their prayers there had no effect. 'Abu 'Ali, who's taking care of the place until I get there, told them their prayers won't been answered while the mausoleum is empty. Some of their needs are dire as well—I could tell from the sheer amount of paper they burnt. But I feel bad for my cellmates, the ozone layer and my lungs.' He drags on his cigarette.

'Can't you get the word out that you don't want them here?'

'Ah, brother Shahed, will you do that for me?' he says sarcastically. 'Trust me, even if I ask them not to come, they'll just think it's some government ploy to get them to stop believing in me. God forbid Nubians stop being magical creatures. Then I'd really be in trouble, and the institution would cut all ties with me, telling people, "The devil is cunning, we have prevailed against the djinn in sheikh's clothing." Tsk. But they'd find another saint. Someone more willing to go along with their schemes.'

'Go easy on the pilgrims,' I say. 'Some people don't know any better.'

'No, no, I'd never give the pilgrims a tough time.' He flicks ash onto the table and wipes it away with his hand. 'They're the ones truly suffering. People trying to make a living to raise and feed kids in a country that wipes out half the day with a ridiculous curfew, telling people to stay inside, not letting them conduct their business—they suffer the most. They shouldn't have to care for my suffering here in the pharaoh's prison. Tsk.' He looks at the ash stuck to his hands and wipes it on his gallabeya. 'People like that shouldn't worry about me going on a hunger strike.'

'Why are you striking?'

'All I said was that I wouldn't eat a morsel of the food they had brought me because it was rotten, so they decided to eliminate the problem. No more food. I responded by using the gas burner in our cell to burn bedsheets and mattresses, which I pushed out through the metal bars. That was when I discovered that burnt mattresses smell worse than burnt paper.' He laughs, coughing out smoke, coughs again to clear his throat, then coughs more loudly, his hand tearing at his chest.

'I have a cheese sandwich I bought at a kiosk yesterday in my coat pocket.'

'No. My body will start expecting food again if I eat, and then I'll definitely collapse on you. I've only just managed to discipline it. Don't ruin my good work.'

All my preparation for this trip went into steeling myself. I didn't give a thought to Nizam's state.

'Apparently, our pilgrims have been bringing food for weeks,' he says. 'It's all been going to the guards, and only the leftovers make it to the people in the town—or to some of them. People like the khabeer out there, profiting off misery. I've just caught wind of it, so I've been given a plate now too. No gas burner to heat up the food, though.'

'No trust.' I click my tongue against the roof of my mouth. 'Not even in the Sufis.'

'Or their Nubian messiah.'

'Shameful,' I add.

'We'll restore that, though.'

There's a pause, and it's clear there are a few paths the conversation could take next. I didn't come here to take the easy way out.

'So, how are you feeling about tomorrow?' I voice the question as casually as possible. We've been circling around it for a while, and it was always going to take a sharp turn to get there. I wanted to be the one to make the turn.

'Did they tell you to ask me that?'

'Did who tell me?'

'You know who.'

He might have sounded paranoid if he weren't right to be wary. I gather that he's referring to the rotba who commissioned his mausoleum.

'You mean General Tala'at.'

Nizam murmurs in confirmation. I nod my acknowledgement and gently thump a rhythm with my fingers on the edge of the table.

On the way here, I asked myself if Nizam was any different from the Brotherhood leaders who hijacked the revolution in Teita's time to try to get ahead in their political competition with the army. People had grown tired of going out to protest, of hurling stones at the police and breathing in clouds of tear gas. The Brotherhood offered them a way off the streets and a reason not to care anymore, as well as a vague idea of reconciliation whereby they alleged they would hold the army accountable. They sold the people 'peace', and it came at the cost of justice. Quite a few of those Brothers had spent years in prison before they took power. I try to imagine Nizam coming out with a furious vengeance, but I can't see it.

'He came and visited me weeks ago,' Nizam says, wiping his hand over the table as if to smooth the grain of the wood. Fixing his eyes on me, he sits back with his hands in his lap, the cigarette still burning between his fingers. 'He asked who I thought should accompany me to deliver the sermon tomorrow, and I gave him the name of the person I wanted by my side.'

'And it wasn't my name.'

'No,' he says, shaking his head. 'Of course not. I wanted them to send Basma. She was at the examination—you must remember her.' He drew a mountain of hair on top of his bald head. 'But Basma is a woman, and so Talaʿat—*General* Talaʿat— refused point blank. When he mentioned your name instead, I balked at the idea. "The swimmer?" I asked. "Yes, Shahed. We trust Shahed." I can see why. Basma wouldn't wear an eagle pin to please anyone, but you would. So, congratulations. You're worthy of their *trust*.' He rests his weight back on the chair. 'I hope you know what to do with it.'

I do know what to do with it, but there's nothing I can say to Nizam. Sweat begins to leak from my pores. He sniffs, and I can only imagine he smells benzene—I still reek of it. He has every reason not to trust me. I'm not his enemy, but I'm not his ally either, even less his friend—the days of finding friends in our enemies' enemies have passed. The hug Nizam gave me on the landing was probably for the khabeer's benefit, to make it look as though he has allies coming to his aid. He doesn't trust either of us, but he knows his fate lies in someone else's hands.

'What about you?' Nizam asks.

'What about me?'

'How are *you* feeling about tomorrow?'

'I'm not entirely sure,' I say truthfully. I notice my breaths have become shallow and my hands are trembling on the table. Is it out of fear? Probably. Out of anger? Definitely. I almost feel ready to self-combust right now, in this room. But what a shame that would be, to have no one but a saintly pyromaniac to see it.

'I've been given a job, and I'll do it,' I go on. 'I'll read through the sermon with you, and I'll be there standing behind you as you talk to the soldiers, who'll all be trying not to squint in the sun or look away from you for fear of what their commanding officers would say. It's all just part of my job.'

'Well, I hope you're proud,' Nizam laughs, and the silence resumes.

I've been given every freedom that this country can offer an ordinary citizen. It isn't enough for me, not anymore. My privileges mean nothing if I can't share them out, and I'd have to step over too many people to climb my way to a position where I could make a difference. This is what this system does to you: it tells you that you're alone. And I know I'm not.

Clearing his throat, Nizam begins a new story. 'You know what they say about people in this prison? "Those inside are lost, those who come out are born."

'On those fishing trips we took on man-made, man-named Lake Nasser, one of my friends—we called him Ghaly, because he was the sixth child and only son in his family, so naturally, he was precious—used to frighten us with stories of djinn. You know djinn usually dwell in the water, right? So, imagine three of us in a cramped boat out on the water, keeping an eye out for poachers, stars laid out all around us like a carpet producing all sorts of tricks of light. Of course we would get scared by djinn stories.

'Ghaly had a smooth, long, ancient face, all sharp corners with high cheekbones, and hairless limbs. He should have been built out of marble, though he would've hated that. "The pharaohs enslaved our people!" he reminded me time and again.

"And still their statues are up everywhere in the north. But what can you expect? The northerners are slaves to the euro, the dollar, the riyal and whatever else they can get their hands on, so if the khawaga wants to see a pharaoh, they'll always roll out their best. The country's in the gutter." He was the son of my father's friend and a few years older than us, so he had to accompany us on our night-time trips whether he wanted to or not. The djinn stories were no more than a childish way for him to get his revenge by making sure our moments on the lake were spent in terror.

'Every once in a while, we would hook a particularly unruly fish that tugged on our boat tirelessly without seeming to move in the water, forcing us to cut the line just to get away. Whenever that happened, Ghaly would say we must have snagged one of the old Nubian houses that had been flooded when the reservoir was built and were now inhabited by djinn. "This is where my ancestors used to live," he told us. I tried to imagine the lost village before it was submerged by the lake, the disrupted lives and abandoned belongings of the displaced community, its dwellings now home to a new set of subaquatic occupants. "That's why you should never use driftwood that you find on the lake," Ghaly would say. "It could have been part of a table, a chair, a loom. Have you seen that big tapestry in Hajj Yassin's house, the one of the celebration, with birds in the sky and cattle grazing in green fields? It was made on a loom right here, and it's a scene from one of the old houses here."

'Our hook caught on overly stubborn fish that were windowsills, dovecotes, stoves, and Ghaly would tell us to cut ourselves loose from his great-grandparents' home. When I asked him what his great-grandparents were called, he told me he couldn't tell me because they were djinn now. It scared me witless, since it made me think I was in the company of a descendant of djinn. That's how I learnt about the horrors that can ensue if you utter a djinn's name by accident.

'Those night-time fishing expeditions came back to me when I was in the city's National Archive. I saw an old photograph of Nubians piled onto a boat, with a sign—written in Arabic—welcoming them aboard. The pier was attached to a sprawling village dotted with doum palms, cypresses and sycamores, with expanses of farmland between each house and the next. In the east, the sun was rising. Cattle stood on the banks, drinking from the water and looking about lazily, as if it were a day like any other. The buffalos were waiting for their human masters to attach them to the mill to start the daily grind, except the humans seemed to be frantically moving all their belongings—blankets, stores of food, clothes, unfinished bits of needlework—and packing all of it onto the boat.

'The image was accompanied by a note from the photographer dated 1956, right before a line was drawn in the sand and Sudan became an independent country. He explained that the soldiers on the boat were clear: no cattle allowed on board. Owners would be compensated for loss of livestock once they reached their destination. But the soldiers had their eyes on those animals and were waiting for the residents of the town to be deposited on the other side of the imaginary line. A few days earlier, a census had declared that all the town's inhabitants had opted to be displaced, from their homes, from their livelihoods, from their cattle—but, again, they were going to be compensated for their sacrifice. So they were assured by a man in camouflage standing with his back to the camera, his head half turned, showing his profile, who told them they had fulfilled their national duty and pushed off the boat from the pier.

'The animals grazed dumbly, looking out onto the water, and the photographer fancied them as confused as the people, though I doubt it. Animals experience confusion, but not in the same way as humans. And when animals see people's confusion, it is of no concern to them, because while people have always looked at animals as kin, animals, recognising that familiarity as odd, feel people as other. Some of the town's residents locked their animals in the barns, thinking they would eventually return to retrieve them. They left plenty of food, and that must have confused the animals. "Why am I being fed like this? Likely, today is my last day, or something is about to change, and I'll need my strength for whatever is to come."

'Of course, none of the villagers made it back. They were deposited so far from any municipal centre that they became residents of no country. When the photographer and the journalist he was accompanying wrote of the plight of these Nubians, the story was buried. By the time the villagers managed to get some form of identification and permission to travel, the 'Aswan Dam had been built, and their village was gone. All that was left to mark it was a plaque touting their sacrifice, written in a language they could not read, and Lake Nasser. It was not a sacrifice they had chosen. How could they have opted to live in one place rather than another if they couldn't write?

'And that's a story that Ghaly only hinted at when we went fishing, that the line I sent deep into the water could only pluck at. Do you think we can switch in our ancestors' pain for today's pains? I feel like I can deal with today, with all its uncertainties, because at least I know that when I lay my head down to sleep, the day will be over, along with its pain. But I can't undo the past, it rolls into today and keeps going ...

'When I rehashed what I saw in the photograph at a public lecture at the institute, it was reported back to the interior minister, the president, the police and the public prosecutor, and I was arrested. After forty days in prison, the public prosecutor finally questioned me about it, and I could barely remember what I'd said. He said I'd accused the army of genocide. "They are guilty of that," I told him, "but I mentioned nothing of the sort during that lecture. I only mentioned that there was a soldier in the photo." And that's true. I don't blame the army today for the sins of the distant past, just as I don't blame Ghaly for his stories about my fishing line snagging a djinn who might pull me down into the water to be eaten by the very crocodiles I was trying to protect, but I do hold both parties responsible for what their lies have caused. Sitting in that archive, reading the photographer's letter, which landed in my lap by some unbelievable stroke of luck, I felt like I'd thrown a line into the star-lit lake and pulled out a Bahamut, and on its back is the cosmic bull, which carries within its singular tear all of existence, the starry night, the years of decay, all of my existence, even you.'

We sit in an easy silence for a few minutes. I believe every last word of his story. Then again, I lose nothing by believing it. I've always resisted easy conclusions, the ones that would carry me away like water. I look for my own direction, and I succeed for a while, but in the end there's no point in fighting natural currents or seductive fables. They're as old as the Nile, except their source will never go dry, and they will always have free passage into people's minds, not out of a lack of imagination but because of its abundance. Maybe that's why he's in jail. In a country and a system designed not to allow its people to imagine existence that transcends basic survival, his words have reach. They echo in the cavernous depths of our minds where all our greatest fears lie, and for a moment, fear doesn't shrink us down to size.

'Are you still pleased to be carrying that eagle pin?' he asks me.

'I'm not carrying it anymore,' I tell him.

'Oh, I know,' he says. 'It's interesting—for a religious institution, the Sufis love to gossip, and do you know what I heard about you?'

I look at him, unsure of what to say.

'I've heard about your races, how you thrashed through the water and overtook that Palestinian boy, who was only competing as a token in the first place, since he belongs to the Bedouin tribes. I have to believe that you're the same person as you were then, and that you want to add tomorrow to your list of accomplishments. Do you see what I'm saying?'

'No,' I say. He's talking in riddles.

'I've given you several opportunities in this conversation to talk to me about tomorrow, about how you're feeling, but it seems you're content to listen to me and be entertained by my stories without really giving any of your own. And like I said, Sufis love to gossip. The company you keep is no secret, and the fact that you're so tight-lipped today when you were so eager to talk before only points to one conclusion.'

I stare at him, frozen in my seat, waiting for him to say his piece.

'This is where you tell me what you have planned for tomorrow.'

*

I put the phone back on the charger as I'd found it, hoping Mama wouldn't realise I'd been snooping.

I had been listening to her voice memos, hours of audio accumulated in short fragments she recorded for herself. Some only had the sound of Mama breathing deeply, as if she were asleep, or perhaps waiting for the moment when the floodgates would open and everything for which she had no language— and about which she could never tell me—would come rushing out. Some were accented by the small *pop* of her lips when she exhales smoke, followed by the crackle of burning paper and tobacco. Sometimes she would speak a few words, almost like a code. *The light bulb, the window, Hilal ... always the light.* Other times she would cry, and that would be all.

It was the summer after my tenth birthday, and Mama and I were visiting Teita from Germany. I had woken up from an afternoon nap a few days earlier to find night had fallen. 'Adhan el-'esha was sounding outside, and the crackling was like electricity in my brain. In a glass on the bedside table, shreds of mint, darkened like burnt paper, floated in water with green lime skins congealing at its surface. It felt warm to the touch and reminded me of algae and stagnant waters.

When the mosque loudspeakers quieted, the sounds of the house returned. I heard the click, slam and slide of 'awasheet moving across the wooden backgammon board, Mama's peals of laughter and clapping hands, and the skittering of dice like an animal escaping capture.

'Sheesh-yak,' said Teita, and I could tell from the dull sound of her piece that she had blocked a khana.

Mama's phone had been next to the glass of lemonade. The table buzzed, and I saw my father's name flash on screen with a notification. I unlocked the phone and found myself looking at a list of voice memos. Not yet fully awake, I pressed play on the last one, thinking I would hear Baba's new message.

It's as though I've attained some sort of balance. The terror always remains, returns, but now it doesn't take away from the possibility of pleasure.

There was a sound in the background of the recording, a musical score, tempo allegro.

I feel the same terror for him now that I felt all those years ago. Can you spend so long in prison that it becomes home? The place where you belong? I think they want us to believe that.

She asked the question and paused, as though listening to a reply that wasn't there.

'I know you'll make it out,' I told myself back then. It was the same soft voice she used to explain the difference between sugar from fruit and sugar from fruit-flavoured candy.

I looked at the date when it was recorded. I was three years old. I could see the flat in Paris with its long corridor and wooden floorboards that creaked and splintered, tearing my socks and scratching my feet. The silence on the voice note lasted for as long as it took for me to jump off the kitchen stool and *pat-pat-pat* down the hallway to the living room, where the television was playing a cartoon about a wily mouse evading the snares of a brutish housecat.

I know he'll make it out too, she said flatly as I entreated her to turn up the volume. Her voice now was tired and ancient as olive pits, tender as the taut skin of figs full of meat and ready for teeth.

The next day, I borrowed Mama's phone asking if I could call Baba, which I did, for a few minutes, before turning again to her voice recordings. I felt ashamed, but I couldn't help it. It made me feel close to her to listen to these messages meant only for her own ears. The words mostly washed over me; I just wanted to hear her voice.

Of course, no secret stays hidden forever, and when I asked Mama what ever happened to her friend Djaber from Paris, hoping she would tell me about his arrest when he went home to Alexandria, it only took a few seconds for her to unravel the truth. That wasn't the first time she slapped me, but it's the slap that stands out in my memory.

'I'm sorry, Mama,' I said, tears already streaming from my eyes.

'Hana-an!' Teita yelled, standing up to draw me close and look at my quickly reddening cheek. Mama grabbed my wrist, pulling me towards her so hard that I felt my shoulder *pop*. I went stiff.

'Why did you listen to them?' she asked, shaking me by the shoulders. 'How do you think that makes me feel? Ask me first before you go prying into my phone.'

I tried to wrench myself away, but she jerked me forward again.

'Answer me!' she yelled, craning her head to meet my eyes as I avoided hers.

'Khalas, ya Hanan, you've scared him enough. Kefaya!' Teita's voice was loud and firm, the same voice she used to impress upon builders the importance of keeping concrete, gypsum and scaffolding timber off her grass. 'Ma'lesh,' she said to Mama. 'What could've been so bad for him to hear? He's your son.'

'My son? My son who goes sneaking into what doesn't concern him? Like a thief?' She turned back towards me. 'I asked you a question—why did you do it?' The tip of her nose seemed to be twitching. I could almost see her face in the van, washed in an orange light that vanished and reappeared with every passing streetlight.

When I didn't answer, she slapped me again. My blood rushed to where her hand landed on my cheek, and when the prickling feeling started, it felt as if her fingers were still there, beneath my skin, pushing for freedom.

*

EL-BAB EL-THALETH

The slums hang heavy in the morning twilight. In the calm, the buildings' darkened edges are drawn in soft lines that blur into the sky as if at any moment they might disappear. I struggle to peel my eyes away from them, worried about what might happen when I turn my back to the town.

Before we leave ʾAbu Zaʿbal, Nizam fills up three plastic bottles with water from the zeirs by the entrance to the ghetto. The canopy covering the earthenware jars is made of dried foliage tied together and weighed down by three upturned chairs, whose legs pierce the sky like rebars or the polished bones of long-dead animals. Nizam reaches his whole arm into the bloated zeir, which seems to expand to accommodate him. I can hear oceans moving inside and air escaping from the bottles as water rushes in. He appears to be locked in communion with the vessel, and as it breathes, I almost believe it could be the embodiment in terracotta of Hakeem, with its broad shoulders and a broken handle recalling the floppy wrist that cost him the race.

I'm getting drowsy from standing outside in the bright early-morning sun, which blocks my vision with glaring white spots. My arms hang useless and heavy. *I slept too well, and good sleep weakens the body.* It's a ridiculous thought, but I can't chase it away. I've lost all the edge that I had when I was talking to Nizam last night. This morning, I don't talk.

'Taʿala zoor,' Nizam motions to me as he fills bottle after bottle. I tell him we have mineral water in the car, which makes him laugh. His good humour annoys me; I want today to be over with. 'Bashrab mayya shaʿbi, bass,' he replies. 'El-maʿdani yetʿebni.' Refusing a drink from a state-sponsored water bottle in favour of groundwater from a zeir. Truly a man of the people.

I think I'll ask ʿAraby if I can drive for a while. It'll keep my mind from wandering. Maybe even give me the feeling that I've got some choice in our destination.

I give Nizam the sandwich that I offered him yesterday, hoping he might finally eat something and gain a bit of energy. He nibbles on it a little before stuffing it inside his gallabeya, which hoards more paraphernalia than the pharaohs' canopic jars hold organs, wine and molasses. He pulls a piece of cloth from his pocket to wash himself, pouring out a little water and wringing it out on the ground. Shocked by the touch of rain, the earth softens, swells and cracks, before drying out again, the softness escaping elsewhere.

'Can't go speak to the soldiers looking this filthy,' he muses as he wipes his face with the wet cloth. 'Do you know if they've got a fresh gallabeya for me? I'd rather not wear these rags in front of the troops. A sheikh is only as pure as his gallabeya.' *Yes, in the boot, laundered and wrapped in plastic*—but he isn't looking for a reply. Finishing his wash by the zeir, he steps out from under the canopy and into the sun.

'Just look at this place,' he scowls, pointing at the run-down, unfinished structures behind us. 'It's disgusting. Same dust we have back in the city, but out here there aren't even enough buildings to absorb it, or people to obstruct it, or water to wash it away. What I'd do for a good monument! Nothing like a mural in bas-relief and some national pride to gather a bit of dust. Where's Ramses, standing tall? The years have broken his back. He would have trampled me under his feet if he'd seen me wasting water like that just now, but where is he?'

He's still standing in the sun.

'Just look at the people here. Scrounging for survival and kicking up dirt for fun. Do they look capable of turning the earth? Raising a crop? They can't even raise a flag.' It feels like something I've heard him say before.

'Do you want to do your wudoo'?' he asks me. 'It'll freshen you up, lift you out of your mood. I can pour some water for you. Might win me a bit of credit from the Chief, helping a disciple stay clean. And you've come all this way to break me out of prison. It's the least I can do.'

'I already did my ablutions,' I say.

'With what?'

'Tayammamt be-l-raml.'

'From the earth itself,' he nods. 'Well done, a real child of the country, able to make do under difficult circumstances when resources are scarce. You'd do 'Abbas proud. But we have water here.'

'It's habit,' I shrug. 'I never use water in the city.'

'Yeah, I wouldn't either. Being out here has done me a world of good. They've already got you doing your ablutions with sand—well, mark my words, before long, they'll start telling you it's safe to drink. "Dust is colourless, odourless, tasteless, it's just sun-dried skin, the remains of all those who came before you will nourish you and cleanse your soul." They'll be selling that next, just you wait.'

My eyes are drawn to the crystal-white scarf draped over his shoulder. It reminds me of the salt I found in the mountains around the Sinai, deposited in thick layers, giving the beige-coloured rock underneath the appearance of a milky hue. I tried to break off chunks of it—discreetly, Mount Sinai being a protected reserve. The crystals might as well have been part of the mountainside; try as I might, I couldn't make a dent.

Squatting over the gap in the rocks, I licked my thumb and grazed it against the salt. The powdered residue on my skin tasted like cleanliness: bitter. I removed the foil from a piece of grilled fish and wiped off the remaining dust from my thumb, thinking it would give it some flavour. Whatever I added was too much and rendered the fish inedible.

I felt cleansed of all my sins.

*

'Koshari?' I asked. 'Fool w-taʿmeya?'

Ramy was fasting, which meant no morsel from an animal could pass his lips. 'I can't decide,' he said.

We were sitting on the railings of Qasr el-Nil Bridge, dangling our feet over the water. Our knees were brushing, but I didn't dare touch his hand where passers-by could see.

I gave him back his copy of *Karnak Café* and told him I didn't like it.

'I didn't either,' he smiled.

'You lied to me.'

'Would you have read it otherwise?'

'What didn't you like about it?'

'The story was fixed from the beginning,' said Ramy, indignant at Naguib Mahfouz's nerve. 'He just stumbled upon the café, and he doesn't know or question why he was drawn there. Who even is he? Why should we care? And the ending, with Khaled Safwan?' He shook his head. 'Just no.'

'I think he's a blank slate for us,' I said. 'The narrator, not Khaled Safwan. I didn't mind that he happened upon the café by chance.'

'But he just let himself get carried with the flow. It felt like he didn't take responsibility for his presence there, when everyone else was using it as a refuge. He just listens in on their conversations. That's it.' Ramy waved the offending book over the water as if he were about to drop it.

'That was my problem with it,' I admitted. 'There was too much schadenfreude. Like he was happy to know all these terrible things.'

Ramy disagreed. 'What's wrong with empathy?'

I knew how fragile our grasp on each other could be, how weak, in the face of a country that can tear people inside out to keep them in line. With one nudge, both of us could find ourselves below the rose-gold water, shimmering in a burning sunset.

His shirt, loosely buttoned, billowed in the wind. Drops of sweat hung on the hair on his arms, reflecting the molten sun. No one could deny us our quiet affection. We felt seen in our shared solitude. Our mistake was that we didn't dream of more. Although, in those days, seeing each other seemed like enough.

Not for me, said Mama, waving her hand as though to clear the air of smoke.

I just can't stand the smell of cooked meat anymore, and he comes back from that shawarma place every night with its stink on his breath.

It's not that I have anything against eating meat, but I can't help but imagine the lumps of flesh hanging on that skewer against the standing grill, layered, uneven, turning slowly, sweating and oozing and turning brown and burning black. I can almost imagine him sinking his teeth into me, biting out chunks of my own flesh.

'Eid is definitely the hardest time. Especially because he loves fattet lahma, which I could never stomach, even when I still ate lahma. When we were back home for the celebrations, he volunteered to bring the meat from the butchers, but I would still have to be the one to cook it. How could he ever understand that I didn't mind the sight of the meat hanging in the windows, but the smell of it cooking made me nauseous? How would he understand that if he didn't understand what I went through? He saw both the burns and the bruises, but he couldn't tell the two apart once they started healing. I still feel every bit of it.

Eventually, I did explain this to him. He leaned over to kiss me on the forehead.

'Habibti, you don't have to do anything you don't want to do.' He spoke as if saying the words aloud makes them true.

The koshari place was one cramped room with white-tiled floors and walls. A young man was mopping when we entered, bringing dust in with our shoes. Khamaseen winds had tunnelled through the city streets a few days earlier, coating everything with fine desert sand. The staff were still wearing surgical masks to keep the dust out of their teeth. Water had been poured to pick up the filth, leaving the ground streaked with sludge.

'This is what I needed,' I said, wolfing down spoonfuls of koshari. I reached for the spicy sauce and sprayed it in thin, even lines over my mess of rice, pasta, chickpeas and lentils and the well of tomato sauce in the middle, which I was waiting for the proper moment in the ritual to tip the rest of the food into.

Ramy had ordered fries and was dipping them into my red well.

'Are you not hungry?' I asked. 'You need to eat, ya-bni.'

'I am,' he said, barely parting his lips to feed fries into his mouth one at a time in quick succession. He seemed to relish spreading the sauce across his lips, coating them in red. The spice was making my lips burn. I imagined that was what his felt like.

Then I noticed they were moving, and the sound of his voice jolted me from my reverie.

'What?' I asked. I was elsewhere.

'How long are your parents here?'

I saw him on the metro.

It was odd. I'd never seen him around the city without me and realised how little I knew of him. He blended into the background seamlessly.

My husband was standing in front of my seat and facing me, to try to keep the other passengers from getting too close to me. He kept craning his head to look around but still somehow missed our son standing there with a group of young men.

It was the swim bag that told me he was my son. His head was hidden under a woollen hat, which my mother must have made for him. It was the same colour she used to make a scarf that I never really wear—it's not thick enough for the weather in Berlin. Then I noticed the sterile smell of chlorine invading the carriage. His mouth was moving quickly; he seemed to be whispering to himself, with his eyes fixed on the windows. He lifted his hand and grabbed the pole on the very spot where another boy with curly, bleached-orange hair was holding it, but the boy didn't move his hand, and neither did my son. They met each other's gaze, and it was then that I realised he was talking to him. His thumb was rolling over the boy's hand. I must have been completely lost in the scene because my husband asked me what I was staring at before looking down the carriage and spotting what had piqued my curiosity.

'Ya Shahed!' he called, waving at him, smiling.

Shahed dropped his hand quickly and pushed his way through the crowd to say hello.

My husband turned to me. 'You didn't even recognise your son, Professor?' He laughed and pulled Shahed into an awkward embrace before fumbling Ramy's name as he shook the young man's hand with a firm grip.

As he thumbed the pin on his mesh bag, Shahed disappeared and became the son I didn't know again.

*

The sky is overexposed; the blue is turning white and burns if I stare too long at the sun. Pigeons streak across to the edges, where the bright horizon drowns them out like static. I've never seen a bird cast a shadow in the desert. Our imprints have never overlapped.

We've been driving for five hours, and I can no longer feel my legs. The combination of benzene and fresh chlorine that lingers on my clothes is burning my skin. I should've taken up Nizam's offer to wash.

Nizam is asleep in the back of the car with his white scarf over his eyes. His legs are crossed to fit on the seat, both feet tucked under his thighs in the folds of his gallabeya. He can't help but pout, pressing his thick lips tightly together with his head propped against the door. No trace of pain or unhappiness, except for an occasional grimace that looks only a whimper away from turning into a sob that I can nearly hear. A muscle works in his cheek as if he's chewing a tough bit of meat. I get the feeling that he's looking at me through the scarf, but I can't tell from where I'm sitting. I retrieve a bottle of water from below my seat and spray him. He doesn't move.

I cried myself to sleep last night, on the floor mattress, next to Nizam. When I told him about my plan, he wasn't surprised. He buried my face in his chest, setting off a powerful and complex dialogue of body, fabric, breath and scent, but no one ever built a revolution with tears or hugs, and the revolutionaries who ended up wrapped in cloth are the ones I don't want to follow. They've found their homes in the desert. Made their beds.

Nizam stroked my hair and told me not to be scared, that it would be fine. I'm not scared of death, I whispered. No, you're scared of living through tomorrow, he replied. You're scared of having to live with the weight of everything that you know, because you know what's right and what's wrong, but that binary only works in the city. Dying tomorrow won't make you good, he said. He was right. Knowing the past and everything that led to today, I worry that giving my life for its sake won't make a difference. The country won't be closer to liberation, and I still won't find peace.

The other option, I told Nizam, is to burn the barracks down. It's them or me—one of us won't survive tomorrow. That's the only way the world can go on. That's not justice, he said, it's revenge. It's the only thing they'll allow us, I said. Revenge against them, and against ourselves for failing.

'Araby asks me for a drink, so I hand him a bottle.

'Finish it,' I tell him. 'I'm fasting.' I'm lying, but it's true that I can't eat or drink. I'm too nervous.

'I'm sorry,' he says and keeps drinking. Liquid ripples and floods into his mouth, and he sighs like a car exhaust. Or perhaps I imagined it. I wake with a sudden start to the sound of the car's gears grinding as we drive on.

'Did I sleep?'

'Only for ten minutes,' he says. 'I could use ten minutes of sleep.' The black soot from the exhaust pipe in front of us reminds me that even machines tire, and when I die, it'll probably be with less dignity. 'You must not have slept well in Nizam's cell last night. Did you get a chance to talk to him? He seems tense.'

'He was awake, but I didn't want to stress him out by talking about today.'

'Why would he be stressed? He's done this before.'

'Still, where he's got to do it could make anyone stressed.'

'Mmm ...' He turns to look at me before continuing, 'You look more relaxed than you did yesterday. Have you finally accepted your fate and realised that the army isn't the big boʻboʻ that people make it out to be? Djinn only exist in your myths, ya sheikh.'

'I've realised that whenever you insult me, or at least when you try to, you call me sheikh,' I comment.

'Because I don't respect you. I don't respect your profession or your people. You try to make the poor people in my neighbourhood feel like you're necessary by throwing around all your stories, without realising what that kind of hope can give to people. You really think that Judgement Day is coming? It's been and gone. We're in the afterlife now. And it's not that much better. Best to accept things as they are, ya sheikhna, and move on with life.

'When I was your age, I heard there was a summit. I heard words were exchanged by men more powerful than you and me and agreements were reached that I couldn't comprehend because I couldn't trace the story back from generation to generation. Don't tell me you'll explain that away too.'

'Only he can do that,' I say, pointing to a passing billboard. *The Army and the People Are One Hand.*

'I'm surprised you can swim with that huge beard,' 'Araby says, ignoring my comment. 'Don't you worry that someone will just grab you by it and pull you down?'

I can tell him to be quiet and drive, but today feels like it should be the start of something new, and I don't want the sour taste of bile in my mouth.

'I don't have a beard.'

'You have a mental beard. That's hardly better.'

'But you respect Sheikh Nizam.'

'Nizam? Yes, ya sheikhna.' He tapped the steering wheel twice as if underlining the words. 'Even if he had a beard, I'd still respect him.'

''Enta 'adeem 'awi, ya 'Abu el-'Arab,' I say, insinuating that he's out of touch with the times. Beards haven't been in fashion since the Brotherhood's fall from power.

'That's why people like you scare me. All those internal scars that you try to tell us we share with you. Should've cut off your heads along with the beards.'

'They did. Remember Rab'a?'

''Ayb el-kalam da, ya sheikh,' he says, shaking his head. 'The army made reparations for what they did back then.'

'What reparations? They slaughtered thousands.' Reparations are not justice. Justice would be if those people were still alive. It would be Mama not being chased out the country and Teita not living out her last years shuttered in her house, thinking of all those who died so she could live a better life.

'Even if they were millions,' 'Araby protests. 'What were they supposed to do otherwise? Your people wouldn't shut up, with all your talk of tyrants and pharaohs. You tried to measure up to the army by imitating their cruelty. How many Copts did the Brotherhood exile? How many liberal butterflies did they put in cages?'

'You're confusing Sufis with the Brotherhood.'

'Am I?' 'Araby grabs my hand and puts it to his chest. I feel his hairs beneath my fingers. 'Please, forgive me, sheikh. I didn't mean to offend.'

I pull my hand away and wipe it on my trousers. 'I don't know how to stop people like you from muddying the water, ya 'Araby,' I say. 'You manage to make everything feel so bleak.' I would have liked to remain hopeful today.

'Is that why you tried to drive when we left the prison? What difference does it make who's at the wheel? We'll end up in the same place. Together. And because I'm driving, we're safe. You can never trust a martyr.'

'I don't believe in martyrdom,' I reply. Showing the cost of life in this country for what it is—death—is not martyrdom. It's profit and loss. I chastise myself as soon as that thought crosses my mind. Profit and loss is exactly how the Armed Forces measure human life. Otherwise, thousands of people would still be alive. Nizam, for all his prodding, was too kind to say what I'm thinking now: *you're playing into the state's hands by killing yourself—saves them doing the dirty work.* But a part of me still believes there's some humanity in the soldiers. That I won't die in vain.

'You can't trust a man who abandons his beliefs either,' says 'Araby. 'Martyrdom is inscribed in the Qur'an, it's sacred.'

'Shouldn't I find my own reason to believe in what I've been told?'

'Some truths are bigger than either of us. Look around,' he says, pointing out the window as we roll into a moving cloud of dust. The road disappears in the sand for a few moments, but we quickly find it again.

'Close your windows,' he says.

'Done.'

'Good man.'

We pass another billboard of the Chief Sufi and the Field Marshal. They're sitting beside each other, turning slightly towards each other, laughing. The president's shoulders are padded, the Chief's humbly and naturally stooped. There are a few rips in the poster, and intermittent gusts of wind reveal the billboard's frame. *We Succeed. Together.*

'What are you?' I ask 'Araby.

'What do you mean?'

'If you're not Sufi, then what are you?' It's a petty question, but he's been throwing around empty words to get a rise out of me.

'I'm on the same path,' he replies. 'We just don't walk together.'

'What's the difference?'

'You should know better,' he hisses. 'Don't make me respect you less by pretending you don't know something to get me to talk. Stop playing me. People like you have been playing me my whole life. If 'akl 'eishi didn't depend on you, I'd leave you to get out and walk. And let me ask you the same question, what if you weren't Sufi, what would you be? Or can you not imagine life outside of your own bubble? Would you just be a swimmer? Would you miss anything? Why are you even making this journey for Nizam?'

Is that what this whole discussion has been about? He is speaking quietly now, as if he expects me to divulge a secret that I wouldn't admit to Nizam, or to myself, about why we're here.

'Have you never felt so close to someone that you wanted to be in the same room as them?' I opt for sarcasm.

'Like we are right now?'

'Yeah, exactly.'

I can't help but answer 'Araby back. He's agitated, and my own agitation takes off and falls again like the cascades of sand thrown by the wind across the windscreen. 'Araby is trying to unhinge me. I would rather let out my rage on him than on Nizam.

*

She signed the contract in a park, leaning the papers on her weekly planner and scrawling her signature. Looking around, worried she would be caught, she noticed her slight frame had barely left an impression on the path, other than a faint softening of the pine needles under her feet. It was mid-October, well into the autumn semester.

I'm not really here. She smiled at the absurd thought provoked by her invisible tread. Something about the impossibility of her own non-existence terrified her, but not without bringing a hint of delight. *Like how children's worlds disappear when they shut their eyes. Opening them again is a gamble.*

For a while, she had thought the university would retract its offer. She had been working without a contract since September. Of course, she'd heard horror stories about academics who worked for months with the promise of a contract only to end up empty-handed. And she remembered her humiliation when they refused to pay her for teaching she had done. She was terrified that it was happening again and that she was powerless to stop it from happening. But things had gone according to plan. The relief now from signing the contract diminished her sense of terror that she would have to ask her husband for money, even go back home. He was going through his own difficulties, and she didn't want to be more of a burden on him.

Bending down, she grabbed a handful of pine needles and stuffed them in her coat pocket.

Diving in a shallow pool, my husband called the move.
   Said I'm better than this path I've chosen.
   I'm sure he meant it as a compliment.

She showed the bunch of pine needles to her therapist.

'I can't stand the smell of pine,' was his response. 'It smells of death. Coffins are frequently made of pine. Ich kann mir aber vorstellen, dass der Geruch für dich nicht ganz das Gleiche bedeutet.'

When she got back to the apartment, her husband was cooking fish rice. Cumin, turmeric and the medicinal smell of cloves.

She boiled the needles in water until the sweet scent of forest and earth passed through the corridor, trying to imagine death in the smell.

When they sat to eat in the dining room, she left the pot on the flame. The husks burned. The smell of rice ash cut to her nose. She could smell the distance, the burning leaves in her mother's garden, and she realised that when she was buried, her mother was wrapped in cloth that probably still carried a hint of the jasmine-scented lotion she used to massage into her well-worn hands.

Mama's skin crawled.

'I taught him how to use a gun,' she said, shaking her head, disbelieving. She imagined what the fingers that she'd glimpsed around Ramy's hand would look like gripping death.

'To keep him safe,' Baba reassured her. 'Should we try and convince him to come and live here with us?'

'No,' she answered. 'I remember I quite enjoyed life back there.'

'Is that a joke?'

*

I lick my lips and taste sweat, scratch my nose and find it warm and oily. I try to close my eyes to sleep, but throbbing flashes of sun land on my eyelids through the windscreen. I must have succeeded for a stretch, because I open my eyes, and 'Araby tells me we just passed the third checkpoint.

'Why didn't you wake me up?'

'There was no need. You looked tired, and I thought you could use the sleep.'

There are dust devils whirling in the distance. They hover like low spectres over the sand, uncertain of which direction to take, before dying before my eyes, leaving me wondering whether they were ever there. I feel nauseous, and not even the cool of the glass against my face stays my stomach.

We take an exit off the freeway onto a two-lane road. There's less wind here, so the dust devils die out. I open the window to get the air circulating. It pelts my face and seems to draw more sweat than it dries, but it feels good. It feels good to get out of the city. For a second, I forget the grim business of our mission. I pull down the visor in front of me, though the sun's still too low for it to be very effective.

I look around and try to imagine how cool the scarf must feel on Nizam's face. When I woke up this morning, I saw him blocking the light from the window where the shirt was hanging, like a scarecrow keeping the buzzards in check. I'm certain that he hasn't looked me in the eyes all morning. There's no way to read him. How he feels shouldn't matter, but it does. I'm transporting him, and he's under my authority. My fists clench and unclench in my lap to feel the pressure of my fingers against my palm. Yesterday, I had a chance to be alone in the pool, to sleep in the locker room, to be as close to the version of myself that I recognise as I can get in the city. There's no being alone in prison. Nizam, in all likelihood, has no idea who he is. I start to feel pity and worry that I've cornered him and now, he's just dreaming of escape, one that can only result in him being back in prison, hopefully alive. Everyone's trying to sell you something, everyone's trying to tell you something, everyone's trying to mould you into a shape that'll fit with their reality.

'I have a pillow,' 'Araby says.

'No, I'm awake,' I reply. He's sitting on the pillow, and I didn't see another one in the boot. 'Thank you, though. How long did I manage this time?'

'Couldn't tell you.'

I have to keep my eyes open; I can't afford any more surprises. Maybe I'll be able to tell something about what's awaiting us at the barracks by the terrain around it. The soldiers learn to master the land, so if I can understand it, maybe I'll understand them. But that's like saying the sea or the water can give an insight into me. And I'm neither that beautiful nor that complex. If I had to be a body of water, I'd be a terʿa. Stagnant, lazy river water cut up into small canals where people wash their clothes and occasionally throw away a dead donkey. Children do enjoy playing in the terʿa in the summertime. Arches of water are thrown into the sunlight, breaking the harshness into a litany of colours, and the blades of glass turn gold with their edges being so thin. Shrubs like bursts of cotton. Rich, weighty water, as if it were a second skin, because of the silt. Don't drink it. Never drink it. Bilharzia, bacteria, islands of rubbish, the aforementioned dead donkey.

We pass petrol stations and rest stops with pick-up trucks and minibuses packed like tins of sardines. One of the minibuses has a rope where the door handle should be, and the first line of people hold tight on the rope, which cuts across the width of the bus, holding the door as close to shut as possible. The door rattles, a wing of a flightless bird that hasn't unlearnt its avian instincts. Adaptation and evolution only change who you are, not what you try to do. It feels like I should be feeling more resistance to what I'm about to do, but there's nothing there.

'Where do you think they're going?' I ask 'Araby.

'To the barracks,' he says.

'How do you know?'

'The uniform the driver was wearing.'

'I didn't see it. What do you think they're doing there?'

'Why does everybody have to be doing something? Why does everything have to have a purpose?' He doesn't even try to keep his voice down. 'Look at where we are. Look at this shit weather. If they're here then they have a good reason to be here, just like us. Don't look at them so closely. They'll burn you. They're probably scared shitless by this car with beige licence plates rolling through. They'll be thinking twice about everything they do or say. Poor women, having to go to the barracks as well. Women don't belong there.'

'But they belong in prison?'

'They're devious, which is why they belong there.'

'And all men are honest.'

'You can tell if someone's a khawal. Te'rafo b-'eino.' He laughs, tapping the steering wheel impatiently. 'Shit, we should've stopped for petrol. Got caught up in our conversation.'

'Too late now.'

'It's not.'

'You said we're late.'

'We'll be infinitely more late if we run out of petrol.'

'They'll definitely have fuel.'

'I can't stay the night there,' he says. It occurs to me that 'Araby may have never spent this much time out of the city. This place might seem as lost to him as he feels. Maybe he's as nervous as I am.

'Same,' I say. 'I don't want to spend the night either.'

'Do you want to drive?' he asks me.

'I couldn't right now. My mind's elsewhere,' I say. 'Maybe on the way back, so you can take a break. How long till we get there?' I feel bad for lying. It's not right.

'Another hour.'

'How are we late?' I look around at the emptiness.

'We're always late. And we've no excuse. No one to fight for the road.'

We pass another billboard.

'Except him,' I say.

I feel condemned to die. Everyone will have to, but as we turn off onto a narrow, freshly asphalted road, I feel my death rushing towards me. A sparse cloud that's barely visible rolls over the car, and for a moment the sunlight turns patchy as if we've found ourselves underwater. The shade's edge washes over us quickly. We break through it, the metal coat of the car again reflecting rays everywhere like a beacon. I always keep my hands in my pockets when I'm not in the water. Otherwise, I end up clenching them around pockets of air that keep escaping through my fingers, which is what I find myself doing now. The air is dry. I push my hand out the window, letting my fingers flutter on the wind. I almost catch a piece of it before it escapes again, and I retire my hand. I pat my breast pocket, feeling the prayer book inside and an unfamiliar stem. Nizam's cigarette. It's the only thing I'm carrying that I didn't have when I left the city.

Will I see the coast again? In the water, if I want to look forward, I look up. When I look up now, an unobstructed sky fills my field of vision. The sun is as low as a streetlight. I can't tell which way it's moving, so I can't tell what direction we're headed in. The celestial movements, the wind, the water—everything is gaining on me. Most of my swimming happens in a pool that tries to remain as still as possible. Nothing can touch me there; nothing can catch up with me except another swimmer. I fight against imaginary currents—crocodiles, my life, my death—pulling the sun down with my own two hands and scattering stars with every stroke. Swimming is not without its drama, which I control.

On a day like this, swimming takes on a skewed meaning for me that I can't escape. I look up to see where I want to go, but there's only sky. An endless dive. I've taken a plunge, waiting to land. I'd kill for a blackout right about now: less sun, more night. I want more time, but I've been living on borrowed time my whole life.

My eyes are drawn to a bird that swoops down and settles into following the same road as the car. In the distance, our destination.

*

I will die today and it won't smell of pine, or eucalyptus, but petrol. I wonder if she will understand.

I hope she doesn't blame herself.

Maybe I should've said something. Left her a voice message.

What should my life have looked like?

Tracing the shadows of leaves on the pavement with Ramy, sohoor with Teita with the smell of slow-cooking fava beans filling the house, the lemon tree on summer nights, the lavender smell of her hand, the hours I spent in the water's embrace ... all of that might not have happened if Mama hadn't lived the life she did.

> *No revolution,*
>
> > *no me.*

I don't know what to do with that thought, but hopefully, today will be enough.

I couldn't believe it, she said. When the doctor placed him in my arms and said, c'est un garçon, I almost wept. The stunned expression on my face prompted the nurse, an Algerian woman, to translate. 'Alf mabrook 'ala ebnek. A thousand blessings for your son.

I was surprised at how heavy he felt. He didn't look real, all swaddled in white, as if he wasn't entirely there yet, which, as a baby, I guess he wasn't. And he just kept crying.

It took all of my strength to let go when I handed him back to the nurse, Wudood. As she took him away to wash him, she whispered, it's fine, dear, don't worry, you'll feel better once you get some rest, I promise. I tried to curl up into a ball, but I was so exhausted. So exhausted. *I wished I could pass out, but I found myself growing more awake. I was splitting in two and I had no way of stopping it.*

My legs were still outspread, I was on the birthing table, and I wanted Mama to be there. No, ya habla, *I chided myself.* She's back home. It's just you, your husband, and your ...

Then again, what good would it have done if Mama were here? She had wanted a grandson for so long that she was bound to love him. And seeing her affection towards him would have destroyed me.

He has destroyed me.

A few years after she caught me looking through her phone, I questioned Mama about it again. I was sitting with her in the stands after a race in Hamburg. Baba was on the phone outside. They had both driven down from Berlin to see me compete.

'What happened to your friend?' I asked her. 'The one who was in prison.' I remembered his name, but I wanted to give her the chance to ignore my question. If I poked her right where it hurt, she'd just swat me away again.

The pool where the race was held was built in the steel casing of a factory. Arches rose above us like ribs, and I tried to imagine how big this Bahamut that swallowed us must have been in life. The windows had frosted over. Steam rose from the surface of the pool in a constant exhale. The beast's body still possessed some heat. It was slowly decomposing around us, keeping us warm. Spectators removed their winter coats and draped them across their knees. The smell of chlorine is something I've never got used to. It reminds me of the odour of embalming materials used to keep the skins of rare books intact.

I didn't top the podium because I let my body float to the wall, my arm outstretched, 'reaching without really going for it,' as the coach said.

'How do you remember stuff like that?' Mama replied. Her amused smile faded as her expression glazed over with recognition. She remembered the slap. The sight of the memory overcoming her brought about a perverse joy. I saw her failure. Failure to remain in control. Failure to be what I needed; what Teita expected of her; what she hoped she could be.

'He was released a year ago. I've not seen him since, though.' She shrugged and looked out at the pool, where swimmers burst and dove in the water with a desperation that I've felt but have tried to tame.

Who am I when I lose control?

'He isn't allowed to leave the country, even now that he's served his sentence, and he always comes up with an excuse to avoid me when I'm back there. So, we just message every once in a while, update each other on what we're working on and promise to collaborate whenever we get the chance, but ... who knows?

'I was always worried ...' she said with an edge in her voice, the words cutting her throat on the way out. 'I always worried about what you would think of my leaving.' She was staring into the distance, beyond the swimmers standing on the starting blocks, waiting for their turn in the relay race. 'I thought I'd come back, I really did, but then I remembered all the reasons why I left.' Her mouth hung open. I could see her mind working, trying to imagine what life would have looked like if she hadn't gone out to deliver supplies at the mosque that night. It was hard—even for her—to think about her departure as being anything more than an escape.

I couldn't leave for fear that I'd forget, fear that life abroad meant leaving the past behind, but there it was, hiding behind her eyes, waiting to reappear whenever she blinked them shut. When her world disappears, where does she go? Is she back in the truck, waiting to pass under a streetlight to glimpse her surroundings? Is she standing with Baba on the sidelines of the hippodrome, waiting to watch the violence she's witnessed mirrored in the eyes of jockeys who would never spare the rod? Is she sitting in Teita's living room, trying to convince herself that the distorted reflection she sees in the darkened television screen is actually her?

I reached my hand out to where hers were nestled in her lap and kissed her fingers. They had more wrinkles than I remembered. She was growing older. I pulled her hands so that they were pressed against my eyes, another gesture I inherited from Teita.

I wouldn't trade my eyes for diamonds, but I would give them up for you.

'Thank you for coming all this way, Mama.'

When I looked up from her hands, she had diamonds in her eyes.

Hamburg itself was a blur. Athletes weren't allowed out without the coach and his assistant crowding us to make sure we weren't let loose on the foreigners. I could barely eat and felt nauseous for most of the trip. I blamed it on the food and said I'm used to eating ʾakl shaʿbi, of which there was none in Hamburg, as far as I knew. I wasn't aware of how I felt about most things in life back then. I didn't even know why I felt anxious being outdoors at night, nor did I realise that I hadn't experienced any sort of nightlife before. Outside, I felt like a caged animal under simulated sunlight, and I was trying to keep myself from falling for the trick. The abundance of city lights brought on migraines, so I was mostly left confined to the hotel room. I kept the blackout curtains closed and the lamps off. My coach took me to a shawarma place and bought me sandwiches there, which filled my stomach. He explained to me that what I felt was 'homesickness'.

Coming back home, I felt like I belonged nowhere. The airport was very well lit, though just outside, monstrous airplanes lurked in the darkness, guided by specks of artificial starlight scattered across the ground. I tried to remember that I held my mother's hands in my grandmother's grip, that I wasn't alone, but surrounded by nothing, it's hard to believe anything but your eyes.

*

Sunlight reflects off the glass surface of the building up ahead, or maybe the blinding glare is coming from my own eyes. 'Araby puts the visor down. I feel dizzy. A headache is coming on. Sand swallows the road behind us. Nizam is sitting up, alert, staring at the glass eye that is staring at us approaching. This place was built to see before being seen. I'm content to blame dehydration for the sudden flashes of light. 'Araby drank all our mineral water. I'm sure they'll have water where we're going, so it's not something I'll have to worry about for much longer. The desert is flat, and it's a straight road to the barracks. There's nothing else around. *Our way is green.*

'Araby's veins are bulging from his temples. I can tell he wants to stop the car to piss. If he does stop, it will prove he's relaxed—and he must be to have drunk all our water in the first place—which would make him one of the army's spies. I smile at how far my imagination stretches, but 'Araby doesn't stop the car. He starts to shake his legs to calm his bladder.

"'Araby, are you okay?'

'Hamdolillah.' The lilt in his voice would suggest a brief exchange of pleasantries in a surprise encounter. He scratches his neck uncomfortably and shuffles in his seat.

The Lada rattles on uneven asphalt, glistening in the sun as if coated in sweat.

'Are you being compensated for this?' I ask 'Araby. 'The long drive, I mean.'

'Yeah,' he says. 'I'm going to buy two new pairs of shoes with the money and wear one shoe from each at a time, so that everyone knows I've got two new pairs.'

The barracks' gypsum-coated walls are riddled with bullet holes in places, and every third window's glass is broken. Exhaust fans are running, giving willingly what the eternal vacuum of the desert would otherwise suck out by force. But what do I know of deserts—I've always lived in the city, and I've never felt more displaced than I do now. I think again of the Bedouin conception of the past and the future as happening elsewhere, time being a geographic location, not an hour, so travellers are equally as likely to find themselves in the past as at their destination. The moral of the story: caution is important when setting out on a journey. I think of Hakeem training without measuring distances, and I remember the bottle filled with petrol in the boot. All hopelessly intertwined.

I beat Hakeem, but I understand his lack of timekeeping more now that I see this awkward agglomeration of buildings. The bullet holes are like needlework, insisting on the place's survival. The flashes of white sharpen the black pinholes, pulsating. They're a way to keep count and weave into this world a past that first launched the bullets. The barracks wears its vulnerability like a shield. I didn't expect that. As we approach the gate, the bullets hit their mark and become visible in their gritty reality. One day, when they get the time, I imagine soldiers digging the bullets out and leaving the holes, then going out to find new homes for the metal they've recovered. It surprises me to think that if I were to put my fingers inside one of them, I'd only feel concrete, rather than the depth of space, the essence of a hidden place, a time when people were not scared of firing guns at these buildings and were close enough to do so. People who trod the same ground we drive on. If nothing happens today, this would all have been for nothing. The stakes are high. I sink further into the passenger seat with sweat pooling around my thighs.

It takes a moment to realise that the people who launched those bullets have probably died, and in this very desert. The car rolls over their unmarked graves. A strong enough wind might uncover them. Maybe tomorrow, maybe in a thousand years. They are long-gone allies, but the mere awareness of their presence beneath the carpet of sand strengthens my resolve. I'm not alone. Others have been here before me, and once I make my stand, others will follow. Let the dust devils dance with the remnants of my body for eternity, so those who come after me will smell my ashes on a wind carried far from the city, traces I've left behind of my minor rebellion, and when they breathe the dry desert air, they will know that I died free by my own hand, believing in freedom and bequeathing to them a dream of a free country. I'm not chasing death because I've given up on life. I believe in life, which is why I don't fear death.

I've come here to find my nest and fight, but faced with these buildings that wear their battle scars so proudly—*I've taken a beating, yet here I stand!*—I momentarily lose hope. The thought crops up again that nothing I do will matter, although deep down, I believe that it will. Yesterday, when I left the city, with its smells of stale river water, jasmine, exhaust fumes and dust, I resolved to be brave. Cowardice won't save me today, and nor will silence—they would only condemn me to a slower death. I refuse to leave my country to these wolves as my parents did. If I am to leave, it will be as dust. If I am to die, let me wash over the city, so that others may breathe me in and know that they don't have to live their lives in fear. I've had an easier time of it than people like Nizam, Ramy, Musa, even Teita, so if I can't summon the strength to make a final stand, who will? Today, my actions will be for my soul. I am the person I've been chasing in the pool. I, not Nizam, am the saviour I've been waiting for.

I must remember that I have not failed. This country has been built to break us, and when it breaks us, it breaks us good. When Musa told me not to go through with this, he said I didn't know how to live, only how to die. Maybe he was right. Freedom is worth dying for. But despite what Musa might think, I never set out to die. If I had seen a way to deviate from this course and follow a different line to freedom—freedom in life—then I would have taken it. But there's no way to topple this military government and live free, no flaw in the system that can be exploited to dismantle it. The state has no flaws; it functions perfectly to serve the people it was built to serve. I'm hard pressed to imagine anything behind these walls that could change my mind about what it is that I have to do.

The car silently approaches the gate, which is really no more than a series of metal rods painted red and white and planted in the ground. Infantry colours, inherited from the Mamluk buildings in the city's medieval neighbourhoods. There are guard towers, but they stand empty. The administrative building, the glass eye of the complex, is set back from the gate by a large expanse of sparse greenery. Signs on the lawn state that the sprinklers distribute untreated water that's good for plants but not for much else. 'Not potable.' Every tree, its leaves dry and frizzy, has been dyed in the colours of the flag. An island of cracked earth sits in front of a building with curtain walls of jaundiced glass reflecting the sky. Even from a distance, it strikes an ancient chord, a temple in reverence of glory attained, glory under attack and glory dissipating, all at once. An illness is growing inside; that much is clear. That's why we're here.

The complex must have been built before environmental regulations prohibited the use of glass facades, and it has aged badly in the desert. The air-conditioning units are struggling against the heat. There are red stripes between strips of plaster near the base of the building, and here the bullet marks are most visible: dark holes surrounded by bright-grey exposed concrete surrounded in turn by deep maroon. Some of the cladding has fallen off the walls and obviously been replaced by a different contractor, giving the impression that the building, like the shifting desert sands, is in a constant process of rearranging itself, and just because it looks like this when we arrive, it doesn't mean it will always carry on this way.

'Private!' 'Araby yells to a man sleeping in the security box by the gate. 'Eftah. We've brought Sheikh Nizam.' Tapping my knee, he says, 'Your ID, ya sheikhna. And put on your shoes.'

I opt for my sandals. We'll have to take our shoes off to pray anyway, and then afterwards ... it won't matter.

The guard steps out of the booth to check our papers. Sifting through the prayer book I carry as a wallet makes me feel more hopeless than I've felt in a while. This is what I come armed with to the gate of a military barracks. I hand my ID to ʿAraby, who pauses to look at it before passing it on to the sentry. His casual intrusion makes me seethe, until I realise I'm being petty. ʿAraby twists around in his seat to reach Nizam, who slaps his arm away jokingly and gives his ID to the private himself. ʿAraby laughs and turns around to open the glove compartment to look for the letter that will grant us passage.

My grandmother's Polaroid slid halfway out of my prayer book as I was retrieving my ID. I heave a sigh and wedge it into the spine so the leaves will hold it in place. I haven't looked at the photo since we left the city, but this isn't the place to bring out something like that.

'Don't worry,' ʿAraby tells me.

'I'm not.'

'Feels too close to yesterday, right?'

'Yes, it does.' I point to the glass building and the lawn. 'Is this it? Where's the barracks?'

'I don't know,' ʿAraby says. 'I've never been here before.'

Behind us, Nizam seems to be whispering, either practising his sermon or praying. His hand is covering his mouth, as though he's muttering into someone's ear, and he has the distant stare of someone whose mind is racing. He strikes me as a different person to the man I saw this morning at the zeir, different to the one who copied out lines from ʿAttar's poem over a year ago, different to the one I slept next to last night. A face at close quarters becomes a confusing jumble of features where no one element fits with the rest. The thought doesn't reassure me. I want to ask him if he needs any food or water, but the bottles he filled are by his feet, and the sandwich I gave him is still in his pocket, though I expect he's forgotten about it.

The private radios someone called Hamdy and asks if Major General Talaʿat is in. 'No,' is the response.

'Well, go look for him. Sheikh Nizam and someone else—Shahed Mustafa Jihan el-Yosry—are here.'

'Araby secures the handbrake.

'Yes, Shahed Mustafa Jihan el-Yosry.'

'Araby switches off the engine, and silence floods into the car.

'El-Yosry.' The private leans against the door of the booth. 'Jihan el-Yosry. Yes, exactly.'

Nizam rolls down his window and wipes his face on his scarf. His eyes dart as he looks around.

'Says here, student. Mawaleed 2012. Alright.' The guard puts the walkie-talkie down and stares at our IDs as if the pictures and words on them are about to move. He gets back inside the security box and sits at his desk.

'What are you here for?' he yells towards the car, to no one in particular.

'Sheikh Nizam is here to give the sermon today,' 'Araby calls back.

The private nods, uninterested. 'What's it about?' he asks. His face lights up at the ingenuity of his question, as if he's suddenly remembered he can be curious.

'You'll have to wait and see.'

'I'm not Muslim.'

'I'm sorry.'

'It's not your fault.'

'Araby asks if there's a toilet nearby. Without a word, the private points with our IDs at the gate, flicking his wrist to indicate that the toilet is behind his booth. 'Araby gets out of the car and asks us if we need to go. I shake my head, and Nizam smiles and pats his chest lightly.

'Terga' be-s-salama,' I say to 'Araby as he leaves.

Nizam is leaning forward between the front seats. I try to put my finger on his scent, imagining his skin glistening beneath his gallabeya. His hand grabs my shoulder, and I start in my seat. He laughs. I cover my eyes, panting.

'How are you doing?' he asks me.

'Hamdolillah. Just hot.' I unbutton my collar and pinch my shirt to try to get a ripple of air going. It might dry some of the sweat.

Nizam clicks his tongue twice.

I turn around to look him square in the face. Up close, he is made of basalt. I don't recognise him.

Seeing my reaction, Nizam leans back to give me a bit of space. 'Just breathe,' he says.

I was glad for the breeze that came with 'Araby opening and slamming the car door.

*

When I first lived with Teita, each night when she would finally leave me in the darkness of my bedroom, fed and warm, I'd bring out a torch and start reading. Teita was instructed to remove all candles from my room; my parents worried that I'd set the house on fire. Not long after she tucked me in, the generator would cease its droning, the walls and doors would stop shaking and my tea would stop vibrating in its hourglass vessel. While the fluid building up behind my eardrum dimmed the daytime racket like the depths of the water, the silence that flooded my room at night lifted me. It was as fragile as the stillness before races, when my pulse would calm to an even undulation so soft that it was ready for touch. Those nights, I rose to the surface as if I were the city's gentle skin.

The absence of noise transformed the words I was reading so that I felt compelled to sound them aloud, as if they were creatures whose names I had to utter to understand, even though I couldn't hear the sounds myself. The thump of my underwater heartbeat rekindled, and I felt the world unwind around me as if a knot had loosened. The line I wanted to follow across the page became apparent, pulling me as if it had its own gravitational force. Night turned into dawn, but without hearing the birdsong, I couldn't tell.

I didn't go to school during those weeks, when everything had to be repeated loudly to pierce my bubble of silence. Instead, I passed whatever time I had outside, drawing the outline on the pavement of the shadows cast by the trees. On their return, my parents would insist on hiring a tutor to help me catch up with the rest of the class, but for as long as they were away, I drifted aimlessly through the days, content to think of nothing but names to give to each chalk leaf I marked on the ground.

As the day progressed, the shadows moved, and my chalk outline seemed to have been exposed to the winds of time. I saw its future blown off to the side, bent out of shape, destroyed. Its tilt reminded me of my flight path when I was thrown into the pool, and I stroked my ribs where a purple bruise had formed. The sting was still there, familiar.

The owner of the kiosk on the corner paid the street-sweeper, Salah, to leave my sketches intact, so I could continue them the next day. On my third day of drawing, Ramy, the kiosk owner's son, accidentally sent a ball flying in my direction. Assuming it was someone baiting me for attention, I barely glanced up. He stopped to pick up a piece of chalk lying a little way away from me and wrote out a word on the pavement. I looked at the letters, then at his feet. Green trainers, old but clean, their shape loose like sagging skin. He prodded his finger on the ground where he had written his name, then gestured to himself, before pointing at me and again at the pavement. The shadow shifted softly across its outline as the sun carried on along its path. I wrote my name down beside an escaped leaf oblivious to the cage I had set for it.

I spent all my time with him after that, aside from my swims and night-time reading sessions. 'Umm Saber, the housekeeper, seemed pleased I had made a friend, though she never invited him in. She used to try to communicate with me through gestures, but despairing of her inability to get her message across, she would sometimes raise her voice so that I would hear. It was an effort for her, so we didn't talk often.

Teita trusted me in Ramy's company, so I trusted him. For as long as I struggled with my hearing, he walked with me around the neighbourhood, holding my hand, interlocking his arm with mine, becoming my ears if I was stopped at a checkpoint or if anyone tried to speak to me. Doormen, drivers, street-sweepers and police officers addressed him to reach me. We developed our own language. A squeeze of the hand: *car coming.* A tap against my wrist: *stop, look up.* Each time I felt his fingers at my joint, my heart would skip and my throat would tighten just as they did when I was launched in the water, and I would hold my breath until my pulse slowed and my throat relaxed. I think I must have squeezed his hand when that happened, because I would feel him squeeze mine back. In my confusion, I'd move closer to him if I was in the way of the road, or pull him closer to me if he was, but there'd be no car, just us.

A thumb rolling over my index finger meant *I'm talking to you*, which would draw my eyes to his. I memorised the sight of the square scar in his pupil, like a bit of dirt, granular and darker than the surrounding brown. I didn't spend long enough in that suspended state of deafness to learn to read lips, but I followed his as he moved them. 'Umm Saber would refill bottles of water from the filter and place them next to us on the pavement, where we scrawled more notes for each other in chalk. The streets were mostly empty, since surrounding checkpoints made it difficult to pass through the neighbourhood, but eventually, Ramy's father insisted that we use a notepad for our messages. On the blank paper, it felt as though we'd been thrust into a room alone together, and suddenly our words seemed foolish, like schoolwork, an exercise with no bearing on the real world.

Whenever Ramy helped his father in the evenings, I would hold my reading session at my window overlooking the kiosk. He would lift crates and top up the generator his father used to power the fridge. I'd observe as he became transfixed by the packets of cigarettes and chewing gum he was rearranging, or while he ran his hands over the newspaper display stand to make sure they were aligned. I offered to sneak him into the pool so he could watch me train, maybe even go for a swim himself, but he pointed to his eyes and then all around, dusted off his hands and waved the air away. *They'd see me and kick me out immediately.*

Most nights when he worked, Ramy would look up through the trees to see me reading by the window. Meeting my eye, he'd smile and wave up at me, before his father called him back to deliver food to the guards at nearby checkpoints: trays of tea, cold cuts, baladi bread and cartons of cheese. I'd stare at the last corner he had turned and wait for him to come back. A few times, he was delayed for long enough to make me worry. Other times, he wouldn't look up at my window but would keep his head down as he walked, staring at the asphalt. On one such occasion, sensing his son's distress, Ramy's father knelt in front of him with a hand on one knee, the other hand pointing into the distance, and spoke words I couldn't hear. Ramy gave him a hug and sat down. He started to make origami animals, braiding and un-braiding a bit of twine until it tore or his father charged him with another task. On those nights, Ramy's father would glance up at me as he got back into the kiosk booth, then quickly glance away.

They were teasing me, Ramy wrote, when I asked why he was upset.

About?

He shrugged and stood up, pulling my hand, raising me to my feet so we could go for a walk.

*

Inside the building, a simple left turn disappears everything outside: 'Araby, the road, the Lada and the desert. There are potted plants in every corner, marble floors, a front desk with no one sitting at it. The desert is but a fanciful daydream that Nizam and I have escaped. Nothing could be that immense and empty. I'm holding the bottle of petrol.

We are led by another private, who introduced himself to us by the steps leading up to the front door, but I didn't listen to his name. He takes us up the stairs to a mezzanine level, where he leads us to a service stairway by a set of lifts.

'They're not working,' the private says before we can ask. 'The doors might open, but there'll be no cabin there. We don't want that.'

The service stairs seem to be the artery of the administrative building. The private takes them two at a time and waits for us on every landing. I keep up, but I try not to go too fast because Nizam is already falling behind. Soldiers are running up and down the stairs with papers in their hands. Voices echo from much further down than where we started, though I'm not counting the floors as we go. A cacophony rises of feet, slaps, laughs, yells—and clicks, since so many soldiers are tapping the handrail with pens that it reverberates beneath my hands like a battle cry. My heart beats loudly in my throat, and I realise I've lost Nizam. I peer over the handrail and see he's two storeys behind us. I call out to the private, and five men turn around before I point to the relevant one and tell him to wait.

As I lean my arm against the handrail, sound from all over the building travels into my body and sends vibrations into the universe in the bottle I hold in my hand. Today, I have a chance to peel back the world's facade and expose it all for what it is. While I'm mulling this over, my mind wanders to Teita's photograph and Nizam's discovery in the archive. People already know that the army has been destroying this country and its people for decades. What difference will today make?

Nizam's voice rises up the stairwell, coloured by a smile on his lips, which push each chanted word upwards like burning incense whose smell travels faster than its smoke. His voice is thick in the air, but I can't hear what he's saying. Looking up, I see the private slowly descending, stopping now and again to look down for Nizam. Above him, more soldiers move and more look over the handrail. Some talk to each other in inaudible whispers, as if they've figured out how to bypass the medium of air and send words straight into people's ears. Further above, I can just make out where light pours in from a skylight.

I think of going back down to find Nizam. The idea that he might be telling someone what I confided in him yesterday worries me, as do the men rushing around me in battledress. They pat my shoulder to move me aside as they brush past. The immensity of this highway through the building, as well as its lack of any distinct smell, the absence of any taste in the air except of Nizam's presence, makes me want to flee. It starts to dawn on me why I've been irritable with Nizam and sensitive around 'Araby this morning. Last night when I talked to Nizam, I resolved to be brave, which is something I've never before had to do. Everything I have achieved in my life till now has been easy, almost pre-ordained, and all my actions have been geared towards avoidance of making the decision I must make today. Now, standing on this landing amid a scrum of soldiers, I feel completely at sea, caught up in this fawda, about to be trampled under the thuds of stomping men. These soldiers must feel fear too, but they seem to march to a different drum, and as much as I try to deny it, they rule over me. The thought occurs to me suddenly that I don't know when I last went on holiday, and I try to imagine the possibility of a life where I'm not subject to these people. Although my mission today doesn't hinge on bravery or strength, it feels significant to accumulate both in a building that oozes one and not the other.

A tune ascends the staircase, interrupted by the hummer's sharp intakes of breath. I see the crest of Nizam's head rise over the horizon of the stairs. He pushes each step down and leans forward, climbing over them, not trusting his body's ability to lift its own weight. He looks weak, and I remember he hasn't eaten. Lifting his eyes to meet mine, he nods at me to continue making my way up.

'Don't wait for me,' he says. 'Teer.'

The private skips past me as I begin my ascent. He briskly crosses the next landing and walks through a door, calling back over his shoulder to tell me that someone will attend to me shortly. The stairwell is overwhelmed again by the sound of movement. I wait patiently for Nizam to appear, but only sergeants, corporals and privates, all in battledress, fly past. I lean over the handrails, but I don't see him.

A hand grabs my shoulder and pulls me back, and my grip suddenly loosens. I let go of the bottle, which rolls to the edge of the stairs and balances there on the brink. From below, a voice calling my name rings out above the rest of the noise, and all the men stop to look around for the source of the abrupt sound: Nizam. The silence from their shock is too much, and the bottle slips over the edge and falls between the railings. I hear it bouncing off the staircase and thumping against the floor, followed by the hiss of running liquid.

'It's all pouring out,' a voice yells from downstairs. My hands feel light and defenceless, and I have to hold on to the banister to keep myself from collapsing. *It's gone.*

As the sharp smell of petrol travels up the staircase, the private by my shoulder pulls me by the cuff, roughly this time. My feet scramble to keep up as he drags me up two more flights of stairs and through a door onto an unlit corridor lined with well-lit rooms. Cold air rushes out of the open doorways of small offices where men busy typing barely look up as we pass through. I see our reflection in the floor tiles, streaked with black marks like disjointed letters—traces of all the others who've been made to run through this corridor. Short, sharp lines; long, dull lines; bearded lines; lines with starched shirts; lines with bloodied suits; lines with blood on their hands; lines with blood on their faces; lines with long, holy faces; lines with crosses on their wrists; lines with black eyes; black lines with no eyes.

'We should wait for Nizam,' I say, unsure of what's happening, or having an idea of what's happening but not wanting to admit it. 'We've left him behind.'

If I'm not a sacrifice, then who am I? The possibility of life beyond today never occurred to me. Now each step I take seems aimed in the direction of a nameless void, where the ground might fall away like sand beneath my feet, or dust in the wind. I will never be dust on the wind. I'll never be apart from this world.

'Nizam will find his way.'

The private's voice is startling. The shapes that his mouth forms clash with the sound coming out of it.

'Someone else will go and get him. Just got to find the right office.'

The noise is hollow, like a ventriloquist's doll, but then who is throwing the voice into this vessel? I look at the brawny soldier and feel my body catch up with my being here, in this barracks, with men who would call me their brother even as they sink a knife into my back. He's shorter than I am, well built but stiff. *I could kill him if I needed to.* The thought is absurd but persistent. *I've battled the sea; I can take on a private.*

He opens the door to a small room where another private is sitting at a desk. Behind the desk, chinks of light shine through the gaps in between a row of filing cabinets. I look up and see a snaking network of interior ducts through the lattice of a suspended ceiling. Nothing hides in this building. A man is coughing loudly inside an adjoining office through a set of double doors. I can smell Cleopatra cigarettes.

'Is General Tala'at in?' the private with me asks the seated private, though the cigarette smoke in the air is enough to make his question redundant.

'Is that him?' the major general calls from inside the office.

'Yes, sir,' my private says. He nudges me to walk through the double doors, and I realise that Nizam isn't coming. How did I lose my way so quickly?

The tiredness of the road journey sets in my legs, and they freeze. The private prods my back with his thick fingers. I lean back into his prod, which only makes him push me harder. I may never have found meaning in life from standing still, but that doesn't mean I don't crave stillness or balance. I want to slow this moment down. I want to pause to scrutinise every detail. I want to stand back and see the moment before this one, when I'm being pushed into a rotba's office having lost a fugitive in an army barracks, not to try and make sense of it, because there is no sense in it, but simply to be able to breathe. I'm holding my breath, and my heart beats so wildly in my chest that my ribs start to pulsate with a sharp pain as if something has broken. The private presses his palm flat against my back now and pushes me forward. My feet stumble, and I tell them to keep moving.

I see the double doors leading into General Tala'at's office, the filing cabinets lining every wall, two chairs in front of a low coffee table that sits between the general and his guests. The furnishings look worn, as if they've been dragged in from outside—just like me—and would be outdated in the city but somehow remain relevant in this place. *It's frozen in time; it will never change; you will never change it.* There is a vast empty space in the corner of the room opposite the rotba, who sits at a desk in front of windows that stretch from the ceiling to the floor. I can make out the gate through which we entered the barracks, but the Lada is nowhere in sight. I realise that the rays of light from behind the filing cabinets in the antechamber must come from similar windows that have been blocked. I wonder if that's from when the bullets were fired at the outer walls. I try to imagine the hunk-of-muscle private hiding behind the cabinets, firing back at the Bedouin outside, digging their graves himself so no one outside this barracks would ever find out the truth. All that's changed in the building since then is the glass. The defences from the siege are still up, the filing cabinets still there to take bullets, but I didn't come armed with bullets—and what do I have now?

Between the deserted corner and the desert behind the glass, I take a seat in the chair facing the double doors, so I can see when Nizam catches up with us, even though a voice in my head whispers, *he won't*.

'I understand you've been to see the barracks of the deceased soldiers,' the general begins. Without glancing up, he solemnly puts down the sandwich he was eating and dusts the crumbs off his hands. 'Fi rahmet rabbak. It was a devastating thing to have happened, especially here. I'm sure you're aware of the history of this base and its importance in the fight against the terrorists. The ghosts of our brave boys now keep us awake at night, but the terrorists have been haunting us for years. The Sinai is teeming with them. Using the name of God to fight for political power ... it's an insult to this country, and to all of humanity, but there's no need to go on about that in your sermon.'

'Sir?' I interrupt, confused.

'This is the assistant, ya fandem,' my private clarifies. 'Not Nizam.'

The general looks up at me and raises his hands in disbelief. 'Where is Nizam?' he asks indignantly, displeased that he was tricked, bewildered that he was mistaken.

'I'll try and find him now, ya fandem.'

'Maybe you should go and find him now, ya-bni.'

My private leaves. Like a stereo, the buzzing static of the stairwell noise starts up when he opens the door to the antechamber and dies when he closes it behind him. It brings to mind the whisper of the sycamore's leaves outside my window, Teita's chapped soles rustling blades of grass, the clicking of her shears trimming back the ivy choking her tree. The memory jolts another, and I think of the cuttings Teita collected from plants in her garden to propagate in small jam jars and plastic cups inside the house.

The night she died, I went into her bedroom when she didn't answer my calls or quiet knocks at her door. 'Umm Saber and I were waiting for her to pray fajr, and as the sun threatened to rise with no sign of Teita, we decided I would have to wake her if we didn't want to miss the prayer. She wasn't a heavy sleeper and usually would stir at the slightest creak of a floorboard. I shuffled in as noiselessly as I could. She wasn't in her bed, so I dragged my feet through the darkness towards the bathroom. A sliver of light radiated from below the door frame. Pressing my ear to the door, I rapped my fingers lightly, in case she had fallen asleep inside.

'Are you doing your wudoo'? It's time,' I said. Worried I was rushing her, I added, 'We're waiting for you, habibti.'

I heard the faintest sound—'*yes*'—and thought she was just taking her time. I should have realised something was wrong from the weakness of her voice, but I didn't want to intrude on her. For most of her life, Teita wasn't allowed her own space. She grew up with five siblings in a cramped apartment, sleeping in the same bed as her sister until they were both thirteen, when she got her own bed only because her older brother was enlisted in the army. Even back then, he was more useful to her in his absence than when he was around. Later in life, the police raided Teita's clinic, and her home was searched and ransacked when I was safely in France with Mama and Baba—she never told them, but she told me. I didn't want to add to this list by asking her if she needed help in the bathroom. Though she was in her seventies, she was still very active and went jogging daily. It would have been belittling to worry about her.

You should've trusted your instincts, I told myself when 'Umm Saber and I managed to get the door open. We found my grandmother lying motionless on the ground. A few plastic cups of pale eucalyptus leaves had fallen with her, forming a ring above her head on the bright bathroom floor.

Teita always loomed large. Hearing about what she lived through, I couldn't imagine adding anything of value to her life or offering anything she might need. I realised then just how mistaken I was. I knew something was wrong, but I'd ignored that voice. If I had trusted my instincts, as she trusted me with her stories, her history, the Polaroid in my prayer book, maybe she would still be alive.

But why do these thoughts come to me now? And where could Nizam have disappeared to? No one goes missing in a place like this out of an exercise of free will. I look around for a clock to try to work out how long he's been gone but only hear a ticking noise coming from the room with the secretary. Maybe the rotba doesn't need to keep track of time. It moves along at his pace and leaves the rest of us trying to keep up.

'And you,' he says, looking up at me. I notice now that he's wearing a watch, but I can't see it for the sunlight in my eyes. 'Why didn't you say anything? Why not introduce yourself?'

Nizam said that Tala'at chose me for this mission. So why is he asking me this?

'I'm sorry, sir,' I say, reaching to retrieve my ID. He shakes his head and laughs. 'What's your name, son? Show your ID to the soldiers. With me you can speak freely.'

I smile and tell him my name. I want to tell him that we've met before, at the inauguration of Nizam's mausoleum, but something stops me. Instinct. Something about this rotba tells me he doesn't forget.

I glance at the empty chair opposite me, its wooden seat bare and polished from use, while mine is covered with a torn cushion. I wonder at the lightness that chair feels and the gravity of its emptiness, as well as the number of souls that have occupied both, which makes me shift in my seat.

Tala'at keeps nodding as he picks up his sandwich and takes a bite. Behind him, on top of another filing cabinet, though this row reaches only to shoulder height, is a charcuterie board of deli meat slices dotted with pieces of olive and peppercorn, alongside tomatoes, pickled aubergines, and a cardboard box of fresh cheese that appears to be struggling to maintain its integrity in the heat of the office. On a separate plate, probably so as to keep the moistness away, is a pile of baladi bread. The general assembles a sandwich and turns to me.

'What do you want to drink?' he asks. 'Have you already eaten?'

'No, sir,' I say. 'I'm fine.'

'Unacceptable,' he says. 'You're a guest. Ma yesahh-sh.'

I think back to times when I've heard that phrase, perhaps after refusing a second serving or a bit of indulgence at a dinner party, and it puts me at ease. *Ma yesahh-sh*, as if there's some decorum I'm violating, as if—even if this man might have massacred thousands of people—a common standard of decency exists that I must live up to.

I wish for nothing more than not to have to make a decision ever again.

'Sayem,' I say, bashfully. 'Sir, should I go look for—'

'Nonsense, travellers get dispensation from fasting. It isn't proper. You have to set an example for the troops you'll be seeing. They see you fasting when you've been travelling and they let themselves grow weak too, because they think it's acceptable. Weak things die out here. Ma yesahh-sh.'

I can hear the rotba's watch and the clock in the antechamber ticking separately, only just missing each other with every passing second.

The rotba gestures to the double doors. 'Is the soldier still out there?' he asks me.

'He's still there,' I say.

'Ya private!' he calls. His secretary comes running but stops outside the double doors. 'Get him some breakfast,' says the rotba, pointing at me. 'What do you want to drink? Shayy? 'Ahwa?'

Each word that leaves his mouth seems to push me forward, nudging me towards an end that I can't envision anymore. The bottle is gone. I heard it fall. And the stench sticking to me from it is worse than just petrol.

'Coffee, then.'

'Sukkar?' the private asks.

'*A-l-reeha*,' I say. 'Sir, what about—'

'Does fool, eggs and pastrami sound good for your breakfast?'

'Yes,' I reply, not really listening to him. Most Sufis are vegetarians, which they must know, but I'm intent on blowing their minds by subverting expectations. *Where is Nizam?*

'And where is Nizam?' the general asks the private. Oh, to hear his name being spoken again. The silence that comes after is thick and heavy as cardboard-wrapped cheese.

'I don't know, ya fandem. My colleague who brought the assistant went to fetch him. Should I go and ask where he is?'

'Maybe go and ask where he is.'

The private runs off only to return a few seconds later. 'Should I go myself or call someone?'

'Maybe just go yourself,' says the rotba. 'Maybe leave the phone off the hook. I'm not going to answer it.' He speaks as if there were an element of uncertainty in his orders, or in the orders that rule this place.

The private does as he's told. The stairwell noise rises and dies, leaving me marooned once more in the silent room with the general. I hope that once Nizam comes back, I'll find a way to get back on track with my plan. *What plan? The plan fell down the stairwell.*

Skidding boot prints mar the floor leading into the rotba's office but die down near the back like waves on the shore. Imagine this place under siege: bullets flying through the glass, littering the office, boring holes in the furniture. Maybe that's why everything looks so worn.

Two sets of tick sounds, just a smidge apart.

'We'll wait for your master,' Tala'at says, smiling. 'I'd rather not make my speech twice. So, best to wait for him.' He holds the sandwich out to me again.

I pat my chest. 'Teslam. I've got breakfast coming.'

'That's right.'

We sit in silence. I feel an instinct to pat my pockets, but I don't want to make any abrupt movements. Thinking I'd be searched, which we weren't, I emptied my pockets and left everything but my ID, and whatever cash I had—can't trust 'Araby—in the glove compartment, including my prayer book. It would have been something to hold on to right about now.

The general puts on his glasses to read some papers on his desk, pursing his lips occasionally as if he's chewing a bone. He coughs over his plate, not bothering to cover his mouth. He's old, with dyed jet-black hair that's long enough to run your fingers through, soft enough that it wouldn't be unpleasant.

After a few minutes, he turns on the air-conditioning. It comes on with a beep, breaking the pattern of ticks. The cold air attacks my body and sends me into a fit of shivers. I clasp my hands together, squeezing, releasing, squeezing again. It's the only thing keeping my blood vessels from bursting in my brain.

The rotba coughs again, this time into his hand.

The private comes back carrying a metal tray with my breakfast. He knocks on the door frame and peers in at us, looking from me to the general, the general to me. *Tick-t-tick. Tick-t-tick.*

'Come in,' says the rotba.

'Sir—'

They found Nizam; he sold me out. Sunlight rushes into my eyes like floodlights. *A bottle filled with petrol? They think I was trying to torch the place. It's all over.*

My heart races and I feel like crying out for mercy before anything has happened.

The private puts a glass of tea down in front of me, and I'm shaken by its rattling in the saucer—*fragile things, breakable things, branches, cars, skulls and bones.* The clear red liquid refracts light on my hand. If I raise the glass to my lips, the shards of light would tear me apart, I'm sure of it. *It's poisoned.* Poisoned? No. Decorum in an army barracks stops at ma yesahh-sh. They'd never shy away from dragging me into a hole and burying me alive. I remind myself of the photos I've seen of Teita fixing the wounds of revolutionaries around Tahrir Square. Subtlety is not part of the army's vocabulary, especially when it comes to death. I also remember, as if it matters, that I ordered coffee, not tea.

Shining platter still in hand, the private goes around the desk and whispers something in the rotba's ear. The rotba doesn't react, but something behind his eyes moves; gears are turning and pieces clicking into place. It seems to have nothing to do with me, because for a moment neither of them looks my way. It's as if I'm not here anymore, which is a comforting idea. I'd like to run out the door, jump back in the Lada and drive back to the city, but there are hundreds of soldiers in the way of my escape.

The sunlight brightens, disappearing the desert outside. I prop my elbow on the general's desk and shield my eyes, which are pulsating furiously. If I could survive without them, I'd tear them out right this second, but I have a feeling I might need them before the day is done. The light reflects off the sand, breaks through the windows, swallows the filing cabinets, the rotba, the private, my breakfast, my tea, my time. There's a ringing in my ears, and I have to keep swallowing back the saliva pooling in my mouth. I turn my head towards the empty corner of the room, but the movement makes me dizzy. I try to listen for my name, but I don't hear it. I can't hear a single thing.

'Fine,' the rotba says, waving the private away.

'Sir,' the private says, pointing to the food.

'Keep it outside with you. The young man will join you shortly. Shahed, isn't it?' I reappear in the room as the general turns and addresses me. 'We've had to send Nizam back,' he says simply, smiling. 'You'll be giving the sermon. Go eat. We'll talk after.' He puts his sandwich down on the plate.

'Why?' I ask, wiping away drool from around my mouth before the general sees it. 'I mean'—I clear my throat—'what happened? Is he hurt?' My voice feels so far away that I wonder if I spoke at all.

'What's with all the questions?' the general asks impatiently. 'What could hurt Nizam here? No, he's just gone through a bad spell, so rather than letting him bake outside in the heat, we've sent him away.'

I swallow back more spit and tell myself not to dab the sweat on my brow.

'I haven't got time for this,' he says. 'Go eat. I'll look over whatever Nizam had planned.'

A practised anger seems to be rising in him. He flips through his papers lazily, then tosses them aside and pulls the plate with the half-eaten sandwich closer to him. He's bored and tired, in a position that has grown dull with age. He bows down towards the plate, too lazy to lift his elbows off the desk to bring the sandwich to his mouth. The secretary passes behind the rotba to leave, and I could swear I see him pocket a few slices of deli meat on his way out.

'Sir,' I say, trying to find the right words. 'I would rather you tell me what's going on. This situation is making me nervous. A man that I'm responsible for is …' I motion to the empty chair. 'It's just hard to understand.'

He nods to himself, and I can tell he has made a decision. Swallowing the last bite of his sandwich, he starts to talk.

*

'Look,' says the major general, smacking his lips, 'Nizam is gone. You seem like a good kid, and I need to ask you for a favour.' He cleans his teeth with his tongue. 'You'll need to pretend that you're Nizam.'

My hand rushes to my mouth to quell a burst of laughter, but it breaks through the dam.

'I'm sorry,' I say, shaking my head incredulously. 'I don't understand.' I measure my next words carefully to avoid the suggestion of a subtle threat or accusation. 'What do you mean, "Nizam is gone"? He was right behind me when we were going up the stairs.'

The rotba shakes his head, amused by my evident struggle to control myself. 'Where he was isn't the issue. He isn't here now, which means you also have a problem. You've lost your ward. He was your responsibility first and foremost, and the letter you delivered at the gate states that explicitly. I have it right here,' he says, lifting a piece of paper from his desk. 'See? That's your name. Read what it says next to it.'

'Sir, I'm aware of my—'

'Just read it.'

My fingers are slick from sweat and attach to the paper.

'Out loud.'

'The bearer of this letter, named above, has sole responsibility for delivering the prisoner to the barracks of the Third Army of the Armed Forces. He must—'

A piece of dust gets stuck in my throat and I start coughing.

'Excuse me,' I say to the rotba, who is waiting patiently for me to implicate myself in something for which I bear no blame. I continue reading. 'He must deliver the prisoner to the commander personally, where his responsibility ends.' I think about Magdy's hammy sense of concern for me when he questions me at the checkpoints, because he's being paid to keep an eye out for me. This general owes me nothing and doesn't hide his disinterest in my survival. He's not paid to protect me. I'm here to serve him, and I have failed.

The sound of the stairwell rises again. The secretary is about to appear once more, and I don't imagine that he bears good news. The clocks tick. Without looking, the rotba leans back and reaches his arm to grab a slice of meat and a tomato wedge, which he places inside a piece of flatbread.

'My boys are handling it. They'll find him. I told them there's an intruder in the barracks. A madman. And that Nizam is safe with me in my office.' He points at me. Then, realising the madness of his own words, he shakes his head and covers his mouth with a look of genuine disappointment and regret.

No, he's just cleaning his teeth.

'It should never have happened, but here we are,' he continues. 'And the mess isn't over.' Patting the desk, he asks me, 'Do you want to go to prison?'

'I just came from prison,' I say.

'That's not what I meant. Listen to what I'm saying. *Do you want to go to prison?*'

'No, of course n—'

'Then this is how it has to be.' He pushes the plate aside and puts both his hands on the table, palms up, cards bared. 'I'll get you out of this mess, but you'll have to pretend to be Nizam. Of course, you're not as dark as he is, and you both have different builds, besides the age difference, but Nizam has always been more of a metaphor for the people. And for the Sufis as well, right? Unless you really do believe in saints. I know you, ya Shahed. I know that you spoke out against Nizam's sainthood—'

'Sir, I contributed to his exam—'

'Don't interrupt me. Do this, for the sake of the soldiers, not for yourself. Let's set silly squabbles aside. And I'll say this plainly'—he launches in without a pause—'I know there's a general dislike among Sufis of the army and people like me who sit behind these desks in these kinds of places, and you, along with a large portion of the population, are a Sufi, no matter what your internal beliefs. Isn't that right?'

My name is attached to Teita's, which is attached to Mama's arrest and her exile with Baba.

'I'll take your silence as a yes,' he says. 'Don't forget your coffee, by the way.'

I pick up the glass of tea, wondering if he'll correct himself. Then I realise that the rotba subscribes to the undying belief that the army makes no mistakes. It doesn't kill civilians, lose sheikhs on its bases or deliver tea when someone orders coffee.

The tea is too hot. I slurp a little and blow on the surface before moving the glass to my lap. A gesture called *patience with tyranny*.

'Hope you don't mind if I smoke? Ya private!' he yells towards the door. 'Hamdy! Get an ashtray. And a coffee for me. Zeyada. I need a boost. Ya Mosahel.' He looks at me and turns the pack towards me. 'Smoke?'

'I've got my own,' I say, remembering Nizam's cigarette.

His arm extends towards me with the lighter, and I notice burns between his index and middle finger. I remember feeling the same callus when he first pulled my hand into his grip in Nizam's mausoleum. Back then, in that dusty courtyard, Nizam seemed too big to die. Today, I'm not so sure.

'But it's for later,' I say, thinking of Nizam's nimble movements.

The rotba laughs. 'Something for the mazag, huh?' He waves his hand as if tickling the air. 'I knew it. Just don't smoke it on site. Smells travel far here in the desert.'

The only reason Nizam agreed to come along on this errand was to have a chance at escape. If he's found, he will die. But death is likely better than prison.

The private brings in an ashtray and a coffee. As he sets them down on the desk, the general turns to look up at him and asks, 'What's this kid's name?'

'Shahed, ya fandem.'

'No,' says the rotba, pointing at me with his index finger.

'This is Nizam. The assistant fell ill, he's been driven home. And there's a madman on the loose in the barracks. Everyone must keep their eyes open. And listen, ya Hamdy. You won't be coming to the sermon. I'll need you to stay here.'

'Hader, ya fandem.' The private scans my face, his brows knotted in irritation. I meet his eyes, which have the colour and ceramic-like sheen of molasses ... I can taste their sharp sweetness and feel the heaviness weighing me down like shackles, drowning me. *I need to go outside. I need to breathe.*

'When are the families of the dead arriving?' asks the rotba.

'Should be here any moment now.'

'Did you place the potted plants in the corridors?'

'Yes, sir. And we cleaned everything. Not a bit of dust inside or outside.'

'Cleaned the desert too?' the rotba smiles.

Hamdy laughs. 'Yes, of course. No grain left unpolished. Glitters like glass.'

'Good man. Now get out of here. Go sit by the phone and tell me the moment they're here.'

It occurs to me that there's a problem in the building that hasn't been tackled. 'Sir, I think the lift was broken when I came in,' I begin. 'But for the sake of—'

The general's face changes. 'Maybe we need to start over,' he orders.

'Start over?'

'Get reintroduced. You're Nizam, now, remember? By the way, hand over your ID. I saw your hand moving around in your pocket before when I asked your name.'

'Why?' I ask, reaching into my pockets.

'It would be more befitting of the situation if you didn't argue with me, okay?' He smiles as he snatches my ID out of my hand and looks at my full name. 'Good, thanks. We'll put this aside in that Lada you drove here.' He places the card in a drawer in his desk and locks it with a key.

I nod. The tea is cooler now, so I manage a few sips. The

empty corner seems to have shrunk, hemmed in by shadow, less light reaching it now than this morning. The sun is higher in the sky, and I can see further out the window than before, up to the horizon. I think about how different life was when I saw the sun's reflection off the glass an hour and a half ago. I was someone else, and now I've just given the last proof of who I was to this rotba. The only other witness to my identity is 'Araby. God knows where he is. Or where Nizam is. *God, where am I?* The questions fall down like a pile of bricks and tears sting my eyes.

The tea is too sweet, but the sharpness of the sukkar calms me down.

'It's almost eleven,' the rotba yells into the next room.

'Yes, sir.'

I hear the private call someone. Moments later, the Qur'an starts blaring outside, in the corridors and through speakers in the corner next to the rotba's charcuterie board.

'We have Copts and even a few Jewish boys and girls working around here, but they're good people, so they don't mind hearing kalam rabbena,' says the general. 'You know, when I was younger, I was this close to going through the Azhar education. Did you know I'm a hafez?'

I shake my head.

'Esm 'ala mosamma, as they say,' he grins, tapping his first name, 'Hafez', on the golden nameplate on his desk. 'In any case, then life happened. We were fighting these terrorists all the way back then, and I felt like I could do more good in the Armed Forces than as a preacher. Of course, I have the utmost respect for your role and what you do for our religious communities. That's why we got you out of jail'—he pauses to look at me, but seeing no reaction, he carries on—'because of the good we think you can do for these boys. Do you know why you're here, why Nizam was supposed to come here?'

I flinch slightly, preferring to gloss over my own reasons for coming here with Nizam. 'To give a sermon,' I reply.

'Are you okay?'

'Yes.'

'What was that spasm?'

'It's just the air-conditioner. It's hitting me straight in the chest, and I was sweating in the car—'

'Say no more.' *Beep*. 'It's off.'

The Qur'an from the speaker is loud enough to rattle the windows and ripple the surface of the tea in my hand. At least it drowns out the ticking of the unsynchronised clocks.

'A sermon,' I say, picking up the word again.

'Yes, but what about?'

I shrug.

'Are you still shivering because of the cold, or did you just shrug?'

'I don't know, sir,' I say, enunciating every word as if it contains a world of its own.

'Ah,' he says. 'You've got some anger inside you. That's good. You'll need that. I told you, I know you. I knew you were Nizam even before you knew it.'

The rotba leans back in his chair and stares at the ceiling with such intensity that I look up expecting to see cue cards, but there's only the lattice of the suspended ceiling and more ducts.

'All the soldiers from the 6th Mechanised Division didn't show up to roll call one morning,' he says, his gaze fixed on the lattice. 'They were a highly trained group, so this was completely unheard of. The dhabet saff went into their room to check on them, and he found complete silence.

'"They escaped, welad el-sharmoota escaped!" he yelled, if you'll excuse my language. But then he noticed a stain spreading across the linoleum floor from the latrine at the back of the barracks. And he noticed that the beds weren't made. Again, these were well-trained, disciplined men who kept strictly to the smallest minutiae of their daily routines. I mean, look at this place,' he says. 'Wipe your hands on any table or surface. Not one bit of dust.'

The general sighs. 'It was a Friday when those boys' bodies were discovered, so the Qur'an was playing from the loudspeakers, just like it is now.' He takes out a sebha and starts clicking the beads through his fingers as he speaks. 'It's on days like that Friday that I wish I had carried on with my religious upbringing.' He looks at me to see if I'm still paying attention.

'We all have our individual paths,' I say, thinking it's what he expects of me.

He shakes his head. 'La', mish 'asdi. I'd never give up this uniform for yours. What you see is who I am. This isn't a costume, it's a uniform.'

'Sir,' I say, touching my hand to my forehead. 'I'm sorry, but it's not my fault that I'm in this chair right now.'

'That's right,' he says. 'I almost forgot. It's *our* fault that Nizam is gone, is that what you mean to say?'

'No, but you're putting me on an opposing side, drawing these comparisons between us. I'm not just a uniform.'

'And neither am I. But there's an appropriate shell for every animal, right? We carry our own shelters with us, always.

'You know, I was completely against you—or Nizam, or whoever you are—coming over to deliver your message to the soldiers. We have a library here, and I was able to look up some of those texts you cite in your speech. Does it surprise you that we have them here? I'll be honest—it surprised me too. Our collection is completely random, and the language in some of those books can be quite loaded. But I had to ask my superiors back in Masr about a few of the titles on your list. Imagine my surprise to learn you were quoting at length from banned books.'

The empty chair taunts me, and I look at it with disdain. It feels ridiculous to try to draw a line between the saint and myself now. The darkening corner seems to be creeping closer to both the chairs. I'm being made into Nizam just to be insulted, when I've suffered insult enough as myself.

'That's what made me think of my past and how I memorised

the Qur'an to become a hafez,' says the rotba. 'You learnt the texts by heart, didn't you, Nizam? Otherwise, the only explanation is that you managed to get your hands on contraband material inside prison, so that you could transcribe those long passages. One or the other.'

I feel his eyes on me, but I can't answer for Nizam.

'I was hoping for more than a smile and a shrug to that too,' he says.

But what else can I do? All he really wants is someone to listen and nod along.

'Sir, I had a water bottle with me,' I say, steering the conversation in a direction that the general can't control. 'It was about this big. When your soldier pulled me into the door, it fell out of my hands and down the stairwell.'

'What bottle? Whose was it?'

'Mine.'

'Was it important?' Tala'at pulls his eyes away from the lattice of the false ceiling and looks at me across the desk as though we're separated by a sea. He's starting to doubt his eyesight, unsure if what he sees is really there.

I almost shrug, but I don't.

'There's not really much to you, is there? You sit around, shrug, look around, judge other people, but you don't seem to be useful for very much. Why was Nizam bringing that bottle into the building? I'll send the private to retrieve it.'

'No, the bottle was mine,' I say. 'It was mineral water.'

'So, what do you want me to do? You've lost your treasured bottle. Was it from your Chief?'

'No, it was a gift, from me.' With the Nile drying up, bottled water is precious. 'My parents taught me that if I'm taken into someone's hospitality, I should show them some of what I expect they'll give me. And my father told me to treat people of the old guard with the respect that they're due.'

'So, the bottle was from your parents?' Disbelief weighs down the general's eyebrows as he tries to focus. His face tells me that he's incapable of imagining a reality where something unexpected might happen to him.

'No, it was supposed to be a surprise. I was just delivering it.' My voice is shaking, and I swallow back more watery saliva. It tastes of nausea. It's hard to call this feeling fear, but I am afraid.

'Is this some Sufi nonsense? Speak up, ya-bni.' There's that anger he so wilfully commands. If only I could do that. 'I don't get it. Mish fahmak be-gad.' He's not the first person to tell me that. 'I've no patience for your riddles, Nizam. I'm starting to think that you might not be on my side. Do you know what happens if you mess up today?'

'I was in ʾAbu Zaʿbal this morning. I have an idea of what might happen.'

'See?' he says, pointing at me. 'This is why I complained. I didn't want you, or Nizam, or any of your ilk here. You can't handle the pressure. But "these are extraordinary times," and "Nizam is a shield against moral corruption," or so my superiors told me.' He laughs scornfully.

'Come in, ya private. Yes, just put the coffee down. No, leave the sheikh's drink. Did you ask him if he was done? Tfaddal men hena, ya khawal. Yalla, barra! And where's the sheikh's breakfast? It must be cold by now.' He shakes his head as Hamdy leaves, disappointed in the tendency of energy to dissipate in the air as it flows towards thermal equilibrium. 'La hawl w-la qowa ʾilla billah.' A typical response when a Muslim senses that they're losing control: hand that control to a higher power, so they're to blame for the trouble you're in.

'You scare me, you know,' he tells me. 'I persevered with the army route because of the security. And I'm not ashamed to say it. It's a good career path. I have six siblings, and my father died young, which meant that my mother had to work. After the 2011 revolution, everything became more expensive, and your Brotherhood—'

'Sir, I'm not—'

'Don't get defensive. I know, that's what you all say, you're not part of the Brotherhood that brainwashed my older brother into thinking they had a right to rule the country using religion. He was a Sufi, but a Brother too. Do you see? Of course, he would never say he was a Sufi. I've never met a Sufi who did. It's an invention. A lame one. Bed'a.

'We relied on the handouts the bearded Brothers gave us, and I am grateful for that. My brother was one of the Brotherhood's guides into our neighbourhood in Maryoteya. Maryoteya was always part of the city—separate, but still part of it. We lived in a small flat in a small alleyway. I never left the neighbourhood, but I knew the names of other parts of the city from whenever the bus passed through, and the conductor would scream *Share' el-Haram, Midan el-Giza, El-Gam'a, Qasr el-'Ainy, Tahrir, Ramses, Ramses, Ramses* with a twang that didn't belong anywhere, like a true showman. You'd think they'd just invented public transport. And my brother would get on one of those buses every single day, and it would bring him back every day. A magic bus. Magic because one day it took him away and never brought him back. Death is a magic trick. You think *you've* seen behind that curtain?'

I shake my head. It's soothing to hear him talk like this. The words sound familiar, and I start to feel like myself again, or I grow more comfortable with the role I'm expected to play. His story makes me daydream, and I remember Nizam's pilgrims. I think about how everyone in the city has a story, a tragedy, all of which are dire, desperate, urgent and made up. They'll throw balls of fire just to be heard.

'My brother would advise the Brotherhood chapters, the Food Bank and other charities on which families to give food to. He was always generous but strong-willed. Neighbours would try to con him by appealing to his gentle nature to eke out more food, more money. One family applied for funding to build five roofs—you would've thought they lived in a mansion. Just because he had a beard and a soft voice and knew kalam rabbena, doesn't mean he didn't know what the neighbours said or did behind closed doors. You remind me of him, you've got a touch of the gentle about you. He knew how to look into people's souls, and when he died, I had to bear that burden.

'I lost sight of the fact other people existed after his death. I was a champion pentathlete, so I left home to train and compete. I was glad for the chance to go. My mother was no longer the mother I knew. My father was dead, and my sisters became walking ghosts, who believed they had to honour my brother's legacy by wearing the long black veil and shutting themselves off from the world. Our family used to be a beacon of light for the neighbourhood; overnight it became a black hole. My mother worked. She cleaned the stairwells of buildings in Garden City, which is where you live, isn't it?'

I nod and offer him a smile. It's one of understanding, not contentment.

'I'm ashamed to say that I didn't go back home for a few years. When I did, my mother and sisters didn't recognise me and wouldn't let me inside. But for the entire time I was away, I sent my family half my salary. It wasn't much, especially as petrol became more expensive, medicine became a luxury, and a militia roamed the alleyway asking people to give up their belongings for the greater good of the neighbourhood. Had I been there when all of that happened ...' He shakes his head to banish the regret, then continues. 'If my brother's death left the family exposed, my absence left them naked. I ought to have done better by them, but I couldn't bear that load. Maybe I should have. My brother died for what he believed in, but he was robbed of the battle he wanted to fight. His "people"—your "Brothers"—hid weapons on site and betrayed their own members. That's why they were killed.'

I don't even feel angered by his explanation; a rotba will always justify that massacre. The Brotherhood were cruel, clumsy rulers, who tried to match the Armed Forces in ruthlessness to prove themselves worthy of power. But in what world could their stupidity and treachery warrant mass murder in cold blood?

'It wasn't what the rumours in the city purport, you know, all that talk about an entirely peaceful demonstration, though *my* brother was peaceful. 'Abdul Rahman ... ah ... ya 'Abdu, they turned you into a "was"! In my mind, whenever I think about him, he's still alive, and then when I remember what happened to him, I have to relive the pain all over again.'

I wonder if he knows I can see right through his spin. I mourn his brother, as I mourn all those who died before me, but someone fired that bullet, and someone gave them a gun and the right to shoot. He may be content to ignore who the guilty party was, but I'm not.

'I feel the pain that the families of our fallen soldiers are going through now, but at least they'll get to bury their dead. My mother, who couldn't write, refused to put her fingerprint on 'Abdu's death certificate. She said she would disown me if I signed it myself. All I wanted was to bury him. Maybe if I'd been given that chance, my life would have been different. As it was, the army was a great place to forget about the city. And it was tough, as it should be, but I rose to the occasion, which is what I expect of my troops. Get that in the sermon, will you?'

I think—though I have no reason to, besides what past experience has taught me—that this rotba knows exactly what was in my bottle and what my plan was. Watching his lips mouth reassurances about his own perseverance and survival, I try to reconstruct what the private whispered to him before I was told to play the saint. The rotba is keeping his last card close to his chest, and I sense that he's holding a trump.

'I did reconnect with my family eventually. I managed to marry off my sisters, so they're someone else's problem now. I never married, which hasn't done my career any favours. But these soldiers are like my children. I survived the loss of my brother, and now I have to survive the loss of my boys.'

His story is nothing more than a shield. He carries it on his back wherever he goes, a snail shell that spirals in a pattern to infinity and contains endless knowledge of how the country functions—all its ranks, factions and movements that seem to speak to a mystical internal mechanism, a natural order of things. And that's where he sees Nizam fitting—the saint is a convenient point of arrival in this order, someone who summons the faith of the people, someone who gets them to believe in the possibility of life after death, so they can chalk up life's misery to a divine test, someone to get the faithful to believe in the power of forgiveness and to tell the living, *justice exists only with the Creator, so make your peace with your brothers in the present, for these are the people who will be walking with you to death's gate*. Nizam has run away with this rotba's peace, and I've been tasked with bringing it back—to him and to the families of the dead platoon of soldiers—in my sermon.

'My mother and sisters got a dog after I left. It barked so much when I returned home that they were terrified to open the door. When I saw that they didn't recognise me, I showed them my ID. My youngest sister was too small when I left to remember me, so she believed it was me, but none of the others did. A few photos I had kept in my wallet finally convinced them. One of my mother that I had taken, and my father's photo—someone else took that. So many other memories won't ever be retrieved. I'm now older than my brother ever was, and though he's still my older brother, his voice doesn't grow old in my head—it just echoes from further away. I lose what he says, the sounds overlap, and I can't keep up.'

But I didn't come here to make peace. When I told Nizam my plan yesterday, he made it clear that our struggles are not the same, that whatever happened, dying in this barracks wasn't part of his plan. Now, he is gone. I hope he found a way out.

'With every strength comes weakness. My strengths are my brother's memory and my boys, and my weakness is my dependency on you.'

I dream of a day when comfort comes not from the memory of those who passed before me, but from the presence of those who surround me.

'My brother was a hafez of names, I'm a hafez of texts. But knowing the ninety-nine names of the Almighty didn't help him save his comrades, and memorising the holy book didn't mean I could rebuild all the memories I lost with my family.'

I want to tell the rotba that I too have gone down that path. I've looked for answers in the past to justify my life in the here and now, but all it brought me was more reason to try to change the future that people like him are leading us towards. I would say this, but the rotba doesn't need me to speak; he just needs an audience to clap to his beat.

'It took a lot of work to reconnect with my family, hours spent over tea and food, as we tried to remember what it was like to share a home together. They accumulated a lot of clutter in that tiny flat. Seeing their life together there, I lost even more of my childhood—and of my brother.' He turns his gaze from the ceiling to look me square in the face. 'So, reading the text of the sermon that was sent ahead, I wasn't impressed by Nizam's ability to recollect all those banned texts. I said to my superior, "Just because they ring true to this man, doesn't mean they'll resonate with these boys." They're my boys and I know them. I know where they came from. I teach them a unified discipline, and that carries them through.'

I look into my tea glass and think of Teita reading my fortune. She would turn my finished coffee cup upside down on its saucer, wait a few minutes, then turn it back over, and read.

'If we can't rely on our memories, then we must rely on our habits. My brother died, and everything became worse. That's all the boys out there can depend on. Each other. And who do you rely on? That godly man? Do you even know him? If your business is the business of the soul, then wouldn't he hide his cards from you? What are you hiding from him? And where's he hiding himself?' He pauses and sniffs the air. 'Do you smell that? There's a stench that wafts in every time the door to the stairwell opens.'

Teita saw me working at a charity, one of the few that remain in the country that haven't been absorbed by the Sufi institute, in something to do with human rights.

'You'll help prisoners,' she said, nodding at the dregs.

According to Teita, time would lead me to realise and accept who I truly am. I'd pick up an instrument for a while, thinking that I needed to mould myself into a new form to become who I'm supposed to be. I'd commit to playing the 'oud in Beit el-Harawy, a medieval Islamic house of music, built out of stone, with mashrabeyas softening the light that enters each room so I wouldn't have to squint into the sun anymore. Calloused hands would guide mine along the curved neck of the instrument, its taut strings holding the promise of everything I want to say but have no words for, until finally I would realise that all I needed to do to meet the future was shift my focus.

'You're a quiet one, aren't you?' says the general. 'Can't trust the children of rich people. Can't trust the children of foreigners, either. I know your parents live abroad. It breaks my heart when the country's people turn their back on her. You have to accept her in all her ugliness. Can't pick and choose what you want from your homeland.'

But there's his mistake: if it were my homeland, I wouldn't have come here to try and escape it. If it were home, I would recognise the people around me.

'You don't know what goes into a hard day's work,' he continues. 'Your habits have nothing to do with survival.'

His attempts to shame me won't work. I never believed I could survive in the first place, and I'm not responsible for the decisions of my parents, just as they aren't responsible for mine. I carry them with me, and Teita is always by my side, but my actions are mine alone. And whether or not I survive, there's no shame in it.

'How did your mother survive?' I ask him.

He smiles at the question. 'My mother refused to move out of her flat to come and live with me, choosing instead to stay among "her people". The fetewat who were blackmailing the neighbourhood's residents were arrested and executed when the Field Marshal brought the country back under proper control in 2013. They were caught dealing in black-market currencies. One of them managed to escape death, but he had to leave the country, so he's out of our hands.

'And that's what disappoints me most about the past. Finally seeing the country liberated and my family coming together again, I looked back at all those other revolutions, at the people who tried to corrupt our Armed Forces with their silly rebellions, and I saw how it all fits together to form one picture. The terrorists in the Sinai, where are they now? We're working with them. How would the army have done that without the foresight of people like me, who realise that you can't remake the past but can only create the future? And we're doing just that. I can't tell how the deaths of these boys will fit into the plan, but I'm embracing them. They're my brothers, they're my children, and they're martyrs. Make sure you emphasise that.'

A plan is forming in my head. It's not well thought out, but I know how it ends.

'Perhaps I shouldn't be telling you all this, but rest assured, we'll know where to find you if you try to run away. Sheikh Nizam himself can't hide in this country. Even the desert will betray you. If I merely whisper to it, the sand will part to form a path pointing to you. Not even your Sufi mysticism can do that.

'You know, when my brother died, my mother and sisters started beating pots and pans with sticks, causing an incessant clamour. My youngest sister was ecstatic that the grown-ups were joining her game to fill the airwaves with noise, but I had to draw the line when she tried to wail in imitation of my mother. Women shouldn't scream like that over the dead. Each scream is a tear in the sail of the boat carrying you from one bank of the Nile to the other. Better to light some incense and wait for it to burn out. Let some smoke into your lungs, hold it, and release, and with it go all the spirits, demons, souls and what have you. But the wailing and the beating and the noise lasted for three days ...' He sighs. 'You know who suffered the most?'

I shake my head, and he doesn't reprimand me for not using my voice.

'It was the birds. On the fourth day after 'Abdu's death, I woke up and saw little pellets scattered all over the neighbourhood. They looked like tiny pieces of dog shit, and I wondered what kind of animal could have disgraced our alleyway to such an extent overnight. It wasn't natural. I soon found out that our neighbour, a tanner who kept large vats of chemicals on his rooftop, had been throwing down these strange lumps after digging them out of the tubs. When I looked more closely at them, I noticed the sharp edge of a beak, a wing, each dyed a different colour depending on which container it had fallen into. The pellets grew clearer, and it felt like I was looking at the whole expanse of the country, at the disease spreading across it that led to the death of my brother, which didn't even leave the birds untouched. Of course, it was the banging that did them in. Each clang threw them into a panicked frenzy until they started dropping from the sky. That was the first time I felt sorry for my brother's death.

'Placing a finger on some of the birds, you could still feel a heartbeat, so the task of finishing them off became the priority. Not even the tanner would do it. He'd had a hard enough time fishing these ones out and said it would probably be years before he stopped finding others. So, I brought out the tub that we washed our clothes in and the one that we used to let them soak. I placed each bird in the first tub and smashed it with a rock, before throwing it in the other. Some were already dead when the tanner found them. I buried all of them, of course. Crows were gathering and started picking at them. Even some of the chickens and ducks our neighbours were rearing—remember, meat was becoming very expensive, people had to make do—started approaching the tub. My mother said animals won't eat meat if blood has rotten inside, but I knew animals can't tell the difference.

'I didn't bury them low enough, which meant my mother had to dig them back up when they started to rot and the house smelt of death, again. I had already left and couldn't do it. When she finally placed me after I came back, it was the first thing she told me about. She showed me where she had exhumed them and where they found their final resting place. Since she never signed the document to retrieve my brother's body, that's where I've always imagined him resting, with the birds.'

*

As I leave the rotba's office, I take one last look around, eyeing the empty corner, which is now completely immersed in shadow. Before he left to greet the families, I asked the major general if I could walk to the barracks where the men died. The official story is that they were killed in an ambush by Bedouin religious fanatics who had been chipping away at the base—a constant threat that the army has been trying, and failing, to quash.

The secretary rips off a piece of meat from a slice in his pocket, and a cat runs in through the door.

'Don't tell the general,' he says as the cat feeds greedily out of his hand.

'I won't,' I assure him. 'Is there any way to get an outside line?'

'Is it'—he pauses and holds my gaze to make sure I grasp what he's saying—'a *private* phone call?'

I nod.

'There's only one private line here.' He points back through the double doors. 'His mobile phone. And it's password protected.'

Hamdy pulls up a chair and places it in front of the cold plate of eggs and beans. 'Please, Sheikh. Sit down and eat.'

I'm surprised to find myself feeling hungry. A tanginess hits my tongue as I take a bite, and I ask the private if he squeezed a bit of lemon onto the beans.

'It's the only way to make it,' he replies. 'It brings out the rest of the flavour. The sharpness of the lemon highlights the earthy, muddy taste of the beans.' He rubs his thumb and forefinger together as if taste were a tangible thing. 'Sitto used to make it like this.'

'My teita made it the same way.' The bread is still warm, and I use my hands to fill it with eggs and beans. I lick my fingers, and the private places a napkin under a glass of water on the table.

'I'm sorry if I gave you a look earlier on,' he says. 'I just'—he takes out another peach-coloured slice of meat and bites into it—'I just wanted to be out there today, to stand with the families of the recently departed.'

'I understand,' I say, though I'm not sure I do. 'The general wouldn't tell me what happened to them,' I add, as I lift my messy sandwich to my lips, hoping he'll take the hint and feed me some answers.

'They died,' he says simply. It's what he's been told to say.

'Nobody drops dead on their own.'

'Some people do.'

An image flashes in my mind of Teita lying on the ceramic floor of her bathroom with a crown of eucalyptus around her head. The smell of dirt mixes with the taste of beans.

'But not here,' I say.

'No,' Hamdy concedes. 'Not here, I guess.' I feel my heart softening, and I almost smile at the joy of finding a comrade. It's only when I remember the reason why Teita died alone, without the rest of her family by her side, that my feeling of affinity dissolves. This private has an inkling that he shouldn't be standing by his rotba, but he can't afford to listen to that voice. Imagine if I told him now that *his* comrades died solely for the sake of the Armed Forces' desire for power. What would he have left? Just the luncheon meat in his pockets.

'If you help me understand,' I say gently, 'I'll be able to stand with the families outside as they need me to.' The families don't need me there giving someone else's sermon; they need their boys to be alive. 'For too long we've accepted that our people should die so that others may live, as if that were a price the dead pay willingly.'

'We're soldiers,' says Hamdy. If not for how obtuse it sounds, I would say that even soldiers aren't supposed to die.

'So, what did they die for?' I ask.

'Whatever is worth dying for.'

'Fighting terrorists?' I take a bite of my sandwich as he takes out his phone and starts to scroll.

'No terrorists,' he says. 'No.'

I wonder what this private would do if he knew better. Would he still salute the flag every morning? Would he carry the rotba's tea to him every hour? Would he want the injustice to end? Would he accept that he could be the start of a change? Would he burn himself alive, shoot his master dead?

'Foreign agents?' I ask, trying not to smile. The excuse is a gift to the Armed Forces that keeps on giving. Anyone who can string together a few words in a foreign language is a foreign agent. With Mama and Baba living abroad, I'm a foreign agent, whether I know it or not.

He doesn't respond to this, and I realise that his silence is deliberate but not malicious. There is nothing he can tell me that will help.

'They killed themselves,' he says finally, still scrolling on his phone. 'It's not the first time it's happened here.' He picks up the cat and puts it on the table. It keeps its back arched for a moment, then stretches on the private's arm as he carries on swiping his screen.

'Why?' I ask. The last bite of my sandwich is frozen in my hand.

'Who knows why people kill themselves? Bad mental health. This place is tough on people.'

The bread crumbles in my fingers and I feel like throwing up all the contents of my stomach.

'Why are the families of the dead being brought over?' I manage to say, swallowing back the sour taste of bile.

'The general is worried about retaliation from the people of the country,' he mumbles, barely moving his lips. 'So, it's easier to bring them along today, get them to sign the death certificates and accept the inevitable.'

'You're going to release the bodies to the families?' I'm unable to hold back the surprise in my voice.

Hamdy shakes his head, rubbing his forehead with his palm. The cat gets up and moves over his tea glass, shedding a few hairs in the liquid. He pushes it off the desk, and it lands silently on the ground and saunters away.

'No,' he adds, in case I didn't understand. 'Their bodies are staying here, on this land. The families are coming here to see you—Nizam. They've come here to find peace.'

*

I regret not choosing my shoes. The desert sand seeps into my sandals and between my toes, scalding my skin.

I had no reason to worry about pretending to be Nizam. Everyone avoids looking at me, to the extent that it's disconcerting.

Walking by my side, General Tala'at is a head shorter than me. A line of officers trails us solemnly, providing a buffer between me and the families, as the rotba insisted. Tala'at walks with a limp, the result of an injury in an assassination attempt on the president a few years ago. He was travelling with the Field Marshal when someone wearing a niqab fired at their car, and his leg was broken in the crash.

'We're not weak,' the rotba declares, nodding at the rows of troops, daring them to have the courage to meet his eyes. Most stare into the middle distance, looking out towards the desert. They stand in fear, and while their minds escape to the open sands, they would never think to run there. There's no surviving the desert. No way out for them, or for me.

'You're silent, ya Sheikh Nizam,' says the rotba, trying to break me out of my reverie. It takes me a moment to realise he's talking to me. His sing-song voice sounds different from how he spoke in the office. Maybe he's also playing pretend in front of his people. He has to sell my ability to heal their loss today, but I didn't come here to heal anyone.

'Not much to say,' I respond.

The general holds on to my wrist, and I tug away for a second before realising that he needs my help. I grasp his hand and his fingers wrap around mine. I'm not going anywhere he doesn't want me to go. Something in me stirs, revulsion at his grip, his sweaty palm, but I can't pull my hand away.

Every soldier has a different face. One looks straight down at the ground, afraid of catching anyone's eyes; one looks ready to tear out someone's eyes; one looks ready to look ready; one is nothing but the upturned corner of his shirt collar, which the rotba adjusts, smiling, inspiring simultaneous fear and joy in the private; one looks like he should be a school teacher; one has the square jaw of a believer; one has no chin; one is sweating, even standing still; one looks like Musa, who is imagining my smouldering corpse and waiting to hear news of today. The army produces a population, not just one nameless, faceless golem. One of the soldiers recognises me but keeps his head from turning, his eyes straining in their sockets. My heart is beating in my throat. There is no other sound, except for the Qur'an blaring over the loudspeakers. I recognise him too, a swimmer who stopped training with the team a few years ago. He has never seen me except in a speedo and swim cap, so hopefully, he'll have his doubts.

'Takbeer!' yells an officer behind us.

'Allahu akbar!' the soldiers boom like a rushing wave.

'Takbeer!'

'Allahu akbar!' I yell with them, and I'm surprised to hear the meekness in my voice disappear. Something different rises with the chorus, a voice with an edge.

'Takbeer!'

'Allahu akbar!' The voices of mothers, fathers, daughters, sons, grandmothers and grandfathers ring out across the sand. A funeral procession for martyrs, thrown by their killers.

My feet stop moving. The rotba tries to pull me forward, but they won't budge. There's a weight around my ankles, and even the sand scalding my feet can't motivate me to lift them.

I don't feel like myself. I envy Tala'at's tale about his personal history, his knowledge that whatever history he dictates is the truth. But I know my truth. Celebrating the dead doesn't wipe the blood from his hands. He might write the history books, but I still have the chance to add a footnote.

They toss the nation's loose change into the Third Army, the people most wouldn't help up if they were sprawled on a pavement cooking in the midday sun. If an attack occurs from the Sinai's eastern border, all that these men are expected to do is stall the enemy, cannon fodder to be crushed below different boots carrying different faces on their way to the real seat of power in the city where the Field Marshal makes his bed.

Kamal—that's the name of the soldier who recognised me. He'll disbelieve his own eyes to avoid breaking rank.

The rotba is speaking, but I'm elsewhere. He squeezes my hand to get my attention. Clearing his throat, he says, 'Let's go pray for the dead.'

A field of light separates the grid of men from the barracks of the 6th Mechanised Division. The building stretches out like a limb discarded in the endless expanse of the desert. In the distance, a brick wall. Behind the wall, the horizon is hiding, and so is the water. If I can reach the wall, I'll see it. The Red Sea. A dip in the sea would make the sun more tolerable. I might even feel like myself again.

I'm to read the sermon from a script marred with black lines that the rotba scrawled across entire passages. The paper sags from the weight of the ink. I looked over it after I finished eating, trying to distract myself and eliminate any possibility of interaction with the families of the dead soldiers. The speech has no substance, just fluff.

As we leave the columns and walk along the sand, a veil falls away, as though the suf has been pulled down from my eyes. The rotba strains to walk; his limp isn't helping him, other than to consolidate his reputation. He leans on my hand with every step. A wind rises, and my footsteps blur in the sand.

I ate the breakfast I was given slowly because my jaw was sore from being clenched through the rotba's story. He talked of his past as though it were a distant bygone era that only he had lived, rather than a history that overlapped with Teita's and with my parents', one that's coloured mine. He's given me more memories, images that pre-date my existence. I came to lay a burden down, not to listen to him speak. How could he draw out his life in abstract lines and with so few details, as if his mind were completely familiar, but I still feel like I don't possess my own? Why does he have the winning narrative? Why is mine unconvincing to my own ears? Maybe if I speak it aloud, it'll make sense, like the Qur'an being played from the speakers—abstract, ancient, perfect, dictated to an illiterate man.

The sermon is folded in my trouser pocket. Nizam's cigarette, a straight-edged twig, is tucked close to my heart. Everything else of mine is in the Lada. My shirt is soaked through and is sticking to me like a second skin. I want to peel it off and let my body breathe again. This heat is unbearable. I want to feel new. I should've done my wudoo' with Nizam this morning. I'm tired and lost.

We're on the edges of the Qur'an's reach, standing by the shoreline where the words foam and fade. We stop a few metres from the barracks where the dead soldiers slept. It's a long corridor leading from one patch of sand to another, enclosed in a single space.

The shrill sound of cheap speakers is dulled by the distance and swallowed by the surrounding desert, leaving me with barely a drop of the Qur'an's honeyed comfort to savour.

I'll hold my book with my right hand on Judgement Day. General Tala'at avoided the question of death and distracted me with his life story. If he can imagine life, why can't he picture death? In describing the scene in these barracks, he mentioned a stain on the floor that I assumed was blood, but then why didn't he say so?

Dying leads to death, but nothing is dead. Memories persist, and only when they fade can anything die. Blood is no indication of life, just a stain on it. At least, according to the Sufi way.

Time to raise the dead and let them testify against their murderers.

I grip the rotba's hand more tightly now. His has gone limp in mine.

'If I had to deal with this life on a daily basis, I don't know what I'd do,' I find myself saying. I want to say something sincere with so many people standing at my back, looking to me for words of conviction, for a reason why their boys haven't risen today from their cots, ready to make their beds and step out into the sun to serve their masters. The real question is by what miracle the rotba has managed to delude everyone around him into thinking that he cares if his soldiers live when there are so many more people in this country willing to die, if only to believe for a moment that they have something to die for.

You're projecting, I tell myself.

'I'm not like these people,' I say aloud.

'Yes, that's why you're in a different uniform,' the general answers. 'Because you're a coward. If you're going to choose a side, at least be on the side that can grab power with both hands, not just wax lyrical about its dangers and responsibilities.'

'So you're content to have blood on your hands?'

'It all gets washed away,' he says, moving his free hand through the air as if it were riding the wind.

'Washed away with what? The Nile's dry, and running water's expensive.'

'And that's the army's fault? What about your cars, all the flights and trains that people take every day? Do you talk about that?' He pushes his hand—the one with mine in it—into my chest. 'I've been saying it since 2012: *we need to cut back, the country will have to tighten its belt.* This sand is burning between your toes because your baba bought two cars when he didn't need them. Because you took a leisurely drive when you could've walked. You want to hear the problems I have to deal with? Go to hell, ya sheikh. But don't think you're better than I am. This is my lot in life. If you can't see me in my struggles as I see you sweating through your clothes, then maybe you've not found your place yet. Or maybe your place was back in prison.'

I release his hand, and his skin tugs mine before I can pull free.

There used to be a plaque with the Field Marshal's name next to the doorway of the barracks. The sunburnt face of the wall betrays the tan-line from where it hung until the building was marked by shame. I try to open the door, but it's locked.

'We're not going in, ya Nizam,' the rotba calls from behind me, pronouncing the name to remind me of my duty here, the performance keeping me out of prison. But this is his precise failure: he thinks I came to his grounds expecting to live till tomorrow. With the way everything has gone, I just want to do one thing to salvage this mess. One thing that would make these deaths less meaningless.

Next to the barracks door is a folding table that looks as though it will rock at the slightest provocation. On top, cold plastic bottles stand to attention, perspiring in the sun. I raise one side of the table and tip the bottles onto the ground, where grains of sand rush to cling to their wet surface. The table is light, and dust is thrown everywhere as I lift it.

'What are you doing?' the rotba asks.

I push the table up against the wall by a high window and jump on top. Its feet sink into the sand as I look through the glass.

'Don't you think what you're doing is indecent?' he calls. 'There's nothing in there. You'll just hurt yourself up on that table.' He wobbles his hands from side to side in a gesture that means, *shaky*.

'This is nothing but a way for you to save face,' I say, too quietly for him to hear me.

The windowpane is dusty. Behind the blur, I make out a row of beds that have been stripped of their mattresses, leaving only the metal frames holding the weight of the air. Empty lockers have been left open as if the place was vacated in a rush. On the other side of the room, a broken window above a bed has been diligently taped over, but for one point where sunlight shines in.

'What, are you going to jump through the window?'

'This one's closed, but there's one on the other side—right there—that's open. Just have to tear away the tape.'

'There's an investigation going on, people died in there, you can't be wandering in—'

I carry the table to the other side as more people run over to join us.

'What are you hoping to accomplish?'

'I just want to see what's inside.'

The tape over the window is firmly affixed in heavy layers. The table digs its heels into the sand as I lean back with all my body weight to pull it off. The tearing screech is drowned out by the sound of men yelling, burying the Qur'an too under their cacophony. As the tape comes away, silence pours out from the window, and I haul myself up to climb inside. It's a tricky business; the passage is narrow, and the window frame digs into my shoulders as I try to shimmy in. Thankfully, there's no glass. With my head inside, I reach for a metal pipe running across the ceiling of the barracks, hold on, and tug. It supports my weight, and I drag the rest of my body through, flutter-kicking the air outside as the metal frame digs into my thighs.

I lower myself down carefully until my feet touch the bare bedstead. My toes can feel the metal, and I realise I lost my sandals in the struggle with the window frame. There is something glittering below the layer of dust on the ground. Broken glass. Barefoot, I tightrope-walk along the bed's outer beam, the cool metal a balm for my scorched soles, until I reach solid ground, away from the remnants of the shattered windowpane. As I glance up to look at the officers gathering at the opposite window near the door, I notice several dents in the wall directly across from me.

I can hear the rotba's muffled speech outside telling someone to bring the key and open the door. 'He's lost his mind.' The walls absorb the sounds, and even the Qur'an quiets to a whisper.

'Let's not judge him too harshly. Just a sensitive soul,' he says, trying to placate the families and the rest of the soldiers.

If they were angry when their sons were killed at the waste of life, then this botched funeral will get their blood boiling—a waste of death.

My clothes have picked up dust from the window frame. I brush off my torso and a cloud rises, and I catch the citrussy scent of bleach on the air. An effort has been made to clean this place up.

'I'll drain his soul from his body when he gets out,' the rotba calls, suddenly changing his tone. I guess selling me as a sensitive soul didn't work on the people out there, so he's reverting to his comfort zone: brutality. 'Haven't these boys gone through enough, ya Nizam? I'm telling you, this isn't right.'

Finding myself alone, away from all those eyes, I take a deep breath but immediately start to cough. The air is heavy with a tasteless smell. I cough it out, but that only seems to draw more in. Whatever it is that's floating around, it's suffocating me.

'Shallow breaths,' I say to myself, and I'm shocked to hear my own voice echoing back to me, not Nizam's. I'm panting.

'What's he saying?'

'I can't hear.'

'Nizam!' There's a steady banging on the door with what sounds like an open palm.

I take off my shirt and cover my face with it. It blocks the dust, but that other smell finds its way through. Sweat covers my skin like dew drops.

From inside, the room looks much smaller than I expected. How did they fit eighty people in here? There aren't enough beds, and the army doesn't allow two people to double up in one. A few long strides carry me across the full length of the room, leaving my footsteps visible in my wake. My eyes follow their path and finish at my feet. They're filthy. I wiggle my toes, shaking sand grains from my skin. Underneath the thick dust are trails of black boot marks where heels scraped across the floor, traces of movement like whispers. A dried puddle still stains the linoleum near the back where the lockers are. I step around it and look into the latrine. Dark. A chill emanates from the room. The air around the doorway ripples in waves as I enter. Water drips onto the tiled floor, where scattered papers have turned to soggy mush. I try to keep my footing, wading slowly through freezing water on the ground. My scalded feet are soothed, but along with the comfort a shiver prickles up my back, making me flinch.

I bump against a table, and on top of it something rattles. I reach out and smash my hand against something rigid.

Teita's face with the eucalyptus crown flashes before my eyes again. I look up and breathe in. There's a bare bulb hanging from the ceiling. On the wall by the door, I flick the light switch.

*

'It's a tad cold out here,' Teita muttered to herself, wrapping her black-and-gold blanket scarf tightly around her shoulders. Behind wire-framed glasses, her swollen eyes betrayed the fatigue of someone just waking up, though she had been up since the dawn 'adhan had interrupted her night's sleep of all of ten minutes a few hours ago.

Galal, the young man who worked at the nearby cafeteria, walked up to her with a tray bearing an assortment of black tea, Nescafé, yoghurts and small plastic cups filled with chopped fruit. The hood of his sweatshirt was up.

'Ya 'asfoor, is it cold for August, or is it just me?' She always called Galal a sparrow because he whistled everywhere he went. The nickname seemed to encourage him, and he came up with more elaborate tunes. Sometimes he'd sing a few words of halting speech, like plodding footsteps.

'You haven't slept all night, you have no energy. I think these shivers are your body's response to the torture you're putting it through.'

'Well, best give me some tea with a bit of sugar then.'

'Won't make up for the lack of sleep, ya doktora.' Clicking his tongue, Galal took a spoon and stirred it into a cup with two quick strokes. By the time Teita reached out to take it, the white of the sugar had disappeared, and the loose tea leaves had started to settle. She felt the heat of the polystyrene against her palm and thought of the slow mornings she used to spend in her kitchen with her husband and their daughter, Hanan, who would insist on holding her tea glass in her palm like the adults, even when it had a handle.

'You need to go home.'

Galal's voice pulled her back into the present. 'Go rest,' he was saying, 'instead of spending your nights camped out here on the streets.'

'But if I leave—'

'Then the rest of us will be here to hold the square,' he said firmly.

Teita reached into her lab coat and pulled out a few bundled notes, but Galal was already walking away, dragging his flip-flops along the pavement and warbling words of wisdom.

'Doktor el-nawm 'al-li, ma tensa-sh el-din. Da el-mahlool elli yenaymak. W-la hatta el-helm yesahheek.'

She looked down and saw he had left a yoghurt for her with a plastic spoon.

''Illa 'iza 'alab kaboos.'

She sighed, frustrated. Not with Galal, but with her own inability even to recognise her body's hunger.

Peeling the plastic off with her fingertips, Teita dug the spoon into the shiny bed of white and parted her lips, only to realise how much her jaw ached from grinding her teeth all night long as she rushed around the field hospital. Her phone beeped a few different tones. She put the yoghurt down on the pavement next to her tea glass and got up to retrieve her phone from her jeans. Swiping away the low battery alert, she saw a message from Hanan: *Where are you?*

Teita looked around. Two young men with blue surgical gloves were collecting rubbish from the field hospital tents in plastic bags, which they were piling up in a corner near the Tayaran Street entrance. The tents were open, the canvas stained from having weathered the city's grime for so many weeks. Inside, bodies upon bodies were lying on jute rugs, mattresses and cushions, so as not to give the Field Marshal a chance to pull them off the streets to clear the way.

There was an unspoken no-smoking rule inside the field hospital, though not everybody respected it. She could see a moustached man sitting at the entrance with a cigarette and a vacant look, similarly scanning his environment, wondering if this was what hope looked like: to see people fighting for a nation that was quickly slipping through their fingers.

'He's reaffirming his faith,' Teita whispered to herself. 'That all of this will not be for nothing.'

She looked back at her phone and pressed the home button. The screen went black.

'Galal,' she called across the street.

'Go home, ya doktora. Orders.'

'Charge my phone so I can reply to my daughter, then I'll leave, I promise.'

He shook his head. 'There's been no electricity this morning. We're having to use the gas stove for drinks.'

She stood up to look for a socket in the mosque next door, but before she could go inside, something caught her eye. A head had risen above the parapets of the Ministry of Defence, just opposite the field hospital. The building's long rectangular facade had reflective glass windows ensuring no one could look inside. Teita saw in the ministry's face the face of every government official, state security officer, ranked army officer, shades-wearing general and—

'There!' she yelped, surprising herself by the high pitch of her voice, her finger pointing accusingly at the rooftop. Was it just nerves or tiredness sketching her surroundings with sharper lines, giving them an edge they didn't have the day before? Were those concrete blocks in front of the ministry new? She was certain those sandbags stacked on the roof weren't there yesterday, sprinkled like nests to shelter the crow who was rearing his head again.

'He has a rifle,' she stammered, choking on her words.

Running inside the open doors of the mosque, Teita noticed the fans that spun lazily twenty-four seven to keep out the smell of wet dog were standing still. Even the usual hum from the speakers had gone out.

'Hana-an,' she called. 'Hana-an, it's happening!'

The last time the scene in Masjid Rabʿa el-ʿAdaweya was this still was a few weeks ago, when the military 'dispersed' the protest outside the Republican Guard, killing fifty people in the process. Motorcycles had driven through to the Rabʻa field hospital, the only sanctuary left for the wounded and hopeful, those loyal to the Brotherhood leader, and those who didn't want the country to fall back into the Armed Forces' hands.

Pulling the charging cable from her pocket, she plugged it into the nearest socket and waited for her phone to react. Nothing. The screen was dark and dumb to her desperation.

There it was. The rapid clanging of pipes on burnt cars, trash barrels, people yelling—*Hold your ground! El-thawra mosta-merra! La ʾilah ʾillallah! La ʾilah*—calling people to—

bang

b-bang

*

The switch produces an empty *cluck*, nothing else.

I take out my lighter and *click-click* it, and the darkness rolls away.

There are corpses in white on the table in front of me. Around me, more trolleys, each carrying two or three mounds of wrapped shrouds like swaddling clothes, as if the bodies inside have reverted to infancy, liable to move an errant limb and hurt themselves or others. Below the white shrouds are blocks of ice, emanating waves of cold that churn my stomach.

Drip-drip.

My flame doesn't brighten the whole latrine. With every movement, breeze or breath, shadows flicker around me. I don't need to see the room's edges to know what lives here.

Names are scrawled across their chests in frantic red lettering, with the country's tricolour drawn on top. A dab of yellowing gold saves a space for the nesr to make its nest in the centre of the flag, which is positioned right where a heart should be beating.

Besides the *drip-drip*, it is silent here.

There are extra white cloths hanging over the cubicle separators, waiting for their turn to be used. Had today gone according to plan, they'd have had no use for a sheet like that for me. *I should have been dust by now.* I wasn't supposed to survive this long, and I start to wonder if I might in fact be dead. Maybe the door to the afterlife is just a passage into nothingness. *But this isn't nothingness*, I remind myself, trying to count the number of bodies I can see, before giving up at twelve. The sting of witnessing this won't be lessened by putting a number on it.

My heart is pounding, and I can hear the rush of my blood like the sound of waves underwater. I wish I hadn't climbed through that window, but it was my only chance to see what they wanted to keep hidden from me. Now that I know, I wish I could go back to standing outside in the scorching desert heat, with only my imagination to suggest what might be inside these walls. *I don't know what to do with this.*

More bleach, and slicing through it, that smell.

As I step forward, the splash of my feet in the puddle winds back the clock. The sound of oars pulling the ferry across the Nile accompanies me as I slosh through the water. Moving deeper into death's hiding place, I find myself back on the river, looking at the lights of the cordon on Qasr el-Nil Bridge, waiting for the slightest sound to betray me, hoping to survive. I place a hand on my heart, trying to remind myself that I am— *against all odds*—alive. I'm just waiting for my boat to hit the concrete pier to signal that I've finally crossed over, so life can move on.

My next step sends relief to my burnt toes and a shudder through my spine. My knees buckle, and I have to grab the trolley next to me to steady myself. I place my hand on one of the shrouds and am surprised by the mossy coolness of its cross-hatched surface. Pressing down gently, I feel the softness of the body beneath.

Ahmad el-Latif.

When I pull up the veil of suf draped lightly over the soldier's face, the form I find underneath doesn't look human. Bloated flesh with stretched features, turned blue and purple, lips split and bloody from where skin has been torn apart. I run my fingers across a light moustache, and the bristles tickle me. Relative to his head, the rest of the man's body seems slight, like a bird.

The front door of the barracks seems to be giving in under the constant battering.

I close the door to the latrine, and the noise from outside almost ceases, leaving only a low whine as if the sounds are coming from my own head.

Mohamed el-Farid has a white neck that is the same colour

as his wrap. His head is a bruise. A paper inside a plastic sleeve lists his occupation at the time of conscription: filmmaker. The accompanying passport photograph bears no resemblance to the mass of flesh in front of me.

Gamal el-Sa'ad, doctor, has no colour at all in his torso. His transparent skin is streaked with post-mortem dissection cuts, his head inflated like a balloon.

Each folder is accompanied by a death certificate, the originals waiting to be signed by the families. *A proper burial has been conducted on the barracks' grounds of the remains of the faithfully departed, who would not have wanted his body to be left uninterred for longer than a day after his death, as per Islamic law.* The cause of death is written in small, hurried cursive. *Asphyxiation*. No details spared, no spare details.

Shams el-Dajani, a café owner. His face is bloated like the rest, a shapeless death-mask.

Naseem el-Youssef, vegetable seller.

Hussein el-Seif has a white patch of hair speckled red near his forehead that seems to have been singed down to the scalp. He worked as an engineer for an oil company.

There is someone squatting on the ground.

It's Nizam. His body is curled up, his left hand holding the hem of his gallabeya, his right keeping count on the joints of his fingers of the noiseless prayers on his moving lips.

I jump at the sight of him and bump into one of the trolleys. It sends ripples through the water on the ground, the splashes echoing off the tiled walls. Nizam sees me now, but his head remains cradled in his knees, as if he can't turn it to look at me.

In the pool yesterday morning, I remember thinking, *I can't go on, I must go on.*

I speak, but my voice is muffled by the shirt I'm using to block out that smell. I uncover my face and ask him again, 'You escaped?'

He nods. 'I'm sorry,' he says in a low voice. 'I just didn't want to end up in a place like this, wrapped in one of their shrouds.'

He sighs. 'And that's what my end will be like if I go back to prison.'

'You left me,' I say, though I don't mean for it to sound like an accusation. Looking around, I can't blame him for doing whatever he could to survive.

'I did.'

'How did you do it?'

'Does it matter?' he asks, dejectedly. 'They've found me now.' He buries his face in his hands and starts to tremble. I can't tell if he's crying or freezing. How long has he been in here?

'They're not looking for you,' I explain. 'They're looking for me.'

'I can hear them calling my name,' he says, a little too loudly.

'Tala'at asked me to take your place. He told me to pretend to be you.'

He lifts his eyes to look at me now, and it's as if he's seeing me for the first time.

'We look nothing alike,' he concludes. 'You've got that olivey skin, and look at me.'

'That didn't seem to matter to the rotba,' I say. 'He found himself in a bind and rushed at the first idea he had to fix it.'

His shoulders start to shake in a fresh burst of emotion. 'And still, you brought them here to me,' he laughs despairingly. 'You've truly been the worst luck for me, ya Shahed.'

My vision grows bleary, and my chest heaves with sobs. *I really tried*, I want to say.

I hear the rush of wind through a wooden hollow and the sound of pecking at a window. It reminds me of the hudhud in Teita's garden.

'That can't bode well for either of us,' says Nizam.

Without thinking, I lunge for a swathe of white cloth resting on a showerhead and grab Nizam by the elbows to drag him to his feet. I pull him to a trolley with space for one more corpse and throw the large square sheet down as though I'm making a bed.

'Lie down.'

Without a word, he does as I say. I pull the sheet taut under him and tell him to stay still and do his best not to shiver.

I tell him to walk east after nightfall. In the distance there will be a wall, which is the boundary of the army's land here. Keep watching the North Star, I tell him, so you don't end up going around in circles. You don't want to get lost before you've escaped. There will be a glow beyond the wall from a port town ten kilometres away. You'll smell the sea air hitting you from the other side of the wall. It's important that you don't let the sand pelting your face stop you from keeping an eye on where you're going. The sand here is soft, so any journey on foot will take time, but it's doable if you keep an even pace and don't waste time going off course. Stay away from any roads you might see. There will be patrols, and with this dead platoon, they'll be looking for any excuse to open fire on people wandering in the desert, Bedouin or otherwise.

When you hear the surf caressing the shore, run towards it. Go for a swim. How long has it been since you've been in the water? Once you've had your fill, all you need to do is follow the coast to the port. The sand will be cool by that point, so the distance won't be as taxing on your body. Just keep moving. When you arrive at the town, ask for a swimmer, a Palestinian from the ʿAzazma, called Hakeem. I raced him last month—just tell him I sent you. He'll take your hand and help you from there.

You're so close to surviving this. I'll have to wrap this tightly around your body so you don't attract attention, but there'll be enough leeway for you to wiggle out of your cocoon when the time comes for your escape. I'll cover your face now with this cloth, and for good measure, I'll write my name on your shroud so it blends in with the rest. Tawakkal ʿalallah, ya Nizam.

I place my hand on his chest and feel the warmth of his body inside the sheet. Faintly, the flutter of a heartbeat. *ʾInna lillah w-ʾilaihi rajeʿoon*, I think to myself. A prayer for the dead to help him pass for dead.

I walk out into the room with empty beds and erratic boot marks licking the floor and accidentally kick a heavy metal cylinder, injuring my bare foot. I stoop to examine the canister, sniffing at its nozzle, and splutter as my eyes begin to stream.

It's tear gas—that's the odourless, tasteless vapour invading the air. This is where the soldiers died, their empty beds standing like blank gravestones. Horror washes over me as I realise that these flittering trails of panicked boot prints tell a completely different story of how they met their end.

I take a moment to look around for something else to hold on to, as if anything here could constitute something of a life. I reach into my pockets by force of habit, even though I know there's no photograph there. I can't tell if I will ever be ready to face what's outside, but here it comes.

Everything falls quiet. A key slides home and twists. Light and shadows rush in through the door.

*

On the journey back, a different driver is at the wheel. I can't see who it is from inside the back of the van. The vehicle lurches forward on the uneven road surface, and I slip off the bench onto the floor. I'm surrounded by soldiers, but they were told not to speak to me. Whenever I nod off, my face lands on someone's shoulder, and I'm immediately awake again. I try to open my eyes, but I can't.

When the door to the barracks banged open, I heard a hissing, followed by the door slamming again. Metal canisters rolled on the floor releasing thin plumes of smoke. I ran to pick them up, but they burnt my hands. When I went for the door, it was locked again. I jumped onto the bedstead and tried to climb back out through the window. A fist hit me squarely in the face, and I fell back inside, bouncing off the metal beams. A loud moan escaped my lips and I writhed on the ground for a moment, trying to breathe in, choking on the gas, the dust and the smell of rotting bodies, which is still clinging to my skin now. I resolved not to die in there.

I used my shirt as a glove to pick up the canisters and launched them back out through the broken window. *He's throwing them out.* More metal flew in, showering me in shards of glass and smoke. I threw out as many canisters as I could, but the smoke had covered the ground in a thick layer and I could no longer see where they had landed, except when I stepped on them as I ran around frantically. The more windows I tried to break, the more quickly they covered them up, cutting off my supply of air and light.

I ran to the toilets and banged the door shut behind me. I looked over to where Nizam's body was lying peacefully. Before he could say anything, I yelled at him not to move or make a sound. Tear gas canisters were soon fired into the latrine. I found a squat toilet and pushed my head as far inside as I could, then sealed off my face using the soggy documents on the floor. I breathed slowly, imagining that I was underwater, that the panic I was feeling was merely the adrenaline rush at the start of a race. The smell of human excrement wafted up from below as though to force me to remember where I was.

As my breathing steadied, I found myself crying at the hopeless mess I found myself in. It was the worst kind of clarity to achieve in a crisis, because it showed that the only way out was death. In the darkness of the toilet's plumbing, I saw all the faces of the soldiers' corpses pass before my eyes as my nostrils filled with the stench from the contents of their bowels. I was going to look exactly like them when my body was found. I felt sorry for my parents, who would never know what happened to me. I had accepted that as a consequence of my own decision, but in dying like this, my choice had been taken away.

I awoke in a fit of coughs to hands tearing at my skin. My eyes were sealed with tears as masked faces dragged me through the latrine door and across the slippery, dusty floor of the soldiers' living quarters. In the ridiculousness of the situation, I tried to stay inside the barracks, for fear of what awaited me outside.

'Araby and the car were swiftly dismissed once they caught me. Noon prayers were running late, he was told, and if he wanted to get back to the city before curfew, he needed to leave now. Nizam and I were safe in their hands, they must have reassured him. *What could happen in the hands of the country's protectors?* He would know the answer to his own question but push those thoughts out of his mind.

When I was brought out of the dead platoon's barracks, the rotba was standing before me, and all I could think to say was, 'Please, please ...' He had my ID, and in my delusional, oxygen-deprived state, I still had hope that I might make it out. I had to keep blinking back tears to be able to see anything, twisting my head in search of a corner of clear vision. Sunlight refracted through the water in my eyes, blinding me. Before I knew what was happening, a fist smashed into my jaw.

'I have to say,' said Tala'at, 'you really must be a saint, Nizam. I can't imagine how anyone could survive that.'

Neither could I. Until they broke my jaw, I thought the blows were misfired signals from my brain as it prepared itself for death.

Bruised and blackened, my skin stretched and split, I let myself be led into a van. People have survived worse, but my hope of survival now seemed too slim for resistance to be worthwhile. My face was slick with wetness, my coughs still brought up the smell of shit, and my swollen eyes let nothing in. Everything was a blur. I held the hand of the soldier guiding me, who seemed to feel genuine remorse for my state, because when I squeezed, he squeezed back. He tried to hold me steady as I climbed into the van, but I tripped and collided with the floor. Pulling me to my feet, he stuffed a slice of something cold and slimy into my pocket and sat me down on a bench.

'Where are my belongings?' I asked.

'What belongings?'

'I had a prayer book. A small prayer book. And a bag.'

Someone ran off and rushed back with a blurry form in their tanned hand.

'Shahed, is that you?' he whispered. 'What are you doing? Why did you do this?'

But all I could do was grab the mesh bag and hug it close to my chest, breathing in the faint smell of benzene and chlorine. With two taps on my arm, a hand extended a small, familiar object, which I quickly stowed in my pocket with the gifted luncheon meat. Something light slipped out of its pages, and I groped around on the floor till my fingers met the glossy texture of the Polaroid.

'Thank you, thank you, thank you, ya Kamal,' I said, suddenly remembering the swimmer-soldier's face. 'I'm sorry.'

'For what?' the voice asked.

I could only sob more loudly.

Bodies piled into the van until I found myself squeezed between bony shoulders, sharp, like teeth.

The drive now is slow and grinding. The canvas covering the rear of the van pulsates, and the wind still manages to lash at my face. My vision must be clearing up slightly, since I can draw my eyelid far enough back to see dots of orange light around me: cigarette tips, flaring up with every breath. The scene is an image of a distant memory. I remember the cigarette in my chest pocket and find it's still there. I bring it to my lips, and a lighter next to me clicks.

'You'll be fine, ya Nizam.'

'None of us could believe that you survived that beating.'

'Truth be told, we regret what the others did. Just know that everyone here stands by your side. Our hearts are with you. You just don't know what it's like there. Life can be so cruel.'

'I know,' I say.

'Do you know where you're going?'

'I know.'

*

ACKNOWLEDGEMENTS

Writing a manuscript might be a personal endeavour, but publishing a book takes a village. To Farhaana and Brekhna, the dynamic duo behind Hajar Press, thank you for your advice, support and camaraderie throughout the editing process. Your faith in this project made me believe in its potential. It's an honour to be on Hajar's list.

Thank you to the Maslaha family and Raheel Mohammed for providing Muslim writers of colour with an opportunity to have their work read by such an incredible publisher through the MFest 2021 Short Story Competition.

I would like to thank my PhD supervisor, Dr Allyson Stack, for reading through numerous 'false starts' to this novel and for constantly challenging me to make sure that this manuscript did not get mired in the trauma and difficulties that gave rise to it.

To my agent, Jessica Craig, who has been a great support and cheerleader for this project, thank you. I can't wait to see what the future holds.

The writings of my sister, Sarah Tonsy, provided me with a deeper understanding of the events of the revolution and helped me to make sense of my own political conjecture. It was through our conversations that I was truly able to imagine the dystopian Egypt where the novel is set—I thank her for being a light in the dark.

I am grateful to fellow writers who have read through different iterations of this manuscript. To the Scottish BPOC Writers Network, thank you for providing writers of colour with a space to share work and for encouraging me to use your platform.

While I tried to rely mostly on my own memories when reflecting on the revolution, *Mada Masr*, *Al-Ahram*, Wiki Thawra, Raseef22, 858 archive and fellow revolutionaries' recollections helped me to fill in the gaps. I wasn't present at Maspero when the massacre occurred, so I relied on archival footage and 'Alaa' 'Abd El-Fattah's writings about its aftermath to reconstruct those events in this book. Similarly, for the Rab'a Massacre, I referred to eyewitness testimonies published by *Time*, *Deutsche Welle*, *The Guardian* and Human Rights Watch. I wrote about the military's so-called 'virginity tests' by reading the accounts of survivors themselves, who, in speaking about their experiences, have pushed back against not just the Armed Forces but also a misogynistic society that to this day does not recognise women's sovereignty over their own bodies.

Finally, my thanks go to the people who stood by me in Mohamed Mahmoud Street on 22 November 2011, who sprayed me with bicarbonate and Coca Cola to try to stop the effects of the nerve agent from taking hold of me, and to the doctor who breathed life into me when I thought I had no more breaths left to take.